The Farmer and the Fury

CHERRY BURROUGHS

Copyright © Cherry Burroughs 2022

ISBN: 9798366059251

Cherry Burroughs asserts the moral right to be identified as the author of this work.

A catalogue record for this book is available from the British Library.

This novel is based on the historical event of the great North Sea flood of 1953. However, it is a work of fiction. The names, characters and incidents portrayed in it, are the work of the author's imagination.

All rights reserved. No part of this publication may be reproduced, stored in a retrieval system, or transmitted, in any form or by any means, electronic, mechanical, photocopying, recording or otherwise without the prior written permission of Cherry Burroughs.

This book is sold subject to the condition that it shall not, by way of trade or otherwise, be lent, re-sold, hired out or otherwise circulated without the publisher's prior consent in any form of binding or cover other than that in which it is published and without a similar condition including this condition being imposed on the subsequent purchaser.

Independantly published by Amazon on 29th November 2022. This book is available for sale and distribution in the United Kingdom.

www.cherryburroughs.co.uk

This book is dedicated to my husband John and all those who were affected by the great North Sea flood of 1953.

Thanks to John, my Beta readers, Sylvia Kent and the Brentwood Writing Circle, my publisher, and all those too numerous to mention.

PART ONE

1

Mid-January 1953

Everyone knew George Hadley. The islanders called him the contented farmer, who always had luck on his side. For most people, luck is a finite force. It arrives by chance one day and then disappears the next, a mere memory of better times.

George Hadley smiled to himself. Yes, he was a contented man and maybe he was lucky too. He leant on his stick, and inhaled the crisp, winter air.

High above him, the wings of the golden plover beat in hushed silence across the still sky. He exhaled. His breath dissipated in a spiral of mist. Streaks of dawn light appeared in the east and the thick, white frost sparkled underfoot.

George looked across the fields of tilled earth. The rows of sown wheat and barley lay dormant as they waited in quiet anticipation for the first burst of spring sunshine.

Aye, you'll be showing through soon enough.

He gave the ground an affirming tap with his stick and turned towards the farmhouse. He smiled to himself. His wife Annie would be bustling around the kitchen as she prepared breakfast, whilst Olive kept a watchful eye on the children.

He began to walk towards the farmhouse, the silence

broken only by the sound of his boots on the crusted earth. He passed a copse of hawthorn trees and crossed the back lane. As he entered the yard, Sam the black Labrador barked a greeting and pulled on his chain. He patted the dog's head and entered the farmhouse.

Butterwood Farm had been in the Hadley family for seven generations and was located on an island in the Thames Estuary. A sea wall surrounded and protected the island and there was one road bridge from the mainland to the island. Before the road bridge was built, the islanders relied on a footpath across the sands, a precarious route guided only by the 'farmer's teeth' or wooden stakes and dictated by the lunar tides.

Each year George cultivated the land, sowed his crops, and brought in the harvest. He maintained his strong herd of cattle and sounder of healthy swine. He knew when the tides ebbed and flowed, the best time to fish and when it was safe for his children to play on the shoreline. George lived and worked within the rhythm and cycle of nature. He was in awe of her beauty, her power, and her ferocity.

2

31st January 1953

The last winter moon hung close to the earth like a giant silver orb in the ink black sky. The spring tide was on its way.

George checked the cattle stalls. The milking cows pulled at the hay as their eyes rolled, and their nostrils puffed spirals of cold air. Out in the gated yard the powerful bodies of thirty bullocks nudged and pushed, in a slow ponderous walk, towards the hay racks and mangers.

The temperature was below zero and forecast to drop another ten degrees. He thumped his arms around his body. A metal bucket scudded across the yard into the wall of a pigsty. He hooked the chain through Sam's collar and attached him to his kennel. The dog's fur lifted in the wind, his nose twitched, and his ears flickered back and forth. He entered his kennel and watched his master walk across the yard to the scullery.

George pulled off his boots, hung up his jerkin and brushed icy droplets from his arms. He entered the sitting room and sat close to the fire. The heat from the flames turned his face a burnished copper.

'You're back then.'

Annie stood in the doorway, her slight frame obscured by the bundle of children's clothes in her arms.

Her skin lay soft in the half light and her chestnut hair whispered around her face.

'Aye. They're all settled. The weather's up, it's squalling out there. I thought of letting Sam come in for the night, but I left him, he's used to his kennel.'

She turned towards the kitchen.

'I'll make some tea.'

He leant back in his chair. The heat warmed his bones, and the flames lulled him into a quiet reverie. When she returned, he was asleep.

The wind gathered pace.

Later, when they had tea together, they heard the wind whip across the yard in angry gusts. By the time they retired to bed the wind was gale-force seven.

Sam's bark came again, like the crack of a whip in a silent night. George went to the window. The moon shone like a beacon and lit up the farmyard. The dog pulled at his chain, his body taut as he straddled the top of his kennel. Furious, squalling clouds sped across the sky and a mist of white covered the ground.

For a few seconds, George saw snow. But the ground shimmered like liquid glass. Then he realised it was water. Silent, unstoppable water, the ground invisible beneath its swirling mass. He thought of his children and a cold fear entered his chest. He rushed to the back window. Water covered the small bushes and crept up the gate posts forming the boundaries of the farmhouse.

'George! What's happening?'

Annie sat up and pulled back the covers.

'The tide has broken through the sea wall!'

She reached the window. Her eyes widened.

'Oh, my goodness!'

The farmyard was covered in a large, pulsating lake. George tucked his shirt into his trousers and pulled on his jerkin.

'I need to break Sam loose. He's trapped on top of his kennel.'

'George! What's up with the cattle?'

Grandpa Moses appeared in the doorway, his long smock white against his lamp.

'The tide's come in and breached the bloody wall!'

'Can we get to the cattle?'

'I'll get Sam and see how deep it is.'

'I'll be down.'

Moses retreated from the doorway. Annie pushed her feet into shoes and pulled a shawl around her shoulders. George fastened his final button and disappeared down the stairs. She ran across the landing. Val had already climbed out of bed and was moving towards the window.

'Why is Sam barking?'

She wrapped a cardigan around her daughter's shoulders and guided her towards the door.

'He's all right, darling. Daddy's gone to get him. Let's go to the boy's bedroom and snuggle up warm.'

'What's going on?'

Nanny Emma crossed the landing, her nightdress billowing beneath a blanket.

'The tide has breached the sea wall.'

'Where's Daddy?'

John sat up in bed, his knees clasped as his eyes scanned the room for an invisible monster.

'He's sorting out Sam. He won't be long.'

She glanced at her twin sons, Douglas and Dennis. They lay in blissful sleep, their pink cheeks suffused from the heat of their bodies. She let herself breathe.

The wind howled and the windows rattled.

'Come on, Val, let's get you into bed. Move over, John.'

She pulled up the covers. Her hands trembled as she

stroked and kissed their faces. She bit into her lip and blinked hard.

'Now, try and get some sleep. Nanny Em is here.'

She smiled at the old woman and left the room.

'Emma is with the children.'

Moses nodded and straightened his braces. Sam's bark came from the bottom of the stairs.

'Get up there.'

The dog appeared, drenched and shivering. Moses grabbed him by his collar, manoeuvred him into Val's bedroom and shut the door.

'Here.'

George threw Annie's rubber boots up the stairs towards her.

'Take care, my darling, the kitchen is full of water.'

She looked down the darkened stairwell and opened and shut her mouth.

'George! Be careful!'

'I'll go with him.'

Grandpa Moses rattled down the stairs.

When Annie entered the kitchen, it was pitch black and the water tipped over the top of her boots. The farmhouse creaked and groaned, like a ship in a storm. She found the candles and matches.

'Oh my God!'

The lit candle cast an eerie glow on the wet walls. Wooden chairs floated in the water and the large kitchen table lifted off the floor.

What do I need? Yes! Yes!

She waded to the pantry, dropped provisions into a box, and picked up the meat cage.

'Mummy!'

A nauseous sensation heaved in her stomach. She balanced the meat cage on one arm, picked up the box and pushed herself through the water to the staircase.

3

'You can't go across with me! The water is too deep and running fast.'

George and his father stood in front of the farmhouse, their faces lit by the moonlight and the lamp. The water level was still rising and reached the top of their thigh boots.

Moses swung the lamp towards the cattle sheds.

'What about the cattle?'

'I'm going across to open the gate. They need to be released before they trample and kill each other. They will have a chance if they can get to higher ground.'

As George spoke, a crescendo of cattle cries crossed the water and the cold fear crept over him. He pressed his father's arm.

'I'm going now! Stay here. I will need your help to guide them once they're through the gate.'

He looked up at the farmhouse.

'I will be back, Annie. I will be back.'

He turned and faced the water. He knew the ground level dipped ahead of him but could not gauge by how much. However, he could see the tops of the fence posts as they curved to the right.

Five fence posts to get to the gate. Yes, that's it.

The moon disappeared behind racing clouds. Moses held up the lamp. George waded towards the first fence post. By the time he grasped the second post, the water reached his waist.

Moses was a cantankerous old man, blunt in his comments and prone to cause upset. But as he watched his son cling to the third post, he saw him as a small boy again. He wanted to encase him in his bear-like arms and heave him out of the water. He lowered the lamp. His shoulders ached, and he could not feel his toes. He flexed his body and raised the lamp.

George left the third post and moved towards the fourth. His movements had slowed, and his body jerked in the water.

'Keep going, son! Don't stop!'

Eventually, George reached the fifth post beside the submerged gate. Suddenly, the low moans of the cattle turned to screams. Then, a heaving mass moved forward and the beasts surged towards the gate.

'You've done it, son!'

Moses swung the lamp from side to side. The cattle staggered and floundered as they tried to swim. He stared across the water towards the gate.

'George! George!

He held up the lamp, but all he could see was the cattle as they swam in all directions.

'Where are you, son? Can you hear me?'

He raised the lamp higher and waded forward in the water, but the swimming cattle forced him to retreat.

'No, boy! No!'

Within a few minutes, the cattle had gone, and the current of blackness returned.

Annie returned to the boys' bedroom. John was awake. Nanny Em rose from her chair.

'I couldn't get him to go to sleep.'

Annie placed down the cage and the box.

'I'll stay with them now, Em. You go get some rest.'

She kissed her mother-in-law and sat on the edge of John's bed. The boy looked towards the window as the farmhouse shuddered and heaved.

'It's a big storm, Mum.'

She touched his tear-stained face.

'Yes, it is dear, but there is nothing we can do until the morning.'

'Where are Dad and Sam?'

'Sam is next door in Val's room and Daddy is checking the cattle with granddad. Now, try and get some sleep.'

She scooped the boy towards her and kissed and hugged him. When he had gone to sleep, she went to the window and peered into the night. She watched the cattle as they clambered over each other and tried to swim. She could not see George or Moses.

Where are they? They should be back by now.

The moon reappeared from behind the clouds and shone beams of light into the yard. She looked again but saw only the cattle. She turned away from the window.

Val lay next to John, her dark, curling hair damp with perspiration. Her only daughter was lovely, busy, and bossy and liked to organise and help beyond her ten years of age. John was nine years old, her first born son and the most sensitive of her children. He was already handsome with his dark brown hair, strong jawline, and vivid blue eyes. And her beautiful twin boys Douglas and Dennis. Just four years old, their mischievous smiles and noisy laughter in hibernation as they slept in silent oblivion.

She lit a candle and sat in her old nursing chair. She removed her boots and rocked back and forth. Her body had warmed but the bottom half of her nightdress remained damp and stuck to her legs.

She streamed silent tears.

George, George where are you?

She turned in her chair, but there was no one in the doorway. She consoled herself with the rhythmic breathing of her children as they murmured and dreamed. She recalled when she married George and left London. Her childhood home, with its neat suburban windows, was so different to the farmhouse. But as the seasons came and went, she fell in love with the island's rugged beauty of open fields and clear skylines.

So much has happened since then.

The open gate lay twisted in the water, torn from its top hinge by the frenzied cattle. Moses held up the lamp and strained his rheumy eyes across the ripples of white light.

'George! George! For God's sake where are you?'

The old man's laments became wild, disjointed, as the water hissed and sucked its relentless tune of death and destruction.

Please, Lord, don't do this to me.

He swung the lamp in a frantic way and the ripples of white light turned to jagged shards. Then, he heard coughing and spluttering.

'Where are you, boy?'

He steadied his juddering arm and leaned forward with the lamp. Suddenly George appeared by the first fence post, his head and shoulders dipping up and down in the water.

'Pa...I can't....'

George gasped and tried to cling to the post.

'Hold on, son. I'll get to you. Just hold on.'

Moses' legs felt numb.

Steady yourself, you old fool.

'Almost there, son, just hold on.'

He forced himself through the treacle of underwater

debris and reduced the distance between them. When he was close enough, he threw the lamp into the water, grabbed his son around his waist and pulled his nearest arm across the back of his own shoulders.

'I've got you, boy. Let go of the post.'

George released his grip and slumped forward, but the old man held him firm, and they staggered through the water to the scullery door. George clung to his father as they crossed the kitchen, but when they reached the bottom of the stairs his grip loosened, and Moses could not hold him.

Annie jolted as the clock on the mantlepiece struck on the hour. A few minutes later she heard movement downstairs followed by the urgent whispers of Moses' voice.

'Annie! Are you there? Quick, come down.'

She pulled on her boots, picked up the candle, and ran across the landing. When she reached the top of the stairs, her heart leapt into her throat.

'Oh, George! Moses!'

She placed down the candle.

The old man's breath came in desperate, strained wheezes as he pushed and shoved George up the stairs. Annie stepped down, took hold of her husband's hands, and pulled him towards her.

'George, dear.'

He tried to speak but she touched and closed his lips. They slumped him into a chair. Moses fell to his knees.

'He got...caught...under the gate.'

He clawed at his throat and held up his hand.

'I'm all right...just get...my breath.'

George groaned.

'I am here, darling.'

She kissed his face and grasped his hands.

'You're shaking. We need to get you dry and into bed.'

His head lolled to one side and his eyes closed. She removed his thigh boots and began to loosen his clothes. They were soddened, heavy and awkward.

'Ready?'

Annie nodded.

Moses heaved George out of the chair and dragged him up and onto the bed.

'I will get the brandy.'

He left the room.

'Thank you, Pa. Dry yourself and get some rest.'

4

'It was such a pleasant surprise, Derek! I did enjoy the evening and the company we kept.'

Derek helped Dorothy with her coat. She smiled to herself. It was their wedding anniversary and she expected to be taken to the Rose Garden Hotel. However, a few days before, Derek had suggested they attend the dinner and dance at the local community hall, but she was reluctant to go. Then, a chance 'hello' in the butcher's shop from the borough engineer's wife, Mrs Bates, swayed her in a different direction, and by the time she got home her mind was made up.

Derek and Dorothy stepped outside. The sky glittered starlight bright with a magnificent moon, but the wind was unforgiving, and they were blown along the street. He opened the car door for her; it was wrenched from his hand by the wind, and he staggered backwards. She held onto the dashboard whilst he grabbed hold of the door and slammed it shut. As they drove home, gusts of wind whipped across the road and caused the car to shunt sideways.

He peered through the windscreen.

'Terrible storm. Our sea wall will be tested tonight.'

'But I thought it was reinforced, Derek. The mainland here is so important. I remember Mr Bates saying that.'

'Yes, it is, and he did say that, but this storm is

powerful and may do some damage although there's been no forecast on the radio about it.'

He parked the car on the driveway.

The wind groaned low.

'I'll get straight out and go indoors.'

She held the door handle in both hands and turned and pushed her body against the door. It opened and slammed shut. She tried again.

'I can't open the door, Derek. The wind is too strong.'

'Wait there. I'll come round.'

He clambered out of the car but was forced to step sideways before he could step forwards. His hair stuck to his face and his winter coat rippled in the wind. He braced his body against the passenger door and turned the handle. He held onto Dorothy's elbow and helped her out of the car. They staggered to the front door.

'Oh, Derek!'

Her body shook and she fought back tears. He fumbled in his pocket for the key, unlocked the door and ushered her inside.

'I have never seen a storm like this one.'

At ten minutes past four in the morning, they were awoken by a loud knock at the front door. Derek got out of bed and turned on the light. The knocks became incessant, and a male voice shouted out his name. When he opened the door, wind raced through the bungalow like a horizontal tornado.

A dark figure blocked the doorway silhouetted by a beam of light from the street. It was PC Talbot. The wind buffeted his helmet and inflated his voluminous cape. Although there was no rain, rivulets of water ran down his body and bounced onto his black boots.

'Mr Brown?'

'Yes, that's right.'

'The water levels have risen and breached the sea wall along the main coastline!'

PC Talbot's voice came out of the dark, stretched, hoarse. Derek pulled his dressing gown around him.

'By how much? Do you know?'

'I don't know. I only know the flood is bad, very bad. People are stranded in their homes, and some have drowned. Mr Bates wants you in now.'

PC Talbot retreated down the path and disappeared into the night.

Annie lay beside George, her head on his chest.

'My darling.'

He kissed the top of her head.

'Pa saved me, no doubt of that.'

George did not tell Annie how the relentless currents exhausted him even before he reached the fifth post. Or when the cattle stormed through the gate and forced him under the water. His breath began to fade, and he saw the blackness again. He pushed the image to the back of his mind and stroked his wife's face.

'How have the children been? And mother, is she safe?'

'They were unsettled but we got them to sleep. And Emma, she must have stayed asleep when Moses brought you back. Sam is in Val's room. I gave him some water.'

He touched her hair.

'Let's get some rest. God knows what tomorrow will bring.'

5

Sunday 1st February 1953

'We need more blankets and clothing. At least five thousand blankets.'

Derek shouted down the line and emphasised the number. Aware he held the only working phone, he ended the conversation and replaced the receiver. Within seconds another call was made, and a voice requested additional coal for the flood victims.

The official headquarters on the mainland buzzed with activity. Derek gulped down his lukewarm tea. Since his arrival, the position became clear. A huge storm had travelled down the east coast overnight, joined the rising spring tide, and caused havoc and destruction in its path. They were attempting to coordinate the rescue services, but the phonelines were down and communication was sporadic.

He pulled out a freshly laundered handkerchief Dorothy had given him and wiped glistening droplets from his brow. He rolled it into a ball and placed it in his trouser pocket.

I hope she stays safe.

As soon as dawn broke George slid out of bed and opened the window. The icy wind blasted in and numbed his face. It was still below freezing, and the flood levels remained high. No sound came from the cattle sheds.

George worried about his pigs. Although the pigsties were on higher ground, he needed to get food and water to them.

He dressed and went downstairs. The door from the scullery to the yard had reclosed from the weight of the water. He heaved the door ajar and squeezed through the gap. The wind unfurled in great swathes across the yard and the speed of the water indicated the undercurrent was still strong. On most days, the main track from the farmhouse took a cart and horses, or a herd of cattle three abreast. But it was difficult to identify the track's location. The barbed wire fences along each side of the track, together with balls of wire used to deter cattle, were no longer visible.

He stuck his stick into the murky depths and stepped into the water. The level came up to his thighs. He was not a tall man and waves of exhaustion swept over him, but years of working on the land had created great physical strength, and the dense muscle mass in his body and limbs gave him fortitude and resilience. As he followed his stick through the water his heart began to pound and the muscles in his legs pulled taut. Items swirled around and past him: a chicken shed, rabbit hutches, small items of furniture, branches of trees and pieces of wood from the cattle sheds. All scattered, misplaced.

All our years of grinding hard work. And for what?

He looked around at the devastation and tears coursed down his face. He jammed his stick into the swirling mass again and again.

Must keep going.

He moved forward and pushed on. He reached the first outbuilding and tried to open the door, but it was jammed shut from the pressure of the water. He put his body weight behind it and gripped its edge, wedged his foot into the gap and forced it open. It was black as tarred pitch inside. He waited for his eyes to adapt.

He wanted one item, and in the gloom, he could just see its shape. It was a raft he built for Val and John, a heavy, wooden float they used to row across to the duck house in the centre of the pond. George collected the oars and placed them outside the door. He returned to the raft and turned it on its side. He took deep breaths, counted to three and dragged and pulled the raft through the entrance of the outbuilding and out onto the water. He picked up the oars, held the raft steady and heaved himself on. The raft submerged, but after a few seconds it bobbed to the surface. As he lay on the raft his body shook, and his breath came in uncontrolled gasps.

Come on! Come on!

After a few minutes, he sat up and positioned the oars. But as soon as he started to row, the oars became entangled in something below the water. He tried to extricate them, but each time he succeeded, they got stuck again until he could not move them at all, and they stood up in the water like fence posts.

'Damn you.'

He slid back into the water; the level reached his waist. He propelled his body forward in a slow, lurching rhythm. Wild rabbits gripped the top of the fence posts, as their terrified eyes scanned the hostile landscape. The corpse of a shire horse floated past; George recognised it as one of a ploughing pair owned by his neighbouring farmer. A cat clung to the higher branches of a tree, whilst a chicken shed bobbed around in the water like a small dinghy.

The cottage of his farm manager was half submerged but he could see the upper windows above the water. He shouted above the howling wind as his body swayed back and forth.

'Josh! Josh! Are you there?'

The wind increased its ferocity. George knew the swell of the tide had not reached its peak. It would become more dangerous, and the relentless waves would continue to crash over the sea wall and onto the island. Eventually he saw the light of a candle and a head appeared through the casement window.

'Get down here, Josh. We need to check the cattle. Bring a lamp.'

The window slammed shut. George shivered in the half-light. He waved and tried to stamp his feet beneath the water. Moments later Josh reappeared at the same window. He slid out of the upper casement and onto the lower roof of the cottage.

'There's no other way,' shouted George. 'You must get into the water.'

'You wanna come round the back, guv'nor. Ain't so deep there. We can use the tractor if we can get her going.'

George raised his hand and waded towards the side of the cottage. Josh was right, the water was lower, and the level dropped to his knees. His wet clothes were covered in filth and mud, and his body felt numb. The men lumbered towards the outbuilding and pulled open the doors. Inside was a petrol paraffin tractor, a Fordson E27N. She stood monstrous and majestic, her huge tyres designed for difficult terrain.

'Let's see how we go,' said Josh.

He picked up the crank, inserted it in position and pulled down hard. Within seconds she fired up and the noise of her engine filled the air. Josh pulled out the crank and stood back from the vehicle. He gave a thumbs up sign to George and adjusted the fuel taps. He heaved himself into the seat, pulled and fixed the throttle lever and selected the gear. George stood to one side as the tractor started to move forward. After a further change of gear, Josh drove the tractor out and into the water. At first, the huge vehicle managed the terrain, but then without warning, she dropped into deeper water and despite Josh's efforts, she spluttered, stalled, and came to a halt. He climbed down into the water and waited for orders. His tall, slim frame was hunched with cold, and his wiry hair plastered to his face.

'Well, that's bloody marvellous,' said George. 'We'll have to get to the cattle some other way. They have been released from the yard, but some might still be alive in the sheds.'

He gestured onwards. As they approached, a terrible silence pervaded the sheds. George was reluctant to enter, but he forced himself forward and stepped into the gloom. The milking cows in the stalls had already drowned. Their constrained bodies floated up and down in the water like toys in a bath. The same ropes used to tether them and keep them safe and warm, had prevented their escape and caused their death. Some cattle had bolted and were killed in the scramble as they attempted to stampede through the gate, whilst others survived and managed to get into the water. However, barbed wire hidden beneath the water had torn at their bodies and trapped and killed them.

George counted the bodies of twenty-eight. He rammed his stick into the water and threw his arms towards the sky.

Why, why, why?

They came across one group of cattle still alive in the water. They had managed to swim some way but stood caught by underwater debris unable to move due to exhaustion. The whites of their eyes rolled, and their fatigued bodies jerked in the water. The men stood helpless as the cattle tried to swim. George recognised the noise. It was the same noise the cattle made before they got into the yard, a low moaning sound followed by screams of terror.

Josh stood beside George, his eyes tearful, his breath shallow, staccato.

'Poor Bertha, Daisy, Gillian...'

He continued the bovine toll.

'Stop that! We need to get on.'

George gritted his teeth and pushed on through the water.

When they reached higher ground, they found two dozen surviving cattle. The cattle stood in a drenched and exhausted huddle and turned their beleaguered faces towards the men in one synchronised movement.

'How the hell, we goin' to get to them, guv'nor? There are big running ditches 'ere somewhere.'

George put his hand to his forehead and scratched his head. They waded on and surveyed the loss. By the time the sun was up the grisly assessment was complete. The men returned to the surviving cattle. They stood huddled in small groups and nuzzled the waterlogged ground in search of food.

'We have to get them off there,' said George.

The cattle required food and water and the cows would develop udder burn if they were not milked.

'We will have to tempt them off with some hay. That higher stack at the back of the yard, I think it's still dry, but we need a flattie, a small rowing boat.'

'Where we goin' to get it from, guv'nor? The nearest one is at the next farm, they've got two there.'

The men stood and faced each other.

'Well, it's no good standing here. We have got to try and get one. Let's go.'

They turned and pushed through the water, but after a few minutes their legs began to struggle, and they heaved themselves onto a bank. They lay side by side, their panting a syncopated rhythm against the sound of the wind and the water.

'Look, over there.'

Josh raised himself on one elbow and pointed to further along the bank. Nestled within the line of goat willow trees bobbed a small rowing boat. George nodded.

'It must have broken free.'

The men held onto the lower branches of the trees and pulled themselves along the bank. When they reached the flattie, they pushed it into the water. They rowed back to the yard and loaded it with hay, ropes, and harnesses. As the boat approached the higher ground, the cattle watched with large, sorrowful, eyes. Josh moored the boat. They collected the hay, one harness and a rope and dropped themselves into the water. The wind changed direction and the cattle smelt the hay. They lumbered forward towards the edge of the water.

'If we can harness one cow and lead her to the boat to feed on the hay, the rest should follow,' said George.

The chosen lead cow was cooperative. They placed the harness over her head, attached the rope and led her into the water towards the boat. The remaining cattle began to murmur, then in one inexorable movement, they plodded into the water and followed the lead cow. When the cow reached the boat, she started to eat the fresh hay.

'Eeeaasy,' said George. 'Nice and slow.'

He stepped into the boat and cast off.

'So far, so good.'

The hay smelt sweet and moreish, and the cattle gathered pace. But their increasing movements caused a tidal surge and water swept over and into the boat. George waved an oar at the cattle and tried to beat them back whilst Josh attempted to herd them away. But the cattle were out of control and George was forced to release the lead cow.

'Damn this wretched flood. Damn it!'

George gritted his teeth and jerked at the oars. As he rowed away, the cattle lost interest, and retreated to the slithers of dry land.

'Let's check the pigs while it's still light.'

George stuck the oars into the mud, and they clambered out of the boat and waded towards the pigsties. Quiet grunts and snorts filled the air. They looked in the pigsties and were greeted with the familiar sight of piglets clinging to their mothers as they attempted to suckle, whilst the male pigs moved their snouts across the ground in search of food. Despite the flood, the pigsties had not changed. The winter bedding, mixed with the pig's own manure, provided warmth and extra height, and remained warm and dry.

Josh turned to George.

'They need fresh water now.'

George hunched his body.

'There's some barley meal at the back. We won't be able to reach the water tanks but there might be some water in the butts near the farmhouse.'

As the afternoon light faded, they rowed the flattie back and forth and transported buckets of fresh water from the water butts to the pigsties. It was an exhausting, cold, and messy business and by the time they had finished, the day was over.

'Thank you, Josh. You mind how you go.'

'Hello. Anyone here?'

A wonderful smell of cooked sausages came from upstairs. George unbuttoned his sodden, oilskin. Annie appeared through the door from the stairs.

'George! I wondered where you'd got to!'

As they embraced Annie trembled. George's wet clothes bore a strong smell of salt, but she could still smell 'her' George. The mingled smells of cattle, fresh hay, sun kissed earth, harvest time and late autumn crops.

'My darling.'

George kissed her soft lips, and they held each other in a tight embrace.

The daylight hours dwindled, and the day came to a close. The Hadley family had enough fresh water, food, and coal for twenty-four hours.

6

When the tidal flood arrived, most of the islanders were unable to reach their front doors and remained in their bedrooms, whilst others removed battens to access their roof space. The islanders who lived on the lower levels of the land heard only crashing, sliding, and screeching for several hours, as the cacophonous rush and roar of water engulfed their homes. Their children cried and shivered, whilst cats in baskets and dogs on leads shook beside their owners.

By one o'clock in the morning the island was plunged into darkness. The temperature dropped to minus ten degrees and the freezing cold numbed their hands and feet and pervaded their bodies. But when the winter sun rose the islanders grew curious and they hung out of windows and climbed onto roofs. A devastated landscape stretched out before them, and an eerie silence consumed the sky and the land. The islanders called out through the murky light and exchanged stories from the perilous night, whilst others who owned flatties rowed to neighbouring cottages to check for survivors.

As the day wore on, an expectation of rescue increased, but as daylight withdrew from the sky, there was no communication or visit from the mainland.

The inexorable tide returned, swept back through the breaches in the sea wall and reclaimed the island.

7

Sergeant Barrett straightened his uniform and turned towards his section.

'Right, men!'

The sergeant's voice boomed out through the freezing, morning air. The soldiers stopped their conversations and turned towards him.

'Last night the east coast and its islands were hit by a large storm made worse by the high spring tide. The seawall here on the mainland has suffered some damage although there are pockets of safety where the wall was not breached. Communication lines are down and information about the islands is awaited. This morning we will be assisting here on the mainland and are tasked with the rescue of survivors from the Nissan huts situated to the east of the town. Most of the survivors will be stranded in their homes and some will have lost loved ones. Apart from the injured, it will be the usual order of the elderly first, followed by women and children. Ambulances will take the injured to hospital and we will transport the remaining flood victims to the local schools which have been turned into reception centres. We will pick up the dead bodies later. Any questions?'

Sergeant Barrett looked around at his men.

'Right, Private Jones and Woodley, you will drive the two DUKW vehicles and lead the front of the convoy. I will follow in my truck. When we arrive at the destination, I will establish the optimal route across the terrain. You will await my orders before you proceed. Jones and Woodley!'

The two soldiers stepped forward.

'Yes, Sir!'

They stepped back as they were.

'Good. We leave in ten minutes. That's all.'

The hum of the soldier's voices returned. They loaded the trucks with first aid, blankets, food, and water, whilst some vehicles had trailers hitched to them and contained a selection of flatties requisitioned from local fishermen and farmers. They checked the ropes that secured the flatties.

'Hey, Charlie, don't forget your manners when you carry any of the ladies.'

Guffaws of laughter ran between them. Charlie turned and winked.

'Don't you worry about me. I know how to rescue a damsel in distress.'

'Yeah, I reckon he does. He did a good job of rescuing that tasty little blonde piece from the clutches of Tommy on Saturday night.'

The men sniggered and nudged each other.

'Get to it,' barked Barrett. 'We have a job to do.'

The men fell silent as Barrett walked amongst them. He knew the location of the huts. They were situated in a shallow dip off the high street not far from the barracks and were used for temporary housing. The survivors would be in grave danger. They had endured a night of sub-zero temperatures and by the time his men reached them more would be dead from exposure, whilst others would be seriously injured, or in the early stages of pneumonia or other respiratory diseases. They were ready. They lifted the green tarpaulins and climbed into the back of the trucks.

The air temperature remained below zero and the ground hard and heavy, but the sun had risen in the east and the sky sketched strips of pale luminous light.

Barrett looked through his binoculars. The huts were submerged, and people huddled on the rooftops, as their clothes flapped in the wind. He counted fifteen roofs and estimated the furthest one as half a mile away. He ordered a soldier to test the depth of the water and nodded to Private Jones to proceed in the DUKW vehicle. However, within minutes, the vehicle sunk into the water unable to move.

Barrett gave fresh orders.

'Unload the flatties two men each. Be quick about it.'

The soldiers scrambled out of their trucks. Barrett looked around.

'Private Woodley, you come with me.'

The soldiers unloaded the small boats, pushed them into the water, and jumped in. They braced their bodies towards the head winds and pulled at the oars. Although the weather was freezing, the morning light assisted them. One by one the boats each stopped at a hut, leaving the remaining boats to be rowed to the next one. Barrett and Private Woodley took it in turns to row.

Sometimes they rowed wide, to avoid an obstacle, at other times they used the oars to push the boat off underwater debris. As they approached the last Nissan hut Private Woodley pointed towards the roof.

'There are two figures up there, Sarge.'

Barrett looked through his binoculars. He saw a woman and a child. They clung to each other and stood on the only flat section of a curved roof.

'Jesus, they must be freezing.'

Barrett swept the binoculars around the surrounding

area. He gestured to Private Woodley.

'Aim for that side of the hut.'

They moved closer. Barrett cupped his hands around his mouth and spoke loud, slow, deliberate.

'Hello! Can you hear me?'

There was no response. The woman and child did not move. The boat reached the side of the hut. Barrett pointed to an open window with an exposed, internal catch.

'Up there.'

They positioned the boat beneath the window. Private Woodley stood and steadied himself in the rocking boat. He threw the looped rope up and onto the catch, pulled it tight and tugged it downwards. However, the proximity of the boat to the side of the hut obscured the sergeant's vision of the top part of the roof. He called out again.

'Hello, Sergeant Barrett speaking, can you hear me?'

Silence hung in the air.

'Hello. It's Sergeant Barrett, Jim Barrett, speaking again. I have Private Woodley with me. Can you hear me? We've come to help you down into the boat.'

After several seconds a female voice responded.

'I can hear you.'

The woman's voice was quiet, terrified, and the sobs of the child travelled with her reply.

'That's good. Can you tell me your name please?'

There was a long pause.

'Daisy. My name is Daisy.'

'And your child's name?'

Her response was quicker.

'Jennifer.'

'Is there anyone else in the hut, Daisy? Or is it just the two of you?'

'Just the two of us.'

The direction of the wind changed. The boat rocked and hit the side of the hut.

Private Woodley pulled and tugged at the rope.

Barrett shouted.

'Daisy, I can't climb up onto the roof, it will not take the weight of three people. We need to get you down one at a time. Do you understand?'

'Yes.'

'Can you guide Jennifer down first?'

Even with Daisy's help, it took time to coax Jennifer off the roof. She held onto the child until she was able to place her feet on the open window ledge and ease herself into a sitting position. Barrett talked to her as she held onto the window frame.

'Ready now, Jennifer?'

She sobbed and nodded.

'Hold onto the rope. That's it. Good girl.'

She held the rope with both hands and lowered herself towards the sergeant's outstretched arms. Barrett caught her and passed her to Private Woodley. He wrapped the child in a blanket and placed her in the boat.

'We're going to get your mummy now,' whispered Private Woodley. 'You keep nice and still in the boat for me.'

The child's teeth chattered. She shut her eyes.

Barrett craned his neck but could not see Daisy. He recalled she wore only a flimsy night dress and ill-fitting shoes and would be at risk from pneumonia or worse. But he knew it would be dangerous to rush her; her limbs would be stiff and numb from the cold and she could fall off the roof into the freezing water.

'Come on, love. Your daughter's safe. Let's get you down and into the boat with Jennifer.'

After a few moments, the sergeant heard Daisy's feet

shuffle a few steps, but she let out a small cry and stopped.

'Take your time, Daisy.'

The men glanced at each other, glad Jennifer was asleep. They waited but no sound came.

'Are you all right, Daisy?'

Barrett craned his head to try and see but the boat began to rock, and he returned to his original position.

'I can't...I just can't.'

Her voice sounded smaller than her daughter's voice.

'What about if you go down on your hands and knees and crawl along to the top of the window. Then you will be able to come down onto the window ledge like Jennifer.'

A few moments later a sound of movement came from the top of the roof. Then Daisy's legs appeared, and she slid down onto the window ledge. She clung to the window frame and stared at the water.

'Don't look down, Daisy. Take your time.'

Suddenly, she swung down on the rope towards the boat. As Barrett caught hold of her, her raven black hair swung out in long, damp curls and her glacial complexion lay smooth like grey satin. Their faces almost touched. A few seconds later, she slumped in his arms. But the sergeant needed to be sure, and he gave her a small, sharp squeeze on her arm. Her eyes flickered open.

'Are you sure there is no one else back in the hut, Daisy?'

He bent his ear close to her mouth.

'My husband...he's back there.'

'Well, we need to...'

'He's gone...drowned.'

She fainted.

Jennifer woke up and started to cry. Barrett wrapped Daisy in a blanket and winked at Jennifer.

'Your mummy's having a little sleep.'

He placed her next to her daughter. Both men removed their coats and placed them over the mother and child.

'Let's go.'

Private Woodley picked up the oars and rowed back to dry land.

8

Eloise stood in the centre of the reception centre.

She had received a visit from a member of the borough engineer's team even though it was Sunday morning. She was the chair lady of the local volunteer services and formed part of the King Canute Rescue Operation.

Her watch showed five minutes past eleven. Her volunteers had made welcome bundles with donations from the local community: food, bedding, clothes, nappies, baby products, toiletries, and toys. They had turned classrooms into makeshift dormitories, checked medical kits and filled tea urns. The flood victims would need a meal and a bed for a few nights, until they left to stay with friends or relatives, or found accommodation.

She noticed the soldier immediately he entered the reception centre. She watched him cross the hall. His step was confident, a combination of military precision and the arrogance of youth. She guessed he was twenty-five years old and from the local barracks. The soldier approached and stood before her. He was close enough to touch. His eyes were beautiful, the darkest brown, with sweeping black eyelashes.

'Sergeant Barrett at your service, Ma'am. I have received orders to report here. My men are on their way.'

The sergeant saluted.

'Ma'am.'

Despite his formality, the sergeant's expression was cocksure, almost brash, but when he met Eloise's gaze, a redness crept into his skin, and he averted his eyes. She detected a thread of anger within him.

She smiled.

'Well, thank you, Sergeant Barrett. Yes, I am in charge here and help is required.'

She inclined her head towards the main doors.

'The flood victims will arrive soon. When they enter the building, their names and addresses need to be checked, also, whether they have any medical issues. Those with serious injuries will have been taken to hospital, but we have a first aid station here for minor injuries, and one of my volunteers is a nurse. The flood victims will need help with their belongings. They will arrive with anything they were able to salvage before they left their homes. Oh, and some will bring their pets.'

'Understood, Ma'am.'

Eloise felt his gaze as it lingered on her breasts, the curve of her neck, her face.

'Thank you, Sergeant. Oh, and if you or your men require refreshments just ask. There will be plenty here later.'

'Yes, Ma'am. Thank you.'

He turned on his heels and left.

She smiled to herself, smoothed down her pinafore and entered the kitchen.

The flood victims arrived from rescue points scattered along the coast. As their numbers increased, the smell of the sea pervaded the hall and saltwater puddles formed like man-made rock pools. Some wore scant clothing covered only by a blanket, whilst others carried bundles of possessions. Small children clung to their parents and clutched toys. Cats in baskets hissed at dogs, dogs tugged at their leads and barked back.

'Where do we go, love?'

'Can we sleep here tonight?'

'I can't find my husband. Do you know where he is?'

'My mother-in-law lost her hearing aid. Can you help her?'

'I've got no nappies for the little 'un.'

'I've lost my false teeth.'

'My children need food.'

'I can't believe we've lost him.'

'Our house was flattened.'

'We've lost everything.'

'He's a good dog. He won't bite you.'

A cacophony of anxiety filled the hall.

The volunteers showed the flood victims the makeshift dormitories and the canteen area. The smell of food caused a murmur of urgency and a long queue formed around the hall.

As the flood victims sat and ate their first hot meal, they talked of their experiences of the last twenty-four hours. They described a normal Saturday evening when they visited friends, sat in front of their fires, or retired early to bed. They were oblivious to the toxic mix of the Atlantic storm and the spring tide, and it came upon them without warning. They spoke of the sheer ferocity and speed of the water, and how it engulfed their homes, floated furniture up to ceilings and swirled up staircases. The moment when beds were surrounded by water, and children cried for their parents, their pets, and toys. The frantic searches for glasses and false teeth. The removal of battens from ceilings to escape the water and get their families into lofts or onto roofs. Their agony, as they comforted the sick and injured, and waited in the dark for the rescue services. The army, police, fire, ambulance services and the local community. The men who waded shoulder-high in freezing water and carried children and the elderly to safety. Their despair for those who drowned including children. The women on the shoreline who provided blankets, hot tea, or donated clothes and their own rationed food. The offer of spare rooms to whole families and their pets, and those at the reception centre.

It was the start of stories that were told and retold down through the generations.

9

Dorothy managed to sleep for a few hours after Derek left. She awoke to the click of the letterbox as the Sunday newspaper fell onto the mat. She was surprised the paper boy managed to get through the flood water at the bottom of the hill and made a mental note to increase his Christmas box. She sipped her tea and unfolded the newspaper.

The front-page displayed photographs of an angry sea together with an article.

The east coast of England has been hit by a spectacular Atlantic storm and an exceptionally high spring tide. Its sheer strength and ferocity sunk the 'Princess Victoria' in the Irish sea with a loss of 127 people, including all women and children. It is estimated the storm has destroyed almost a third of the Scottish fishing fleet and uprooted and decimated several million trees across the Scottish landscape.

Overnight it made its way south down the east coast of the country. The northerly winds increased the hurricane force of the wind. The predicted sea levels rose and the tide hardly ebbed. No warning was given by the authorities, and it caught everyone by surprise.

The effect of this weather phenomenon can be seen today along the east coastline. It is a scene of devastation, destruction, and loss of life.

She closed the pages and emitted a small cry. She wanted to telephone family and friends to check they were safe, but the phone lines were dead. She got dressed and cleaned the bungalow, ironed Derek's shirts, and cooked a meal for him. But by seven o'clock in the evening she was still alone. She took a hot bath, made herself a light supper of cheese on toast and turned on the radio.

The local news reader spoke of the plight of lives lost in the flood. The destruction of homes and how the rescue teams were hampered by a lack of communication. The efforts of the emergency services, the volunteers, and the soldiers. The report reminded Dorothy of the civilian effort during the last world war. However, the most concerning aspect of the broadcast was the report about one of the islands, the one she always visited with Derek when it held its summer fete.

Despite several attempts today, rescue teams were unable to cross the road bridge, the main access way onto the island. At three o'clock this afternoon a reconnaissance plane was sent out to locate any survivors. The pilot reported the island was submerged, buildings destroyed and the farming community devastated.

There was no sign of life.

10

Monday 2nd February 1953

The clock struck one o'clock in the morning.

George lay in bed. His red rimmed, unblinking eyes refused to surrender to sleep. Two hours earlier the barometer showed minus eight and forecast a further drop in temperature and gale force winds throughout the coming day. Their supplies were limited and there was no sign of any rescue or even contact from the mainland.

He sighed.

He wanted to hear the familiar sound of his cattle, their early morning remonstrations for attention and their evening calls before they settled for the night. But they had gone from the farmyard and only his pigs remained bedded down in the safety of their pigsties. He considered getting out of bed to check the yard again, but it was pointless; he was already familiar with the featureless landscape of black water. The tide, with its easy rhythm and inundation, had once again flowed through the breaches in the sea wall and covered the land for a second night.

We will get out of this. We will make good.

Strokes of silver and pearl streamed through the window and lit the room.

He cradled his head and leant back on his pillow. His

thoughts returned to his surviving cattle marooned on high ground, in freezing conditions and without food or fresh water. He loved cattle. He remembered when his father brought his first herd to the farm. They had been excellent breeders and produced healthy calves for the next generation. His own herd was just as strong, with their quality strain of stock and easy temperament. Somehow, he must get them back to the yard. He could not bear to lose any more.

He put his hands together and prayed.

He opened his eyes and followed the plaster cracks in the ceiling. He smiled as he recalled Annie's complaints, when loose particles fell and woke her during the night.

If only our problems were that easy now.

He looked across to the window.

'Out there is my life. There is no other life for me and my family.'

He spoke to no one and yet he spoke to everyone.

He turned towards Annie. Despite her deep sleep, the muscles in her face were tense, and her breathing came in small gasps as if she was seeking out air. He recalled the first time they met. She was the girl from the big capital city, who had never set foot on a farm and knew nothing of the country way of life. But he was captivated by her the moment he saw her, and a year later they married.

Annie, our children, mother, and father. I must keep them safe.

His eyes misted. An image of the submerged gate in the cattle yard entered his head and the cold fear began to rise within him. He suppressed the sensation.

I must keep them safe.

He wondered how his father's smallholding fared in the flood. The cottage and land were occupied by tenants, a plan invoked by his father as he advanced in years. At the same time, he had handed Butterwood Farm over to George and Annie, although his parents continued to live with them in the farmhouse. His father required time to let go of Butterwood Farm.

He forced himself back to the present.

Yesterday should have been our family day.

Every Sunday the whole family attended church. And after the service, whilst Annie and his mother spoke with the vicar, he slipped away with his father to the public house, to 'reflect on the sermon', before they returned home for lunch. Then in the evening, when the children pleaded to stay up and were shooed upstairs by Annie and his mother, he sat with his father, a bottle of brandy between them, as they caught the last warmth of the fire.

We will get out of this. We will make good.

11

Within a few hours, streaks of light appeared in the east. George's body felt leaden. He heaved himself out of bed, splashed his face with cold water and pulled on his clothes.

As he rowed across the yard, the dawn light evolved into a dim, cold murkiness. The dank air permeated and chilled his body and caused a dull ache in his bones.

Josh had arrived and stood by the pigsties. George moored the boat and waded towards him. Josh spat out a slither of straw and nodded to the pigs.

'They're doing fine.'

The pigs put their snouts to the ground and nuzzled for food.

'Aye, one good thing.'

He brushed droplets of water from his oilskins. They checked the water buckets, mixed up more meal and placed the containers in the pigsties.

'Did you hear that?'

George walked a few steps and looked up, but the dull morning sky revealed nothing. And then it came again, a distant, incessant hum, like a droning bumble bee. The men scanned the sky. He turned to Josh.

'Do you think that's a...'

'I think it might be...yes!'

The sky filled with the unmistakable sound of an aircraft engine. There was a pause, the men shouted at each other and began to wade towards the boat.

'It's getting closer,' said George. 'He needs to see us.'

He clambered into the boat and trailed a leg in the water as Josh pulled hard on the oars. The noise in the sky continued. George stood up, shaded his eyes, and scanned the bland blanket above him. He pointed into the distance.

'There he is!'

He jumped up and down. The boat rocked from side to side and Josh drove the oars into the mud.

The plane increased in size, its wings square as it approached the farm. The men drew in great gulps of air and filled their lungs. Then they waved their arms wide and frantic, and shouted until their voices became hoarse. The plane got closer and its engine roared. Within seconds, it dipped down, flew over the farm, and climbed back into the sky. The men watched as the plane receded and disappeared into the grey horizon.

The sky was silent.

'Do you think he saw us?'

Josh scanned the sky with squinted eyes.

'I am sure he did.'

But George's jaw was set rigid, and a deep furrow crossed his brow.

Derek had been in the operations room at Essex headquarters since he left Dorothy in the early hours of Sunday morning. His adrenaline and the intense activity of those around him had carried him along, but he craved to return home, and slip between the cool, clean sheets of his own bed. Suddenly, a buzz of excitement replaced the subdued conversations of his colleagues, and a report was placed on his desk.

He eyed the document for several seconds. He placed

his hand on the report and turned the first page. The report contained information from the owner of a private light aircraft, a local man who knew the island, was aware of its geography and the location of the populated areas. Within the last hour, he had flown over the island and checked for survivors. At first, he saw an island submerged with no sign of life, but when he flew low over other parts, he saw desperate people scattered on rooftops or sat in boats.

Derek did not hesitate and with one final burst of energy he actioned a rescue plan. Whilst the tide was out, military DUKW transportation together with army trucks and medical transport, would attempt to cross the road bridge onto the island. If that was not possible or too dangerous, then the flatties would be deployed to rescue the islanders.

The tide was due in four hours.

'Go now,' said Derek. 'We can't leave them another night.'

12

George opened the bedroom window and looked across the submerged fields in the direction of the sea wall.

A dot of something appeared on the horizon. He picked up and focused his binoculars. A speck of a boat showed on the distant waves. He refocused his binoculars and muttered under his breath.

'Come on! Move!'

The boat seemed to stand still on the water. He kept his binoculars fixed on the boat. After a while, it got closer, and came across the submerged fields towards the farmhouse.

George ran out onto the landing.

'Annie! They're coming! Get the children ready!'

She appeared in a doorway, her eyes anxious, expectant.

'Are they coming for us, George!'

'Yes, my darling, they are. Thank the Lord. Get the children ready.'

She moved from one room to another and took a last look at their home. She stifled a sob, picked up her bag and ran into the children's bedroom.

'Children, we are going on a boat ride this morning.'

She fixed her face into a smile.

'Now, find your favourite toy and bring it with you.'

The children scrambled in all directions. Val looked for her story book. John searched for Bun, his toy rabbit.

'Where's Olive? I want to play with Olive.'

Dennis began to look under the bed. Douglas crawled in front of him.

'Olive is with her brothers and sisters. Now, where's your bear Dennis? And Douglas, I can see your blue tractor. Look! It's over there.'

She pointed and guided the boys towards their toys.

'Come here, children.'

She dressed them in their winter coats, wrapped scarves and pulled on hats and mittens.

George spoke to his father.

'We will row out to that first hedgerow and guide them back to the farm. What with the weather and the muck underwater, they'll need our help.'

He looked at his watch. It was just after half past nine in the morning. They pulled on their oilskins and waded to the flattie. George rowed out of the yard. As they travelled between the tops of the main gate posts his mouth became dry and he began to perspire. He licked his lips and pulled hard on the oars. They crossed the submerged track and entered the first field.

The rescue boat crept towards them in the morning light.

'They will take time to get to us.'

Their own boat rolled and dipped, and he felt the taste of salt heavy in his mouth as the east wind whipped across his face. They watched as the rescue boat drew near. It contained two men; one turned and waved. George shaped his hands around his mouth and shouted as loud as he could.

'Avoid that big tree.'

He pointed to his right. The top half of a large ash tree was visible, but its lower trunk lay submerged surrounded by barbed wire. One of the men raised his hand in acknowledgment as their boat lurched and veered in the water.

'We've got the worst weather for this,' muttered George.

'Good morning, gentlemen.'

His voice rang out through the air, bright and confident.

'Good morning to you, Sir. My name is Bill.'

The man was of middle age and possessed a certain stoutness. His face was rough and red from exposure to the elements. The man gestured to his companion.

'Arthur.'

Arthur nodded. He was young. His eyes were dark holes drawn in his face and stubble covered his chin. He rowed and chopped at the water with the oars, to keep the boat alongside George's boat. George waited for the men to regain their breath and pointed across the submerged track to the small wood of poplar trees.

'The farmyard is beyond those trees. We will lead you back through there. The water gets shallow near the farmhouse, and you will be able to get everyone into the boat.'

The men nodded.

'The sea wall is still intact back there,' said Bill.

His breathing heaved and caused his body to shudder.

'The road bridge is submerged...the DUKW and army trucks were unable to get this far inland...we had to carry the boat up and over the sea wall and row her across the fields.'

He forced air into his lungs.

'We must get you back to the sea wall... before the tide turns. There's a fishing smack waiting on the other side. It'll take you and your family over to the mainland where the rescue services will be waiting for you.'

'Righto,' said George. 'Let's get going.'

He began to row and led the small convoy across the submerged track, between the gate posts and into the farmyard. As they reached the back of the house, Annie appeared in the doorway.

The men dragged their boats onto the higher ground. They entered the kitchen and followed Annie upstairs. George bent down to his children and scooped them towards him. Four pairs of large, unblinking eyes looked at him.

'Now, children, you are going in the boat with Mummy and these nice men.'

George nodded towards Arthur and Bill. Arthur winked and waved at the children. George felt his throat constrict; he coughed and pulled air into his lungs.

'Be good and do what they tell you. I will stay here with Nanny and Grandad, but we will see you in a few days. And don't forget, be good for mummy.'

John and Val started to cry. Annie kissed the tops of their heads. Douglas and Dennis stood silent, their faces blank.

'You're not going to let them go in that boat son, are you? They will be drowned before they get to the sea wall.'

Annie gasped and raised her hand to her mouth. Moses continued.

'Tis a sad thing, but they won't make it.'

George pressed his children towards him. For the first time in his life, he held no respect for his father and looked away from him when he spoke.

'They will make it across. Yes, they will.'

John and Val clung to their father, their faces screwed tight, their sobs inconsolable. He took a deep breath and unpeeled their limpet fingers.

'Come on, my darlings.'

Annie moved their unlocked fingers away from

George. Val and John grasped hold of their mother's hands and continued to cry. Emma comforted Douglas and Dennis.

'It's only for a couple of days. Daddy must stay here and do a few things on the farm. You'll see him soon.'

George took off his cap and ran his fingers through his hair. He brushed his hand across his eyes and replaced his cap.

'Let's get you into the boat. Arthur and Bill will look after you.'

Within a few minutes Annie and the children were seated in the boat with the two men. George and Annie kissed. He whispered in her ear.

'Keep safe, my darling. I will be with you soon.'

They forced themselves apart.

Emma kissed Annie and the children and Arthur picked up the oars. George waded through the water and guided the boat between the gate posts. He gave the boat a final push and let go. As Arthur rowed across the submerged track, a helicopter suddenly appeared and hovered above them.

'Reconnaissance,' said Bill.

The helicopter swerved away and disappeared over the poplar trees.

George watched the boat leave. His heart hung like a lead weight in his chest. Although he had contradicted his father's grim prediction, he did not speak to Moses for the rest of the day. He thought of Annie and the children in the boat, her small frame and slight build and the children so young. The temperature was minus twelve. The force and speed of the wind had increased, and when the boat reached open water, fierce cross winds would make the journey even more treacherous. There was a risk of regression, even capsize. He prayed his family would be able to cope with the elements and tried not to think of the exhausted faces of their rescuers.

When the boat reached the edge of the field, Annie saw the expanse of water across to the sea wall for the first time. Her stomach churned up and down a mountain. She pulled Douglas and Dennis tighter into her arms and smiled at John and Val who sat opposite.

'Keep warm, my darlings. Cuddle each other, that's it.'

The gale force wind pulled the boat off course several times, and when Arthur rowed ten yards, he was pushed back five yards. His eyes showed dull and red, and he struggled to coordinate his arms and legs, but it was too dangerous to change places with Bill and the tide was due within the hour. Suddenly, a large wave hit and soaked the boat. Arthur heaved at the oars to counter the swell. Annie scanned the horizon but all she could see was a fearsome expanse of water stretched out before her.

The children locked their eyes on their mother.

'We're getting there,' said Bill.

They crept closer to the sea wall. She could see a group of policemen and soldiers as they stood and waited on top of the wall. Arthur wrenched at the oars, his arms as taut as piano strings.

'Not far now,' said Bill.

She looked for the fishing smack but could not see beyond the wall. She watched Arthur as he tried to row faster, but his arms did not respond, and a faint tremor ran through his body.

Suddenly, the boat hit the lower, grassy part of the sea wall. Strong arms held the boat steady whilst others lifted John and Val out of the boat and onto the surface of the wall. Annie helped Douglas and Dennis out of the boat.

'All hold hands, my darlings.'

She turned to both men; her eyes pricked with tears. 'Thank you. Thank you, so much.'

Arthur waited whilst Annie and the children were helped up and over the sea wall. His hands were covered in chilblains and blisters and his body seemed to deflate. He spent the last twenty-four hours up to his waist or shoulders in stinking, brackish water. He had rescued families trapped in their homes and coaxed, cajoled, or lifted them into his boat. On one occasion, when he rowed down a street, he saw the dead body of an elderly man lodged in the branches of a tree. And when he reached his destination and entered the house, he met a father who held his dead child in his arms.

Arthur's hands started to shake. He tried to stand but could not control his arms and legs.

Distant voices shouted.

A blackness engulfed him.

13

'Thank goodness you're here!'

Bessie hugged and kissed Annie and the children. She was a lady of generous proportions, and her hugs enveloped them with large cushions of soft, warm flesh.

'You've had a terrible time. Come and get warm.'

Annie and the children crowded around the fire. They were a beleaguered group, with their bedraggled clothes and exhausted expressions.

'Here you are.'

She gave Annie a cup of tea.

'You drink that, and when the children have warmed up, I will take them up to their rooms. We will have lunch soon and then you can rest.'

Annie gave a wan smile.

Within minutes Tom arrived. He was a small slim man with fair hair and a smooth complexion. His physical appearance was a stark contrast to the rugged, dark features and muscular body of his brother George, but their blood link showed in their identical mannerisms.

Tom hugged Annie with his thin, muscular arms.

'George has stayed behind on the farm with mum and dad. They will join us in a few days.'

He gave her another hug.

'George will be fine, Annie. The worst is over now.'

Annie did not contradict Tom. However, she knew

until the sea wall was repaired, the daily tides would run back through the breaches and the island would remain vulnerable to the higher spring tides that came every fourteen days throughout the year.

She accepted a second cup of tea from Bessie and sat by the fire. She was no longer cold and wet, but her body felt drained. She yearned for a warm, soft bed, where she could pull the covers over her head and have a dreamless sleep. A sleep free of life-threatening flood waters, destroyed houses and death. And when she awoke, she would be back at the farmhouse, by her fire and in her kitchen as if the flood had never happened.

She was distracted by the excited shouts of the children from above, followed by footsteps and the soothing tones of Bessie's voice. She leant back and closed her eyes. The last thing she remembered was the sound of muffled whispers and giggles, accompanied by the pad, pad, pad of small feet back and forth across the ceiling.

The midday tide re-entered through the breaches in the sea wall. George noticed the flow of the water was not so fierce and there was a slight reduction in its level. The high spring tide had gone but the next one was due in fourteen days.

'Let's have another go at the cattle. Get them off that high ground and back to the yard.'

Josh rowed to the surviving haystack. It stood on elevated ground and still held dry hay. They cut into the side of the stack, bound the hay into bundles and placed it in the boat.

The cattle showed little interest when their visitors arrived. They had endured another night exposed to the elements and looked dejected. George counted thirty cattle.

'Good, they've survived the night.'

He pointed to a fence post.

'Moor up there.'

Josh placed the oars in the bottom of the boat and hooked the rope over the post.

'Here.'

He passed Josh a length of rope and pushed a bundle of hay towards him.

'Strap it to your back if you can. We must get them through this water and herd them back to the yard. And remember, keep well away from me. The cattle will be hungry and might crush or trample us if we get too close to each other.'

They checked their bundles and waded through the water. As they approached the remaining herd, one heifer stepped forward. The rest of the herd followed and lumbered into the water.

'Steady, steady.'

The cattle's pace was slow and hesitant, and one unfortunate beast got trapped in barbed wire and could not be rescued. But the smell of the hay attracted the remaining cattle, and they followed the men back to the yard.

'We've lost those stalls at the back of the farmhouse. We must try and double them up in the remaining stalls. Ready?'

Josh nodded. The cattle stood in small groups; they could smell the hay and began to move.

'What about if...No! Wait!'

The cattle gathered momentum and began to climb onto a half-submerged midden.

'Stop! Stop!'

The men waved the bundles of hay at the cattle and continued to shout at them. However, the weaker cattle fell beneath the hooves and bodies of the stronger ones, and by the time, the men had pulled, shoved, and slapped the cattle off the midden and into the stalls, ten lay dead.

There were nineteen left.

Bessie cooked Annie and the children a lunch of lamb stew and apple pie. As they ate, John and Val told their own stories of the flood, their impression of the great sweep of water and their description of the farmhouse and yard. Tom pushed back his chair.

'I need to check the cattle.'

The children left the kitchen and played in hushed quietness or slept in clothed heaps around the sitting room. Annie defied the call to sleep and attempted to help.

'You look "all in" love,' said Bessie, as she cleared the plates from the table.

'Why don't you go and have a lie down. I can watch the children for you.'

Annie forced a smile.

'I am a little tired, Bessie, but I'm fine. It would be nice to be able to give the children a bath before they go to bed.'

'Of course, my dear, but you must rest. Just for an hour. You need to look after yourself. It has been a terrifying and worrying time for you.'

'Yes, you're right. I'll go up in a moment. And thank you for the bath. I will sort out the children later.'

She accepted the tea Bessie pushed towards her and warmed her hands around the cup. She wondered how George was coping at the farm. They had waited hours to be rescued, then when it did happen it was so quick, with rushed hugs and hurried goodbyes.

I might not see him again.

She fought back tears and finished her tea.

'Actually, I'll get the children bathed now.'

She stood and pushed her chair under the table.

'I'll be back down.'

'Don't you worry about coming back down, I'll come up in a bit and see if you need any help. The towels are by the tub and if you want extra bedding let me know. Then promise me, you'll get some rest.'

Annie nodded. She corralled the children and followed them up the stairs. As she reached the last few steps, her knees wobbled, and she stumbled. She gripped the handrail and stood still for a few moments. She was glad the children were ahead of her.

'Val, darling, you don't need to do that.'

She waited whilst her daughter stopped folding some towels and placed them back on the chair.

'Will we see Olive again?'

Val had the same penetrating gaze as her brother John.

'Yes, of course we will, Val. Why don't you show me our room? Wait...'

Noises came from the boys' bedroom.

'Douglas! Dennis!'

Annie ran towards them as they bundled and scrapped on the floor. Their fighting was vicious; arms punched, and legs kicked as cries and shouts rolled into one frightening brawl.

'Stop it at once!

She separated them.

'Now, no more! Go and sit on your bed.'

The twins slumped onto the opposite ends of the bed, their faces wet with tears, their arms folded. She sat next to John on his bed and put her arm around his shoulders.

'You're very quiet.'

He did not reply. She hugged him.

'Your bed looks nice and comfy.'

His lower lip quivered.

'What's the matter, John dear?'

'We left Bun behind. We left him there.'

He started to cry. She hugged and rocked him.

'My dear, I'm so sorry. Yes, we did forget Bun, but he'll be fine. Daddy will look after him.'

'But I want him now!'

His cries turned into loud wails and sobs.

'Well...there's nothing I can do now. But he is safe with Daddy, Nana, and Grandad. We'll see Bun when we go home.'

She kissed him, smoothed his hair, and cupped his face with her hands.

'Now, as my eldest and favourite boy, I think you should get in the nice warm bath first.'

Later that evening, John asked again for Bun. He wanted his rabbit with the smooth velvet fur and wobbly head. Whose bright bead eyes followed him around the room as he waited to be picked up and cuddled. Somehow Annie and Bessie persuaded him to take a corduroy cushion to bed with him instead. And when Annie entered his room the following morning, he lay asleep, the cushion clasped to his chest.

14

Eloise's body ached, her energy was wrung out and her mind a turmoil of emotion. It had been a busy day at the reception centre, but most of the volunteers had gone home to their families, the chaos of the last two days a stark reminder of how one's life could suddenly change. A quiet momentum ensued as parents recited bedtime stories, tucked their children into makeshift beds and kissed them goodnight.

Eloise cast one last look around the reception hall and entered the kitchen.

It was half lit but she could see it was tidy. Cleaning rags soaked in a bucket of bleach and crockery and cutlery lay in rows on the serving counter, ready for breakfast the next morning. As she hung up her pinafore, she sensed the presence of another person. Barrett appeared from the unlit shadows and stood before her. She jumped and put her hand to her chest.

'My goodness! What a surprise!'

The sergeant's dark complexion was pale, and his uniform was spattered with muddy water stains. He took off his cap.

'I'm sorry, Ma'am, I didn't mean to frighten you.'

'Well, good evening, Sergeant Barrett. What can I do for you? Have you eaten?'

He answered both questions with one answer.

'Not since midday.'

He rubbed his eyes. She moved past him and pulled out a chair.

'Here, sit down. I will find you something. It won't take a minute.'

'Thank you. Oh, and please call me Jim. I know your name is Eloise, one of your volunteers told me.'

She smiled as he slumped onto the chair. His eyes followed her as she walked across the room. She returned to the table and placed a glass of fruit squash in front of him. He drained the liquid from the glass and wiped the back of his hand across his mouth.

'You've had a busy day.'

She picked up the empty glass. He gave a nod and half closed his eyes. She walked back to the counter and disappeared through a back door. A few moments later, she returned with the remains of a cold joint of beef and a half-loaf of bread. She cut two thick slices from the joint and broke off a hunk of bread.

'Here you are.'

She placed the plate of food and a fresh glass of squash in front of him.

He stared at her breasts. She returned to the counter. Her heels clattered on the tiled floor and the hem of her skirt rhythmed with her hips. He waved a partially eaten piece of bread in her direction.

'Thanks for this.'

'Hard, dirty work, what you've done today, Jim. I'm sure many people will be grateful.'

She reached the table again and placed more bread on his plate.

'Sorry, there's no beer. A stiff gin and tonic would slip down a treat too.'

She giggled and put her hand to her mouth. He continued to watch her, his mouth full of food. She reorganised the crockery on the counter. Then she reorganised it again and patted the sides of the plates. A few moments later, she returned to the table.

'Here you are.'

She placed a slice of apple pie in front of him. As she collected his empty plate, her fingers brushed the back of his hand.

Butterflies danced in her stomach.

'Thank you. I like something sweet.'

He looked at her as he bit into the pie and brushed the crumbs from his chin.

'Yes, a nice end to a meal.'

She smiled and shrugged her shoulders. He placed the last piece of pie in his mouth and pushed the dish away.

'What time does your husband expect you home?'

She picked up the empty dish.

'Oh, when I get there. He doesn't fuss about me.'

'You don't have to rush then.'

Before she could answer the kitchen door swung open. A young boy stood before them.

'Sorry, Miss. Me mam is asking, can we have more blankets *please.*'

He added the word 'please,' as if he suddenly remembered his manners. A colour rose in his cheeks, and he shuffled his feet.

'Oh! Why yes, of course!'

Her face developed a competitive pink glow.

'Well, I will be off. Thank you for the food.'

Barrett winked and replaced his cap.

When Eloise returned home, she found Fred sat by the fire alongside his stamp collection. He looked up, smiled, and nodded, but said nothing. No comment about the extraordinary events of the previous forty-eight hours, or any enquiry of her whereabouts away from home. Later, when she made hot cocoa, they sat together in silence and sipped their drinks, until Fred drained the dregs from his cup.

'Well, love, I'm off up now. Early start in the morning.'

He kissed her cheek, patted her shoulder, and retired to bed. And when she followed, she found him asleep, his snores in rhythm with the rise and fall of his body.

Eloise could set her watch by Fred.

Every night at six o'clock he arrived home from work, kissed her on the cheek and went to the bathroom. A quarter of an hour later, he reappeared with his tie removed and his shirt sleeves rolled-up. He sat down at the kitchen table and waited for his evening meal. On Fridays he finished work at five o'clock on the dot, and when he arrived home, he placed his pay packet on the kitchen table. Sometimes he complained about his bad back but said little else about his day at work.

They had nuptials every Saturday night, but within minutes he rolled over, and before she pulled down her night dress, he began to snore. Their conversation revolved around practical issues: the rationing of food, the shortage of abattoir workers, a puncture in his bicycle tyre, and Christmas shutdown at the meat factory.

Intimate conversation was never on the agenda.

Dorothy looked at the clock on the mantlepiece. The hands showed just after eight o'clock in the evening. She was still alone. She sat by the fire, a magazine on her lap, her hands folded on the open pages.

Every Monday evening, Derek took her to the Plaza Club for their ballroom dance lesson. She felt disappointed they would miss it, especially as she had saved up her allowance and purchased a new pair of dancing shoes. She drummed her fingers on the arms of the chair. They last danced on Saturday evening, but for her, the highlight came when she met the new doctor from the local surgery. She adored his crisp English accent and impeccable manners. She could not recall his wife's name but remembered her dress; it was unspectacular in colour and style.

She listened to the updates on the local radio station. People remained cut off from their homes; the telephone lines were still down, and the electricity supply unrestored. Her lower lip trembled, and a quiver of anxiety ran through her. She closed the magazine, placed it down the side of the chair and sipped her second glass of sherry.

I must check Derek's supper.

She opened the oven door. The minced beef pie, carrots, and rice pudding looked dark and dry. She sighed, retrieved the dishes from the oven and placed them on the table. She returned to her chair, took another sip of sherry, and let out a small appreciative hiccup. Her thoughts fluttered like a moth around a light. The local radio mentioned about the female volunteers who helped with the flood effort.

How did they manage to leave their homes and not return for several hours, without a complaint of neglect from their husbands?

Darts of envy pricked at her. She had wanted to train as a nurse before she married Derek, but her mother disagreed.

'Marriage my girl. Marriage, having a family and looking after your husband and children. That's the path for you.'

Her mother's response had been final, and they never spoke about it again.

And now? Her mind turned one way, then the other.

She had played her part within the marriage, cared for their two sons, and ran the home. She looked around her. She had a nice kitchen and a nice house, and Derek was a good man with a job that opened some doors for them.

Things would have been so much better if Derek got promotion. But it's too late now.

He rarely spoke to her about his work, and when he did, it was a light, watered-down version so she was able to understand. She finished her sherry, rose from the chair, and patted her hair. She crossed the room in a slow, careful, manner and retired to the bathroom.

Derek turned his key in the front door and stepped over the threshold. The still, dark hour suited his mood after the noise and chaos of the operations' room.

'Derek!'

Dorothy wore a pink winceyette nightdress, and her hair was set in rollers and covered by a net.

'I cooked dinner but...'

He held up his hand, walked past her and entered their bedroom. He took off his glasses and removed his clothes and shoes. He slipped between the bed covers and pulled them over his head. Dorothy let out a small sigh, patted her rollers and checked her net. Her unbathed husband lay asleep in their bed. She stepped forward and removed her pillow, checked it was clean and retreated to the spare bedroom.

15

Tuesday 3rd February 1954

Jake and Reggie set out at dawn. They had always walked the wall together to check for repairs and George Hadley readily gave them time off to do so. But this time it was different; they had to report back to the army officers on the island to enable the information to be collated and for the repairs to begin. The men rowed and punted the flattie to their allocated section. When they were unable to take the boat any further, they plunged into the freezing water and waded towards the wall.

Jake nodded to the left.

'The "farmer's teeth" have gone.'

The line of wooden stakes had disappeared beneath the fetid water, lost to the elements.

'Mind the barbed wire,' said Reggie. 'If you get trapped in that lot, it will tear at your feet and pull you under.'

The barbed wire had been used to secure and fence in livestock, but all that remained were coiled, hazardous loops, some visible, some submerged. They clambered onto the wall and walked along the top.

'We can get across this one.'

They jumped across the small breach.

'These sections of the wall have held up against the first surge of the tide, but the scouring out at the back of the wall was caused by the receding waves.'

They studied the damage. After several minutes they continued along the wall. Suddenly, the men stopped.

'By Christ! Look at the size of it!'

The breach was hundreds of feet wide and surrounded by crumbling rocks. They peered into the huge, bottomless crater.

'In all my time of doing this work, I have never seen anythin' like it.'

Jake's eyes widened as he studied the breach.

'Imagine the pressure from the tidal surge to create a breach like that, said Reggie. 'It's goin' to take some work to get that filled.'

The men stood in silence, their respect for the sea a mixture of admiration and terror. The next spring tide was due on 14th February and would reach its peak a few days later. If the wall was not repaired to hold back the tide, it would bring further flooding and destruction to the land.

Dorothy hesitated. She knew Derek was exhausted, but also, she knew he despised rising any later than half past eight in the morning even if it was Christmas Day. She took a deep breath and opened the bedroom door. He was still asleep. She placed a cup of tea on the bedside table. He lifted his head and tried to focus but dropped back onto the pillow and closed his eyes. She sat on the edge of the bed and watched his body move up and down as he took each breath. She felt nervous and twisted her handkerchief in ever smaller knots. She tried to think of an explanation as to why she had let him sleep on, or why she had not awoken him earlier, in readiness for either mood when he woke up.

The muscles along his jawline were tight even in sleep, and the lines around his mouth etched deep and long. After a short while he put his hands to his face and rubbed his eyes. He propped himself up on one elbow, reached across for the cup, and sipped the lukewarm tea. She shifted her position on the bed.

'Sorry I did not return earlier yesterday.'

He replaced the cup.

'I intended to come home late morning but got held up. I couldn't get away.'

His smile made a gradual appearance. She gave an inward sigh of relief. She simpered and patted the covers. By the time she had collected his empty cup and saucer and crossed the bedroom, he was asleep.

Dorothy's reflection in the hall mirror showed a stout woman with a round face and green eyes. Although her eyes were her best feature, they expressed disapproval so often it was difficult to remember them for any other reason. She wished she could be less fierce, more gentle and inviting towards people, but only harsh words came from her lips and somehow the right words never came out. She smoothed her hair and placed her hat into position; she pushed the pin hard through its fabric and rolled her lips together.

The weather was still bad, but it was Tuesday and on Tuesdays she always cooked minced beef and fried onions for dinner. She buttoned her wool coat, pulled on her gloves, and picked up her basket. She recalled her mother's advice.

'Learn to cook and you will make a man happy. They like regular meals and a pretty wife to come home to.'

She received further advice on other occasions.

'Men need looking after. You must spoil them, meet their every need, then they will stay.'

Dorothy felt a sense of doomed entrapment as if she was stumbling around a lifelong maze. She shut the front door and walked down the path. The lower road was still flooded, but the upper road to the shops was clear of water. Her face pinched cold, and her brisk pace caused the flurries of snow to separate.

The high street was busy with shoppers and a different atmosphere hung in the air. She reached the butcher's shop but did not enter. Instead, she followed the crowd of people, walked to the top of the hill, and sheltered under the canopy of a building. Opposite, people bustled about in front of the main entrance to the school. Soldiers delivered boxes whilst others spoke to members of the public. She recognised some of the women who helped the soldiers.

'They need more blankets in there. Here, take these.'

'Those potatoes look heavy, let me carry them for you.'

'The baker is bringing more fresh bread this morning.'

'Let the ambulance through, please.'

She watched as the ambulance men ran into the school with an empty stretcher. A few moments later they reappeared carrying a young girl, her face white, as her mother walked alongside and held her hand.

'Can I help you, Madam?'

The soldier's brisk, polite manner reminded Dorothy of her youngest son.

She looked towards the entrance.

'I was wondering what was going on.'

'The school has been turned into a reception centre for the flood victims, Madam. Were you looking for someone?'

Dorothy shuddered and shook her head.

'No, I'm not thank you, officer.'

As they spoke, three women walked past carrying bundles of clothes in their arms. They crossed the road, entering the school. The soldier anticipated her query.

'They are delivering clothes and blankets for the flood victims. Are you interested in helping the flood victims, Madam? I can introduce you to the lady in charge if you wish.'

He gave an encouraging smile. Dorothy felt an inward quiver.

'Yes! No! Well...I don't know. No, I could not possibly....my husband would not...'

The soldier waited. His smile had gone but his eyes were enquiring and gentle.

'Well, if you change your mind, Madam, just go into the school. You will receive a warm welcome.'

'Yes, thank you, I will think about it.'

She retraced her steps.

Yes, I would love to volunteer, but what would Derek say? How could I cook his dinners and iron his shirts if I wasn't at home? What would the chief borough engineer, Mr Bates, and his wife think? Perhaps I ought to find out if they know anyone who has volunteered and what they think about it.

By the time she had returned to the parade of shops, the idea of becoming a volunteer lay buried beneath layers of excuses. The butcher's shop smelt of ageing meat and unwashed bodies. Customers huddled together and chatted as their hot breath steamed up the windows. She made her purchase and hurried home. She turned the key in the lock and crept into the hallway. She heard movement in the lounge and opened the door. Derek was dressed, but he was oblivious to her presence and paced up and down the room. She felt the creeping nervousness return. He stopped mid track.

'Oh, there you are.'

His voice was perfunctory, and he looked at his watch. Dorothy gave an apologetic smile.

'Sorry. I...'

Her voice faded away. She pulled off her gloves and removed her hat. When she unbuttoned her coat, a slight tremble ran through her fingers, and she began to fumble.

'Sorry, I...'

She gathered the items together and left the room.

An hour later she placed a dish of minced beef and fried onions on the table. She served the food and pushed a plate towards Derek. They ate in silence.

16

5th February 1953

George waded back to the farmhouse. When he reached higher ground, he removed his cap and scratched the top of his head. He replaced his cap and swirled the toe of his wader boot around in the mud strewn water.

Three days earlier, Annie and the children crossed the perilous flood waters to the mainland. Since then, he had heard nothing, no information about whether they got across and reached a safe destination. And the alternative?

No! I can't think of it.

The cold fear returned. He pushed it away and tried to keep himself busy. Moses did not approach him and stayed in the shadows all day and by early evening his mother took to her bed with a chill. The following morning, when he checked the open fields, he saw thousands of white threads floating on the water. When he got closer, he realised they were dead earthworms, drowned in the flood and driven to the surface.

The farmhouse roared silent in the morning dawn, its doors and windows closed, and no light came from within. Before the flood he rose in tandem with nature, heard the cacophony of the dawn chorus as it wrapped around the sunrise, and the cockerel's piercing alarm call as the bird strutted big and bold across the yard. But now, when dawn arrived, it was a quiet and introspective affair. There was no dawn chorus or cockerel, only a few muted birds warbled in the desolate landscape, whilst rabbits remained trapped in trees and dead livestock lay half visible in the water.

Josh arrived.

George waved at his manager and beckoned him over.

'How are you this morning?'

He raised his eyes.

'Oh, no electric, no telephone, the fire barely burning and the wife, well, she's miserable.'

George nodded. He thought Josh harsh on his wife and felt sympathy towards her. As his farm manager, Josh was allowed to stay on the island and work on the farm, but his wife was left alone in a flood damaged home and expected to get on without support or company.

Josh turned to George.

'I saw the wall walkers earlier this week.'

He turned up the collar of his jerkin and pulled it tight around his face.

'And the Mosquito planes. There were a few of 'em about. They were flying below the cloud. Suppose that's why they used them.'

'Aye, that must be right. They need to get those repairs finished. If they don't, that next spring tide will cause more havoc.'

He swirled the toe of his boot in the mud.

'They have started the repairs. My Uncle Peter who lives down by the creek, he rowed over this morning. He said the army was down at the wall yesterday, volunteers as well. There's a hell of a thing going on down there.'

He blew hard into his cupped hands.

'Good job the army is involved. Once we have sorted out here, we'll row over and look.'

Their conversation was interrupted by voices. A few moments later a flattie appeared. George recognised the man rowing the small boat, he was a local man who lived on the mainland. But the second man was a stranger to the island. He wore a thick woollen scarf wrapped around his neck and face, exposing only his eyes and the top of his head. He carried excess weight and clutched a clipboard.

The boat came to a bobbing halt. The second man stood up in the boat and looked at the surrounding water. He stepped forward, as if to get out of the boat, but hesitated and stepped back. The boat tilted and the rowing man dug the oars into the mud.

'Good morning to you,' shouted George. 'Can we help you?'

The man with the clipboard adjusted his balance. He lifted the bottom half of his overcoat up, as if to make a curtsey, and stepped out of the boat. Water topped his wellington boots.

George whispered under his breath.

'Has he got any sense?'

He suppressed a laugh as the man hugged his clipboard into his armpit, kept his coat hitched up and made tentative steps through the water. He could not understand why a man dressed in such attire would visit a flooded farm in the winter months. However, he was cautious, the man pulsed importance.

'Is this Butterwood Farm?'

'Yes, that's right,' said George.

'I am looking for a...a Mr George Hadley.'

George folded his arms.

'And why would you be looking for him?'

The water became shallow. The man dropped his

coat down and repositioned his clipboard. He walked across the final stretch of water and stopped in front of them.

'Anderton is the name. I am part of the Post Flood Operations Team. I oversee animal welfare.'

The man opened the clipboard, took a pencil from his pocket, and started to scribble.

'Well, I am George Hadley. This is my farm and Josh is my manager.'

The man's eyes flickered upwards. He nodded at George and ignored Josh.

George did not take to civilian workers; 'pen pushers' his father called them. He wanted to ask the man questions, questions which had been travelling around in his head like a merry-go-round all his waking hours. He wanted to know whether he would receive help to get his remaining livestock to safety and how they would be kept alive, and whether he was going to get any financial help from the government. But despite his worries he kept quiet. He was wary of officialdom and knew better than to appear to be causing trouble. The man pulled his scarf down from his face and pushed his chin free.

'I have come to check on your livestock, Mr Hadley.'

He scribbled and looked up.

'I need to know whether any have died and if so, how many. There is also the issue of water contamination. There are certain health regulations that require compliance.'

He continued to scribble. George lifted his cap and scratched his head.

'I have lost a lot of my cattle. When the flood hit, some drowned, some got killed when they tried to stampede, and some got stranded on higher ground. Then, when we got the stranded ones back to the yard, they panicked, and I lost a few more. My pigs are safe for the moment, but they need fresh food and water. My cattle need hundreds of gallons of fresh water every day. Can you help me with that? If my cattle drink any quantity of sea water, they'll be in trouble.'

'How many cattle have you lost and how many are still alive?'

The man continued to write.

'Before the flood we had seventy cattle. And now? Now we have no more than twenty. I have lost my best heifers they...'

'I don't need the detail. Just numbers, so I can report back.'

George seethed, but he zipped his mouth and looked straight ahead. The man marked his notes.

'I will have a look at your surviving cattle, also your pigs if they're nearby. I don't need to see any dead ones.'

George set off across the yard, and when the man slithered in the mud and almost fell, he did not slow or offer to help.

'Here they are.'

George made a sweeping, flamboyant gesture with his arm towards his surviving herd. One or two cattle twitched their ears, the rest remained inert and ignored the men. The man gave a cursory glance towards the stalls.

'Twenty out of seventy. Is that right?'

'Yes.'

The man counted the cattle.

'There are only nineteen here. Which is it nineteen or twenty?'

George scratched his head.

'Oh yes, I forgot. We lost one before we lost ten in the midden. Nineteen it is.'

'Where are your pigs?'

'This way.'

The man followed him to the pigsties. George leant over the gate and waited.

This man holds my future. How are we going to survive?

'That's it.'

The man drew his pencil across the page.

'What happens now?'

'Well today is Thursday. The animal welfare officers will be here next Thursday, and if you cannot show you can sustain your livestock, they will have to be destroyed.'

He looked at his watch and checked his notes.

'You have a week, Mr Hadley.'

George's eyes widened; this time he did not hesitate.

'I don't understand. If you slaughter them, I will have nothing! Our livelihood will be gone! As I said, they need fresh water every day and winter feed. We are too far inland to get them off the island. They need to stay here and be kept alive. I cannot... '

'The animal welfare officers will assess the situation when they visit next week.'

He nodded to the man who brought him in the boat and turned back to George.

'Mr Hadley, if the animal welfare officers determine you cannot sustain your livestock, they will be destroyed and removed from the island. As I said earlier, water contamination caused by dead animals, is a serious risk to public health and you must comply with the regulations.'

He tapped the clipboard and placed it under his arm.

'Now, I have other farms to visit. Good day to you.'

He pulled his scarf back across his face, straightened his overcoat, and made his way back to the waiting boat.

'Bloody fool.'

George kicked through the mud.

'I reckon that's the first time he's ever been on a farm. He hasn't got a clue. Not a bloody clue. He doesn't know and he doesn't care.'

17

Annie slipped out of bed and pulled the covers over Val's exposed shoulders. The child murmured but stayed asleep.

She crossed the landing to the boys' bedroom.

How peaceful they look.

She was relieved the children had slept well since their arrival at Tom and Bessie's farm, but a growing worry niggled and gnawed at her. John had reverted to the behaviour of a much younger child. He had chosen to bring Bun with him and shed inconsolable tears when he realised he left him behind. And the fighting between Douglas and Dennis, she had never seen such aggressive behaviour between them, and their unforgiving kicks and punches expressed a real intention to hurt. But Val's behaviour had not changed at all, and she continued to offer help like an adult with no outward sign of trauma.

Her suffering could be the worst of all of them.

Annie covered her face with her hands.

If only I knew he was safe.

She missed George's friendship, easy conversation and humour, his touch and most of all his love.

And Moses and Emma? Are they still at the farmhouse? Maybe they have left and gone to their smallholding. Or is that under water too? And Olive? Is she alive? What do I tell the children? She's been part of the family since John was born.

The sound of Tom's truck broke her thoughts. She watched from the window as he alighted from his vehicle and crossed the yard. It was just another day for him. Her intake of breath was sharp and pained her chest. She tried to breathe but her uneven gasps created a feeling of suffocation and overwhelmed her. Then the tears came; a wet flow of bitterness and resentment as she thought of their plight and the good luck of others. She took a deep breath, patted her chest, and dabbed at her face.

Bessie appeared in the doorway.

'I brought you some tea, love.'

Annie turned towards her hoping the dull morning light would hide her tear-streaked face.

'Oh, how kind, thank you.'

'Did you manage to get some sleep?'

'Yes, I did thank you, and the children did too.'

'There is bacon and eggs for breakfast, but don't rush, come down when you're ready.'

'Can we go outside, Mummy?'

'Can we see the cows?

'I want to see the pigs?'

'I asked first!'

Bessie untied her apron.

'Give me ten minutes and I will take you all outside to the pigs and cows.'

'Thank you, Bessie. Now, children, I want you to go upstairs and play while I talk to Uncle Tom. Aunty Bessie won't be long. And no squabbles or fighting!'

Annie did not have to ask Tom about George.

'I am going to try and get over to the island this morning. I have borrowed my neighbour's flattie and will take a box of food.'

The high street was busy. Women carried bundles of clothes and the men boxes of food, whilst soldiers from the local garrison mingled amongst them. Tom nudged his truck forward and followed the throng. When he arrived at the local school, he parked his truck and approached one of the soldiers.

'What's going on here?'

'This is the local reception centre for the flood victims, Sir. Are you delivering supplies for them?'

Tom blushed.

'No, no not this time. I am looking for my brother. The last I heard he stayed on the island at his farm. I need to get across to see him. Our parents are there too, they are elderly, I...'

'You won't be able to get across, Sir. The road bridge is manned by the army and not open to the public. I suggest you try again in a day or two.'

Tom pushed his way back through the tide of people and returned to his truck. When he reached the road bridge, a young soldier stepped out and signalled to him to stop. He wound down the window.

'What's your business, Sir. The public are not allowed on the island. The water levels are too deep.'

'My brother lives on the island with our parents. We farm Butterwood Farm together and I need to get across to deliver some food and to help with the livestock.'

Tom kept his gaze steady. He could not think of another reason to give other than joint ownership of the farm, even if it was not true. The soldier looked at his face and clothes and ran his eyes over the truck.

'I have my orders, Sir...'

'What about if I leave my truck here and one of your soldiers gets me across to the farm.' He gestured behind him. 'There's a flattie in the back. If I go now, I will be back before the tide turns.'

'Oh, very well. But make sure you are back, or I'll be for the high jump.'

Ten minutes later they were on their way.

'Good grief! I did not realise!'

Tom swivelled around in his seat and peered through the windows of the army truck.

'Yep, it's bad.'

The soldier wrenched at the steering wheel and caused them to jolt in their seats.

He eyed the soldier.

It's worse than bad, sonny, it's bloody devastation. Can they recover from this?

He curled his hands into fists and tightened the muscles in his arms; the tension travelled up to his neck and jaw.

The soldier stopped the truck.

'The water dips down deep from here, even with the tide out. I'll help you with the flattie.'

He checked his watch.

'I'll drive by at one o'clock. Make sure you are here.'

Tom stood beside the bobbing boat and looked around.

Right, which way...ah, yes.

'How is mother this morning?'

George wiped a piece of bread around his plate and soaked up the remains of the sausage fat.

'Oh, all right,' said Moses. 'She's had her tea.'

'I'll go up and see her in a while, but first, I need to see Josh and tell him about the pigs.'

The old man stacked the plates in the sink.

'It's just a little cough.'

Emma gave a weak smile. The tea was cold, untouched. Moses searched her face. His wife was not a vocal woman. Her message was in her actions, her looks, her behaviour. But in all the years of their marriage she had never stayed in bed and rose with him each day, even during her pregnancies. He swallowed hard.

'We are going to leave as soon as we can, Em. You need to be away from this wet and damp.'

He pulled the covers to her chin and kissed her cheek. It felt hot and feverish. He went downstairs, pulled on his thigh boots, and waded outside. A stiff breeze blew and caused fresh ripples on the water.

'Damn this weather.'

As he hunched into his oilskins and stamped his feet a small boat appeared in the far corner of the yard.

'Tom! Tom! How wonderful you are here!'

He pointed across the water.

'Come around this way.'

Tom rowed, then waded to the farmhouse.

'It's so good to see you.'

He slapped his son's back and hugged him like a bear. Tom gasped and laughed.

'How are you? Where is George? Is mother well? I've brought some food.'

'She's got a chill. Go up and see her.'

When George saw the empty flattie, his chest began to tighten.

Not another visit from that man, Mr Anderton. I thought he gave me a week.

He scratched his head. He had left Josh a few minutes before and not seen anyone on his return.

Maybe they are inside.

The farmhouse was quiet. Then he heard men's voices and a clatter on the stairs. Moses appeared followed by Tom. George felt the cold fear start to rise and tried to suppress it.

'Annie and the children are safe, George. They got across the water and are with us on the farm.'

For several seconds there was silence. George began to sway, and shuddering sobs rose in his throat. He gripped his brother's arms.

'He wanted to row across to the mainland to see Annie and the children, but I stopped him.'

Moses gave George a gentle shove.

'I told him he was no use to Annie dead in the water. But their leaving haunted him, I could see it in his face.'

George passed the back of his hand across his eyes.

'There's talk of allowing the farmers back and forth to the mainland,' said Tom.

'If that is true,' said George. 'I will be able to visit Annie and the children and bring back supplies.'

'We need to get your mother off the island. It's too damp here. She won't get better stuck upstairs, without warmth and proper meals.'

'I can loan you a vehicle, George. And you must come and stay with us, father. I don't know why I did not think of it before, but it has been so hectic, what with Annie and the children and running our own farm.'

George gripped his brother's shoulders.

'Thank you, Tom. Thank you for everything. I must go up and see mother. Tell her about Annie and the children.'

18

Barrett drove as close as he could to the sea wall, parked his truck and jumped out. He could see his men in the distance as they approached in a convoy of trucks. He was desperate for a cigarette. He exhaled into the freezing air, stamped his feet, and flexed his numb fingers.

The soldiers of the Royal Engineers had arrived on the island before daybreak and commenced work by flood light. They marked and dug out new culverts and ditches, to enable the daily ebbing tides to drain away from the land. However, they did not work on existing drainage systems, they were left to the local farmers.

'Get that drag moving!'

Barrett heard the farmers further along the sea wall, as they shouted at their farm workers. They were skilled in opening sluices, and clearing blocked ditches and culverts, and worked with little rest. Also, they were aware that when the blockages were cleared and the flood water drained out, they were a step closer to completion of repairs to the sea wall and a return to the island with their families.

His men arrived in their DUKWS and trucks. They unloaded wooden planks and formed makeshift tracks, ready to transport wooden piles and sandbags to the sea wall. The sergeant had been allocated a group of 'civvies' to assist him, civilian male volunteers who arrived from the mainland and reported to him each day. Private Woodley organised the men into gangs and kept them to task throughout the morning.

'Get to it, men. Heave...Get your shoulder to it.'

The men strained every muscle and limb as their laboured breathing, grunts and groans performed a duet with the screaming seagulls. They heaved, and pulled the wooden piles through the thick, knee-deep mud, up onto the wall and into the breaches. Other gangs mixed gravel, chalk, and hard core to fill the scour holes in the back of the remaining parts of the wall, or shovelled clay or sand into sandbags.

The final gang formed a line to get the sandbags to the breaches. They juddered and slithered in the suppurating mud, as they passed the sandbags along the line to the last man, who dropped each sandbag into the breach.

Private Woodley shouted down the line.

'We break in five minutes. For thirty minutes, men. No more.'

Barrett watched the women volunteers arrive and set up their stall next to the army trucks. Their hot soup and bread would supplement the civvies' own food and the soldiers' food brought from the barracks. Barrett walked amongst the women volunteers. He scrutinised their bodies and faces; as always, there were possibilities.

Eloise supervised the unloading of the hot soup and bread. When she turned around, Barrett stood in front of her.

'Good morning, Ma'am.'

His voice was professional, detached.

She felt a hot sensation creep up her neck and across her face. She tried to speak, but her throat constricted and strangled her words. She took a deep breath and exhaled in one slow release.

'Good morning, officer.'

She remembered not to mention his name.

'My men will be over in a few minutes.'

He turned to the women and winked.

'Now ladies, my men will be hungry. I'm sure you will look after them.'

Murmurs and giggles arose from the group. The sergeant's gaze lingered on the woman next to Eloise. She returned his gaze, her look was bold, a challenge. He walked past Eloise and spoke to the woman, just a few words about the wall and her voluntary work, enough to secure a future conquest.

Eloise understood why he spoke to her in a detached way. She was a married woman. But his lack of kind words and acknowledgment stung her, and when he spoke to the woman next to her, she felt tears prick the back of her eyes. She dropped to her knees and became busy under the stall as she looked for something, anything.

Barrett returned to his men. They had voracious appetites. They ate their own food, and the hot soup and bread, and returned to the wall with renewed vigour.

The afternoon darkened and the tide flowed back through the remaining breaches in the sea wall. The civvies returned home for a few hours' sleep, but when the tide ebbed in the early hours, they returned and started again. The shouts of the men cut across the 'bomp, bomp, bomp' of the Track Field Marshall tractors as they transported sandbags, and the exhaust embers showed orange and red against the flood lights in the night sky.

'There she goes,' said one farmer.

'What a beautiful sound!'

The men continued their endeavour over the hours,

days, and nights. They worked around the smaller daily tides. They worked in fog, sleet, and snow and through their own exhaustion. And when they returned to their families and spoke of their work on the sea wall, the older menfolk tapped the floor with their sticks and recalled their own youth, when they stood in the trenches, knee deep in mud, for a common purpose that would alter their lives forever.

19

It was a dull afternoon and the clouds hung motionless, like resting giants in the grey sky.

Barrett crossed the half-lit street, his step light and buoyant. He recognised a passer-by and stopped and spoke a few polite words. He liked to mix with the civilian population, it enabled him to assess their attitude to the army, and whether they were likely to cooperate during practice manoeuvres.

He tapped his top pocket; he needed a refill of 'baccy'. He walked further along the street and was about to enter the shop when a woman appeared in the window. She had her hands on her hips and swivelled her body as if to check the space around her. Barrett recognised the woman. She was one of the volunteers who helped Eloise at the sea wall a few days earlier. He whistled a soft, quiet tune and positioned himself under the nearest streetlamp.

The woman tucked a large roll of paper under her arm, hitched up her skirt and climbed a couple of steps up a small set of ladders. She was not his usual type. Although she was pretty, she was solid in the body, with thick set legs and muscular arms. But he recalled the bold glances she gave him when she stood next to Eloise at the sea wall, and he was confident she would remember him.

He wondered whether to enter the shop, make a

purchase and speak to her, or wait, and surprise her when she finished work. Barrett smiled and ran his fingers across his trouser fly. He was off duty until tomorrow afternoon. He leant against the lamp post and rolled his last cigarette.

The number of people in the street dwindled. It was dark and cold, and beyond the streetlamp lay a dank gloom. The sergeant lit his cigarette and drew the nicotine into his lungs.

As he pondered, he was distracted by a movement further along the street. A woman and child emerged from the pet shop, accompanied by a small dog. The woman stood in front of the shop door and appeared to continue a conversation with someone who was still inside the shop. The sergeant guessed she was talking to Mrs Stirling, the widowed owner of the pet shop.

Mrs Stirling had taken in and cared for stray cats and dogs separated from their owners during the flood. The sergeant's men had helped to rescue the animals and deliver them to her. He recalled how some of the animals were barely alive when they arrived.

The child bent down and stroked the dog. The dog shook its body and sniffed at her feet. The woman finished her conversation and turned; the streetlamp bathed her face in a soft, golden light.

'Well, well,' said the sergeant in a quiet voice. 'It's Daisy and Jennifer.'

Daisy waited whilst Jennifer stroked the dog. After a few moments, she took the child's hand and tugged on the dog's lead.

Barrett extinguished his cigarette, took a deep breath, and curled back his shoulders. He waited whilst Daisy and Jennifer walked towards him. A few moments later, he stepped in front of them.

'Good afternoon, Ma'am.'

Daisy stopped, took a step backwards and pulled Jennifer towards her. The dog sat and scratched the side of his body.

'Sergeant Barrett, Ma'am – I rescued you from the Nissan Hut.'

'Why yes, yes, I do recall being rescued. But I...'

'It's good to see you both looking so well.'

He nodded towards Jennifer.

'That's a sweet little dog you have there.'

He knelt and stroked the dog's head.

Jennifer joined him.

'What's his name?'

'Buster.'

The child pulled at the dog's ears and stroked him under his chin.

'He's not our dog. He belongs to Mrs Jackson who lives next door. They lost each other in the flood, and we are taking him back to her.'

Jennifer stroked the dog again and her tone became wistful.

'I would like a...'

'We ought to be going,' said Daisy. 'Mrs Jackson will be wondering where we are.'

Barrett straightened up.

'May I escort you both home Ma'am? It's getting late, it's not safe to be wandering around in the dark.'

Daisy looked at him with clear, cool eyes.

'No thank you, Sergeant.'

She nodded towards a small lane further down the high street.

'We are almost home.'

'Very well, Ma'am, but are you sure? It's really no trouble at all.'

'I am sure. Thank you, sergeant. Come along Jennifer. We need to get Buster home to Mrs Jackson. She will be wondering where we are.'

Daisy smiled at the sergeant. She placed her arm around Jennifer's shoulders and pulled on Buster's lead. Barrett stepped to one side and gave an exaggerated salute. He placed his hands on his hips and watched them as they walked down the high street and turn into the lane. When they had gone, he kicked the ground hard.

Daisy is an ungrateful woman. She doesn't understand what she is missing, but I will teach her, and she will learn.

A few moments later, he shrugged his shoulders, and returned to the shop.

He leant against the lamp post and re-lit his cigarette. Someone within the shop pulled down the shutters and turned out the lights.

20

George unlocked Tom's car, picked up the written note from the passenger seat and read the address.

Yes, just as I thought, the road is behind the high street and close to the shops.

Annie and the children had moved into temporary accommodation, a large, rambling, Victorian house loaned to them by Tom's neighbour. Although they were still on the mainland, they were closer to the island. He turned the engine of the car, changed gear, and whistled one of Annie's favourite tunes.

Annie eyed the pile of dirty clothing on the floor. She sighed, pulled on her rubber boots, and tied her apron.

There is so much to do!

She placed the washboard in the sink and began to beat and scrub the clothes in the hot, soapy water.

'Mummy, when will we see Daddy?'

Val stood in the doorway and scuffed the linoleum with the tip of her shoe.

'I don't know, darling. Soon, I hope.'

She wiped her brow and smiled through the steam.

'Why don't you go and play with your brothers.'

'I don't want to.'

She scuffed the linoleum for a second time.

'Don't do that, darling. We must look after the house and keep it nice while we are here.'

'Why can't we go home? I want to go home!'

The child's voice rose to an unfamiliar pitch.

'The sea wall is still being repaired, darling. It must be safe for us before we can return to the island.'

'But I don't like this house. I want to go home!'

She started to cry.

'Val! Wait!'

But it was too late. The door slammed shut and angry footsteps ascended the stairs. She stared at the soapflakes as they slithered down the washboard into the sink.

She's right. We do need to go home. But when?

She wanted to sit down and have a cup of tea, but the wet washing had turned the kitchen into a giant hothouse. She dragged the clothes into fresh water and rinsed and wrung them out by hand.

If I can get them hung out in the garden, they might dry a little bit.

She pulled on an old Macintosh given to her by Bessie, loaded the wash basket and walked to the line at the bottom of the garden. The garden lay still in its hibernation and most of the trees were leafless, their branches thin in the bare landscape. The sky was grey and there was little sun, but a strong wind made the clouds race and kept the snow away. She began to peg out the clothes. They weighed heavy from the retained water and were destined for a place in front of the fire later in the day. She folded back the sleeves of the Macintosh and worked as fast as she could aware the children were in the house on their own.

'Annie, Annie.'

The tone and two calls of her name rang a familiar memory; it came from her courting days. She turned towards the house, squinted, and gasped. Her heart began to pound. She threw down the pegs, her small frame fighting against the voluminous folds of the Macintosh as she ran up the wet path, across the dormant lawn to the steps of the house. By the time she reached the back of the house her breath came in hard bursts and her exhalations created a white mist around her. And then strong arms lifted her off the ground and swung her around. She buried her face in his neck and soaked his collar with tears.

'Annie, my darling.'

He kissed her lips, her face, her neck and murmured her name again and again.

It was an embrace they never forgot.

'Daddy, Daddy.'

The children surrounded them in one whooping, crying circle. George knelt. He ruffled their hair, kissed their faces, and gathered them towards him.

'It feels like we have been apart for a long time.'

Annie leant into the curve of George's arm as they sat on the sofa. The children had gone to bed, their exhausted excitement a guarantee of sound sleep.

He squeezed her towards him.

'That's because so much has happened.'

'Did you bring Moses and Emma across? Tom told me he offered to let them stay at the farm.'

'Aye, I did. They will stay with Tom for a while, but they spoke of going to their smallholding when they do return to the island.'

'Oh! Why not with us at the farmhouse?'

'I don't know. There's a change in the old man. I haven't asked him or mother why, but we need to respect their decision.'

Annie left the subject alone. She wanted to revel in George's return and shied away from family issues. She kissed him on his cheek as if to seal her decision.

'I have got the use of Tom's car or truck for as long as I need it. And today the army stated they will issue passes to farmers so we can travel back and forth to the island. I can drive Tom's vehicle across and use the flattie to get to the farmhouse until the water recedes.'

'Does that mean you can stay here with us?'

He kissed the top of her head.

'Yes, it does, my darling. It does indeed.'

That night George crept into the children's bedrooms and watched them as they slept. He listened to their soft breathing and gentle murmurs and stroked their faces.

Thank God they are safe.

'I'm off now. I will be back later.'

George kissed Annie and padded down the stairs in the still darkness. He drove towards the road bridge.

If only I could have my farm workers back.

He had seen Jake and Reggie and some of his other men when they volunteered with the army. But when he did speak with them, an air of expectancy hung over their conversation as they waited to be offered work back on the farm.

'I will have you back as soon as I can.'

Jake stepped forward. He was a tall, strong man and his large hands looked as if they had been hewn from granite. The rest of the men stood behind their spokesperson.

'And when will that be guv'nor?'

'As soon as I can.'

George remembered his own awkward smile.

I must think of something. They need to feed their families.

He parked the car on a verge and pulled the flattie into the deeper water.

'Morning,'

Josh helped George drag the boat towards the scullery door.

'Oh!'

'Hello, Mr Hadley.'

George looked blank. He could not think why Josh's wife, Bertha, was at the farmhouse.

'You asked me to come over and sort out some toys for the children.'

She smiled.

'Ah, yes, I remember now. Most of them are in their rooms as far as I know. And thank you, Bertha. If you put them in a box, I will take them back with me this afternoon.'

George turned towards his manager.

'Have you fed the animals, Josh?'

'As well as I can, guv'nor.'

'Righto. Let's have some breakfast and see if we can repair some of the fencing in the yard. There's nothing more we can do for the livestock.'

The men ate their food as Bertha's footsteps crossed above them.

'Let's get on.'

George put on his cap and pulled on his oilskins. The men worked until dusk and rowed back to the farmhouse.

'Here you are, Mr Hadley.'

Bertha gave George a large box.

'There is something in there for each of the children.'

'Thank you, Bertha. I will see you in the morning, Josh.'

'Yes, guv'nor.'

George arrived at the house, placed the box on the

kitchen table and called out to Annie and the children. As he removed his boots, Val, Douglas, and Dennis pulled their toys from the box and kissed and hugged them. However, John knelt on a chair by the table and waited until the other children were gone. Then he peered over the top of the box and lifted out Bun. He looked at the toy rabbit for a few moments, clasped him to his chest and ran from the room.

'Wonderful,' said Annie

Her eyes moistened. George clasped her hand, pulled it to his lips and kissed her small fingers. Her skin tingled from his touch, a combination of soothing overlay and subtle sexual undercurrent. She collected plates and moved around the kitchen. Gentle snores pervaded the room, and she quietened her step.

She thought about their farmhouse, its rambling rooms, uneven walls, and ill-fitting windows. She knew repairs to the sea wall progressed each day. George spoke of the breaches being filled and the lower tidal flood waters, which reduced the water levels running onto the land. And when she entered the local shops, the women spoke of their loved ones who volunteered to work with the military. They consisted of farm workers, agricultural students, professional men, and tradesmen; anyone who was physically able, undertook the work.

A flurry of excitement arose within her. If repairs to the sea wall held at the next spring tide, they could go home.

21

12th February 1953

It was a week since George had received the ultimatum from Mr Anderton about his livestock, and although he knew he would not be forgotten, he comforted himself with the fact he heard nothing.

George arrived at the checkpoint to the road bridge just before seven o'clock in the morning. He let the car roll to a standstill and joined a small queue. He hovered his foot above the accelerator pedal, wound down the window and held out his pass. His breath mingled with exhaust fumes in the cold morning air.

'Okay, Mr Hadley.'

A soldier waved him through.

Although it was now possible to drive on the road bridge when the tide was out, it was still covered with some water and travel remained slow and hazardous. Several sections of the road required careful navigation, and the last part of the journey still had to be completed by boat. He parked the car on a piece of high ground next to his flattie and pulled on his thigh boots. When he entered the farmyard, he was surprised to find two men already present. The men stood close together, spoke in low tones and checked their watches. They wore thick wool coats and carried large duffle bags strapped to their backs. The duffle bags were bulging and misshapen, and as the men spoke, they hoisted and heaved them into position. When they saw George, they stopped their conversation.

The first man spoke.

'Is this Butterwood Farm? Are you, Mr George Hadley?'

The second man pulled out a clipboard from his duffle bag.

George's eyes narrowed

'Yes, that's correct.'

'We are here about your livestock, Mr Hadley. We are government animal welfare officers. Mr Anderton informed us you have some surviving cattle, also some pigs. Is that correct?'

'More or less. At the last count we had nineteen surviving cattle out of seventy. The pigs are fine and in their pigsties. Look, all I need is fresh water and more time, that's all. We have some hay which was not ruined in the flood, but fresh water supplies are scarce. I need more time to source a fresh water supply.'

The man with the clipboard spoke for the first time.

'I have read Mr Anderton's notes. He informed you last week if you could not sustain your livestock they would have to be destroyed. He also informed you there must be compliance with public health guidelines.'

The man ran his finger along the edge of the clipboard and tapped the paperwork. George felt his jaw tighten. The first man continued the conversation.

'We do understand, Mr Hadley. But unless you can show us how you propose to source your own fresh water supply, your livestock will have to be destroyed. It is government policy. There are strict guidelines that must be followed. I have the regulations here if you would like to...'

'But that's absurd! The whole country needs food, and meat is still rationed. I can get my animals through this, but I need help. Can't you wait another week? The flood waters have already started to subside and the repairs to the sea wall are well advanced. Have you seen the wall?'

'We are not here to see the wall, Mr Hadley. We are here to deal with your livestock. We have a destruction order here.'

A document was placed in the man's outstretched hand; he held it out towards George.

'You must sign this document, Mr Hadley.'

The man held up his hand.

'If you refuse to sign it, Mr Hadley, my colleague will witness my signature, and it will be a valid legal document. However, I advise you to bear in mind that if you don't sign this document, it will hamper your chances of a successful claim for compensation from the government. Now, I suggest...'

'Damn you. Both of you. I won't sign it!'.

George clenched his fists; his knuckles protruded like bony promontories.

'I will not sign a death warrant for my own animals. This is madness! Utter madness! My animals are perfectly healthy.'

The man withdrew the proffered document, folded it in half and pushed it into his pocket.

'Very well, Mr Hadley. I suggest you leave us to do our job.'

The man nudged back the edge of his coat sleeve and looked at his watch.

'We will be finished by early afternoon.'

The men turned away and spoke to each other in low tones.

George felt as if his feet were rooted to the ground, stuck in the mud, like huge anchors caught in an early tide. He knew there was nothing he could do. He was no longer a legitimate obstacle to the destruction of his livestock, merely a disgruntled farmer whose objections no longer mattered.

The water picked up a slight swell. The men hoisted their duffle bags and moved towards the cattle stalls. He fixed his eyes on the undulations in front of him. He felt nauseous.

I've got a half a stack of hay, a small pot of savings and nothing else.

Somehow, he got into his boat and rowed out onto the lane. He flagged down a passing tractor.

'Thanks, Eric.'

He climbed up into the cabin.

'They are shooting my livestock today.'

'Sorry to hear that, old chap.'

Eric changed gear.

'They destroyed mine yesterday, although we rescued a few cattle and most of our sheep. We also saved the piglets, and the smaller pigs. The army managed to gain access and we drove and carried the smaller animals onto the trucks, but the heavier ones have gone. It's a difficult time for all of us George. As I said to Anita this morning, the only consolation is we have all survived, including our children.'

'Aye, tis a saving grace to be sure.'

George shifted his position. It was a bumpy ride. The increase in farm traffic, along with the army vehicles had created huge ruts in the ground which filled up when the tides ebbed and flowed through the remaining breaches in the sea wall.

'It will be good when they finish repairs to the wall and these wretched tides stop covering our land,' said Eric.

They drove in silence until they reached the sea wall.

'I'll be back in about an hour if you want a lift back.'

'Thanks, Eric. I might take you up on that. But don't wait for me, I could be here for a while.'

He jumped down and stood back from the tractor. As it pulled away, its huge wheels churned up spirals of filth.

He walked towards the sea wall; he did not notice the numbing cold. He wanted to revel in the exposed wild spaces and let the sea air and coastal winds clear his mind.

Several gangs of volunteers and soldiers stretched out along the wall. Alongside the gangs, a smaller group of men worked the huge diesel pumps supplied by the Royal Engineers. He watched as the pumps pushed the sea water out through the remaining gaps in the wall and recalled when Jake drove his dragline digger a few days earlier, to clear the ditches and move the soil.

'That's it, men.'

The officer's voice came from further along the line. 'The pump out is done. Let's start those final repairs and get this wall finished.'

The order pulsated along the gang lines like an electric charge and the men called on one final surge of energy.

He walked further along the wall, past the Royal Navy floating barracks where some of the volunteers were billeted, until he came to the spot where Annie and the children crossed the flooded fields in the boat. Either way, as far as the eye could see, the wall stood tall and strong with its repairs of wooden piling, rocks, stones, and sandbags.

The men have repaired the worst of it. Now we must wait and see if it holds against the spring tide.

As he returned to the checkpoint, the slate sky reflected eerie shadows of fading light.

The pain is over for my animals. I must start again.

22

'You are early.'

Eloise smiled. Barrett held her arm and kissed her cheek. She blushed and felt small quivers of pleasure run through her body. She pulled away from him, aware one or two volunteers remained in the main hall and patted his hand.

'I'll get you a sandwich.'

He rolled a cigarette and lit it.

'How are you getting on with the repairs to the sea wall on the island?'

He exhaled and walked towards the counter.

'Oh, they're coming along.'

She nodded towards the reception hall.

'It's less busy here. Not so many new flood victims, but we are making sure everyone has somewhere to go.'

She placed the sandwich on the counter.

'I'll get you a drink.'

He returned to the table and balanced his cigarette on the ash tray. By the time she provided a cup of tea only crumbs remained on the plate. She removed her apron and hung it up.

'Come.'

Barrett gestured for her to sit on his lap.

She hesitated, then hitched her skirt a little and positioned herself on his knee. She could smell his body sweat through the layer of cigarette smoke. He stroked her hair, then her face and kissed her on the lips.

'You are a very attractive woman, Eloise.'

His tongue searched her mouth, but she pulled away.

'I had better be going. Fred is always home early on a Friday; he will be waiting for his dinner.'

Barrett released her from his arms and held up his hands in mock surrender.

'Will you be here tomorrow?'

'Tomorrow, yes, but not Sunday.'

She straightened her skirt.

'Sunday is my rest day.'

After he left, she went to the bathroom. Her eyes were ablaze and her lips a pillar box red. She felt so alive. She reapplied her lipstick and smoothed her hair. A fleeting image of Fred entered her head, the way he looked at her the day before when she returned home. She sighed and dismissed it from her mind.

Barrett returned to barracks, took a shower, and put on civilian clothes. He adjusted the belt on his trousers and took one last look in the mirror. He had slicked his hair back with pomade and his face felt smooth and soft after its shave. He slipped his comb into the pocket of his jacket and smiled to himself. He decided to go to the public house and turned into the high street. He had visited Eloise at the reception centre every evening that week and things were progressing well.

It won't be long now.

He stopped by a shop window and looked at his reflection. He took out his comb and raised it to his head, but his hair was nicely slicked back, and he returned the comb to his pocket.

As he walked, he wondered whether he should visit his mother. His parents had left Ireland after they married and moved to East London where he, and his two younger brothers were born. The war years had turned many of the houses and tenements into bombed out shells, but his family was still there, in that same tiny house. He had not been back for years but managed to keep up with family news; his mother included a short note when she sent him birthday and Christmas cards.

He recalled his younger years.

The lack of food, the overcrowded rooms and two small bedrooms. The shortage of money made worse by his father's heavy drinking; his shouts of anger, the vomit on the doorstep, followed by his collapse in the hallway or on the stairs.

They were the better nights.

The worst nights came when his father had insufficient money, and was unable to reach a barely conscious, inebriated state. On those occasions he returned home in a vengeful mood. As a small boy Barrett sat on the stairs and listened to his father's aggressive tones and his mother's careful, quiet response.

Then it happened.

His father's screams of abuse came, followed by the thump of his fists as they hit the soft, curved ball of his mother's flesh. Barrett remembered how he cried, crept back to bed, and shook with anger and fear. Fear his mother would not be alive the following morning. Anger at the injustice of the wicked strength of evilness. But his mother did survive. She appeared the following morning and gave him breakfast, her body covered, her movements slow and painful.

As he grew up, he began to think it was his fault. Maybe his father assaulted his mother because of him, or perhaps he had done something wrong and upset his father. But as the years passed and conversations with friends and their families alluded to his father's behaviour, he noticed their horrified looks as he rationalised the cause of his mother's bruises.

'Your father's a drunken bully, he should be locked up for what he does to your mother'

Barrett was fourteen years old when his friend's older brother made the statement. He left them, walked down to the river Thames, and sat and looked across the estuary. He could not deny the truth of the statement.

It was almost midnight that night when his father arrived home from the public house, his drunken voice loud, uncompromising as he searched for his mother. And when the assault began, he ran down the stairs, entered the room, and jumped on his father's back. For a few seconds he felt a surge of power when his father's punches ceased, but he was no match for the strength of a drunken man and his father flung him aside and grabbed him by the throat. Then came the sound of bone on stone, as his father smashed his head into the wall and caused him to slump to the ground. When he regained consciousness his father's distorted face was in his face. The hairs from his nostrils stood out like bristles from a yard broom and the acrid smell of alcohol swamped his airways.

'You little gobshite. I'll feckin' kill you if ye ever try dat agin.'

His father spat in his face and roared with laughter. As he lay helpless on the ground, the proximity of his mother's body provided a cinematic view of her plight. Her body bounced from the impact of his father's punches and her exposed flesh turned blood red. His father staggered, dropped to the floor, and fell asleep. And his grunts and snores sung like the trumpets of angels. Barrett remembered how he tried to help his mother, but she did not respond to his young, endearing hands and lay in silence on the cold, stone floor.

Her submission was complete.

Years later, when he left to join the army, the parting words of his mother rung in his ears.

'Don't come back, Jim. It's not safe for you. I'll be all right.'

But his life had already changed many years before when he first saw his father assault his mother. From that day on, he spoke like his pretty, dark haired English mother. He adopted her accent, her habits, her history, and culture. He was his father's son in name only.

He missed his mother. He wanted to sweep her into his arms, hear her soft, endearing voice and feel her maternal, nurturing warmth. But he couldn't go home. He knew if he went home and saw his mother's bruises and pummelled flesh again, he would kill his father.

23

15th February 1953

George awoke early on Sunday morning. He had last visited the island the previous Thursday and was anxious to return. He dressed in the winter darkness, crept downstairs and stepped outside. His stride was quick and long as he side-stepped patches of ice and moved along the street. He reached the car, wrenched at the handle, and released the door from its frame of ice.

'You're an early bird.'

The soldier's familiar voice rang out through the cold air.

'Aye, plenty to do today. We had a full moon yesterday and the next spring tide is due tomorrow.'

He pulled away fast and caused his back wheels to slide. He slowed the car until the image of the soldier disappeared from his rear mirror. He parked on the familiar mound of stones and debris and changed into his thigh boots. The water level had reduced, and he waded and pulled the boat for most of the journey.

He knew what awaited him when he entered the yard, but he wanted to see his animals for the last time before they were finally removed from the farm.

He had not spoken to Annie about the visit by Mr Anderton or the pending slaughter of the livestock. He planned to tell her when the grisly job was complete, and the dead animals removed. He had not seen his pigs since he gave them their last feed and convinced himself their slaughter was for the best. A quick and efficient solution carried out in difficult circumstances.

For the first time since the flood, the yard was almost clear of water. But in its place lay a sea of thick, sludge and mud interspersed with oozing trails of slime. The lower water level revealed a strange mix of items: tendrils of barbed wire, a smashed chicken house, a whole rabbit hutch, animal food bins, a dining room chair and an old coat that belonged to Annie. All lay scattered alongside uprooted bushes and small trees. He placed his feet with care and picked his way across the yard. The landscape was more hazardous than when it was submerged and contained unstable, slippery surfaces, and random, misplaced objects. It took him almost as long to make the journey on foot as it had by boat.

The gate to the pigsties was padlocked. He hoisted himself onto the top of the gate but was distracted by a flicker of movement.

'What...?'

He stopped, his leg poised mid-air. Another flicker caused the straw to move. He jumped down into the stye and blinked hard.

'What...the hell...'

As he advanced towards the back of the stye he heard quiet moans and murmurs accompanied by further movement in the straw. His stomach somersaulted. His pigs lay on their sides. Their breathing was laboured and came in short rasps, as their bodies twitched and shuddered on the verge of death. He suppressed a surging bile at the back of his throat. He turned away; he looked again. He visited each stye and found the same scenario. The captive bolt pistol used by the animal welfare officers had stunned the pigs, but the subsequent bullet failed to kill them.

'No! Not my beauties.'

He sunk to his knees and faced the nearest sow. Her sad eyes opened, then closed and her groans echoed in his ears. He crawled across the stye. The exposed brains of the pigs veered towards him and away from him. But he could not put them out of their misery. He had no gun or knife with him and could not perfect their slaughter. Black spots appeared before his eyes. He knew, if he tried to stand, he would come to harm. He lay supine in the straw and splayed his arms and legs like a crucifix.

A fury grew inside him.

He rolled towards the edge of the stye, grasped the railing and pulled himself up. He swayed for a moment, steadied himself and stamped his feet. He left the stye and forced one foot in front of the other. When he reached the farmhouse, he went straight to his gun cabinet and took out his twelve-bore shotgun. He returned to the styes and climbed over the gate.

Then, he took careful aim and fired clean, precise shots. He slaughtered every one of his pigs.

The air hung oppressive, like a huge black coat.

He shouted out.

'Better see what those bastards have done to my cattle.'

He crossed the farm and turned onto the main lane. His breath drew sharp. His remaining bullocks and heifers, the cows, and their late born calves, all lay in funereal rows along the verges of the lane. A few days before, he had watched them as they waited for food. Their magnificent, strong bodies solid to the ground, their tender eyes on their young as they nudged them towards the hay. But now they were inert hulks of muscle. Their hind legs were still, their tails passive, and their large, soft eyes, were dark, blank orbs.

He straightened his legs and pulled his muscles taut. He was determined not to collapse again. However, the mud caused him to slip, and he fell forward. His hands took the force of his body weight and prevented a fall flat to the ground. But his knees and hands got stuck in the mud, and when the freezing cold forced him to try and move, his hands behaved like obstinate suckers. He pulled hard, released his hands, and fell backwards. He screwed up his eyes, but wetness forced through, and his eyelashes dropped a stream of tears.

His voice was a whisper.

'You flood our home, strike us down, crush our livelihood. You are too cruel! I cannot fight you, anymore.'

His body shuddered and he was afraid to open his eyes. He tried to understand. Was it a warning? Was it a test? Or was it both? No answers came.

Eventually, he pulled his body out of the mud. When he got back to the car, he slid onto the seat, gripped the top of the steering wheel, and placed his head on his hands.

24

17th February 1953

George was wide awake, even though it was still dark outside. He had felt Annie tossing and turning beside him all night, and he was unsure how much sleep he managed to get himself. He was about to close his eyes when he heard his wife's voice.

'Are you awake, love?'

'Aye,'

They rolled towards each other and made a warm cocoon. After a few minutes they pushed tiredness to one side, got out of bed and went down to the kitchen.

The full moon had waxed to its biggest size two days earlier and had begun to wane as it travelled through its equinoctial cycle. The tide tables predicted the spring tide at two o'clock overnight with a smaller tide later that day. George planned to drive over to the island at seven o'clock, after the tide had ebbed for some hours, and there was sufficient light to check the sea wall and water level.

He lit the fire and drew two chairs in front of the hearth. As they drank their tea, he put his arm around his wife's shoulders, and in a hushed voice, told her about the livestock. When he spoke about the plight of the pigs she cried. They held hands and sat in silence, but when the clock hand approached seven o'clock, he became restless. She sighed and dabbed her eyes.

'I had better get going, it will be light soon.'

He patted her arm and rose from his chair.

She stood in the doorway and watched him pull on his boots. When he was ready to leave, he pulled her towards him, steadied her shaking hands and kissed her forehead.

As he arrived at the checkpoint, the night sky retreated, and glorious grey, and pink streaks appeared in the east. He looked ahead and in the rear mirror. He did not recognise any of the other vehicles in the queue. He inched forward, his breath forced through clenched teeth, shallow and syncopated.

'Come on.'

He jabbed his fingers at the steering wheel and shifted around in his seat. Minutes later he arrived at the front of the queue and drove onto the island towards the farm. His driving became erratic, and the car zig zagged along the road.

'Come on, my girlie.'

After he had parked the car in the yard, he walked towards the tractor.

'Now, my darling, let's get you started. I must get close to the shoreline.'

He picked up the crank, and with the full force of his body, turned it several times. He jumped back as the tractor spluttered and roared into action. He adjusted the fuel tap, turned up his collar, and climbed into the cabin. He fixed the accelerator throttle, changed gear, and patted the vehicle.

'No engine failure this time, my sweet.'

He drove out of the outbuilding and dropped into the mud. The tractor was easy to manoeuvre, and her huge wheels churned through the terrain. When he got onto the main road, he avoided the water-filled ditches and dikes and turned towards the sea wall. He smiled to himself as he felt the familiar rhythm of the vehicle beneath him. The leaden sky showed a flurry of snow, and the seagulls called loud and sharp as they circled above him. He noticed that since the flood, the gulls flew inland rather than out near the shoreline.

'Ah, yes.'

He realised why the birds changed their habits. He remembered each year when his farm machinery turned the soil. The seagulls followed him and picked off the exposed earthworms and other insects. But in the winter months when he did not operate his farm machinery, the seagulls stayed close to the shoreline and sourced crabs and molluscs.

Of course, the flood and the salt levels on the land. They have changed everything.

He turned around in his seat. Whichever way he looked, he saw the white threads of thousands of dead worms, an edible graveyard strewn across the fields.

You are lucky, gulls. You have an extra food source this winter.

He could see Eric walking ahead accompanied by two men. He swung his legs over the steering wheel and jumped down.

'Hey, Eric.'

Eric stopped and the men turned towards him. He quickened his pace, his last steps a run.

'Morning, all.'

The men murmured and nodded a greeting. George recognised the other two men. They were brothers and farmed in the south of the island.

'We have just arrived,' said Eric.

One of the brothers spoke.

'It was the big one last night.'

'Aye,' said George. 'The tide tables said it would be a spring tide and the BBC forecast that too. Let's go and have a look. We should be able to see in this light.'

They pulled down their caps, thrust their hands into their pockets and trudged in unison towards the shoreline. They walked in silence, absorbed in their own thoughts. Fragile, tentative thoughts of hope and possibility accompanied by a fear that when they reached the sea wall, those same thoughts might be dashed against the rocks. They walked to the headway and the tide ebbed in the dawn light. The men stood in a line alongside the wall and searched its surface for clues.

'There it is.'

George kicked the line of flotsam and jetsam: seaweed, pieces of pallet, driftwood, dead rabbits, chickens, and wild game birds.

'That is the flood water level. You can see it was not disturbed by the spring tide last night.'

He moved more flotsam and jetsam with his foot.

'The tide this afternoon, and those that follow, each of them will be lower until the next spring tide, right through to the bird tides.'

The men continued to look at the wall until each one of them was satisfied that what they saw was strong, complete, and whole. George took off his cap and smoothed down his hair. His voice wobbled and made a strange crackling sound.

'They have done it. Thank God, they have done it. The wall has held.'

Within a few hours news of the wall reached the mainland.

A swell of excitement grew amongst the islanders. Their conversations buzzed as they ran between houses, congregated on doorsteps, and leant over garden fences.

They queued to speak to government officials, questioned the local 'Bobby' and asked strangers in the streets.

'When can we return?'

'What about the looters?'

'Will the army still be there?'

'Will we need passes?'

'How do I get a pass?'

'We have lost everything. Where do we start?'

'My Johnny wants to go back to school.'

'I will see my Auntie again.'

'We need the shops open.'

'Our homes are full of stinking mud and debris.'

'How do you get rid of the damp and salt lines?'

'Will we get any money from the government?'

Most of the islanders and their families had lived on the island for generations and the flood had severed those links and destroyed their livelihoods. But now they had a way back. They would be able to reconnect with their community and re-establish their way of life.

25

A line of light outlined the shut door of the storage room.

'No, not here. Someone might find us.'

Eloise felt Barret's hot breath on her face as she attempted to pull his hands away from her waist.

'Come on, baby.'

He pulled open his shirt and unbuttoned his fly. She smelt freshly dug earth and salt air, and her cheeks tingled from the stubble on his face. As he found her lips her head filled with fleeting images; her teenage years, her parent's acrimonious divorce, her first date with Fred. Barrett freed the buttons on her blouse and touched her breasts. She felt his excitement and let out small gasps. For a few seconds he fumbled as he searched under her skirt. Then his fingers traced up and over her stocking tops until he reached the prize of her smooth, soft flesh. He pulled up her skirt and lifted her onto a table.

She cast caution aside.

What would they say now? Why shouldn't I? They don't care.

Later, they fumbled for their clothes and dressed.

He tucked his shirt into his trousers.

'We will finish working on the sea wall this week. The borough engineers will take over after that and organise the permanent repairs.'

She felt a niggle of anxiety.

'Where will you go?'

'Oh, just back to barracks.'

Her anxiety hovered.

'If the wall is finished, the reception centre will be closed and revert to being a school.'

She wanted him to caress her, reassure her. She slipped into her shoes and straightened her skirt. A silence hung in the air.

'What time does your husband get in from work?'

'Well, about six except Fridays when he is home earlier...Jim, I...'

'Then I will come to your house, during the day, when I am off duty.'

'I am not sure...I must think of the neighbours, why can't...'

'He's a man of habit, you told me so, yourself.'

'Yes...but...'

'Well, that is settled. There is no other place we can go if we want to, well, you know.'

He slapped her bottom. She felt a mixture of irritation and anxiety. She checked the seams of her stockings and buttoned her cardigan.

As he opened the door, a shaft of light fell upon them.

'It's all clear.'

He took her hand.

26

April 1953

It was early April and the day of John's first return to the island.

He awoke in the early hours and tried to imagine what the island would look like, but his excitement spilled into his thoughts and gave him a fuzzy head. By the time Annie came to wake him, he was out of bed and dressed. He ate little breakfast despite Annie's cajoles and stood by the front door waiting for his father.

Annie tugged at Bun's ear which protruded over the top of John's coat.

'Don't lose him.'

She smiled at John, adjusted his scarf, and gave him a hug and a kiss.

'Now, you're ready.'

George appeared in the hallway.

'Come on, son, don't tarry.'

She stood in the doorway and waved as they left the house.

The boy jumped over puddles and ran and skipped alongside his father.

'Here you are, lad.'

He scrambled onto the passenger seat of the car. He stretched his legs across the burnished leather and sat Bun on his lap.

When they reached the checkpoint there was one truck ahead of them. A soldier leant in through its window and spoke to the driver for a few seconds, then stood back and slapped the roof. George winked at John.

'All right, lad?

He nodded and pulled Bun towards him. His stomach fluttered with a thousand butterflies. The soldier shouted a greeting and waved them through. They pulled away and drove onto the road. As they travelled, the wheels of the car hit a large trough of water and caused a fountain of spray to wash over the vehicle; for a few seconds it buoyed the car, as if it were floating up and over the water.

Lit by a pale, weak sun, the sky sketched an iridescent palette of brushed silver and pearl. The seagulls called across the sky and their large symmetrical wings soared and dipped as they looked for food. John turned in his seat one way then the other, his eyes wide, his mouth open as the bold gulls swooped past the car.

They turned onto the back lane. Uprooted trees and bushes still lay along the lane. It was the same lane where birds and rabbits had sat alongside each other in the branches of trees during the flood, as if nature always intended cooperation between the species.

John recalled the mighty power of the water as it covered the land, the dreadful warning from his grandfather to his father when they got in the boat, and the anguish on his father's face when they left. But nothing surpassed the fearful trip across the water to the sea wall, and the look of relief on his mother's face when they reached the mainland. Years later, he recalled those memories; they were vivid, stark, violent, as powerful as nature herself.

He jolted in his seat.

'Here we are, son. Wait there.'

George opened his door and jumped into the mud. He laughed, and with steps large and ridiculous, walked around the front of the car. John stood on the seat and climbed onto his father's back. The farmhouse stood silent and eerie and when they stepped inside, the smell of stagnant water almost overpowered them. The rugs and floors lay covered with thick mud and the salt lines showed like chalk marks along the walls. George flung open the windows.

'Now, let's have some eggs!'

He took four eggs from a box, placed lard in a pan and turned on the gas cylinder for the cooker. The transparency of the eggs turned white as vicious bubbles of fat spat and leapt from the pan.

'Sit at the table, son.'

He filled the kettle with water.

'We will eat our eggs first, and then go down to the wall.'

As they ate, the heat dissipated from the cooker and air blasted through the open windows. John finished his eggs and pushed the empty plate towards his father.

'Dad, can we see the pigs and cows before we go down the wall?'

George paused; he placed his cup down on the table.

'No, no lad, not this morning.'

'But I want to see them. Why can't we see them?'

The boy's unblinking blue eyes fixed a determined stare.

'Because they have gone, lad. They are dead. They all went in the flood.'

He rose from the table, collected the plates, and placed them in the sink.

'It's all right, lad.'

He pulled his son to him and squeezed him into a big

hug.

'We will get some more pigs and cows when we get back on the farm. Now, let's go and have a look at the wall!'

The seagulls escorted the car to the coastline. George noticed the surface water had reduced further, and for the first time the wheels of the car felt solid to the ground. He watched from the corner of his eye as John stroked Bun.

I am glad I brought the boy over today.

He hated himself when he lied about the cattle, but it was the best he could do. He knew returning to the island would be traumatic for his children, and their home would look and smell different for many months. He pulled up the handbrake.

'Leave Bun here, son.'

He held John's hand as they bent their bodies against the gusting wind. After they had reached the wall and climbed onto its flat, broad top, he turned him towards the sea.

'No waves until high tide, son. The moon is still pulling the tide back and making it ebb.'

He crouched down and pointed to the seascape, his finger level with John's line of vision.

'Do you see? The water is out by about two miles.'

The boy turned to his father.

'Will the sea be bad again Dad?'

'A flood is not the sea being bad, son. It is nature's way. We must work alongside nature and be grateful for what she gives us.'

The boy wrinkled his brow and flickered his eyes towards and away from his father. George held him by the shoulders.

'Look around, son. See the colour of the sky.'

He turned the boy again.

'Look at all the different shades of blue and grey.'

He took his hand.

'Now close your eyes.'

John's eyes flickered beneath his eyelids as his hand tightened, then relaxed in his father's hand.

'Taste the salt in the air, lad, smell the seaweed, and listen to the gulls.'

The boy licked his lips; his nostrils flared and twitched, and he lifted his face to the screeching gulls.

'Use your eyes, ears, and nose, son, taste the air and you will find nature. Nature is everywhere. She says what will happen to the land and we must listen to her.'

John opened his eyes and blinked hard.

He looked at the sky, out to the horizon and beneath his feet.

'Aye, son. That's it. You've got it.'

PART TWO

27

May 1953

'It will be hard when we return, Annie, hard for all of us.'

George scratched his head and pushed a pile of paperwork aside.

'Our income from the livestock has gone and the fields are saturated with salt. Nothing will grow in the fields this year. The soil is so damaged, I am not sure if anything will ever grow on the island again.'

He tried to keep his voice calm. He did not tell his wife about the grip of panic he felt when he thought about the flood damage. Nor how he heaved and surged within himself, despite his presentation of a capable man ready to overcome their difficulties.

'But, George, it is our home, and besides, your family has farmed there for generations. We can't give up on Butterwood Farm. We must try.'

'But the farmhouse, Annie, the state of it. We have tried to clear it but...'

She reached across the table and squeezed his hand.

'It is all right. Don't...'

A hissing sound came from the cooker.

'Oh!'

She stood and removed a large, bubbling pan from the gas ring and opened a small window.

'We have some savings, and we need that money, but I must pay Josh. He is a good man. I do not want to ask him to leave.'

He sighed.

'And the rest of the workers, Jake, Reggie, and the others, I have seen them down at the sea wall. They all want to come back, and I want them back. I need them to help clear the farm, but I do not know how I will pay them. Josh and I, we cannot do it all.'

'We will manage, George. Somehow, we will manage.'

In the final days before their return, George travelled to and from the island every day and did not return until it was dark. And for Annie? Every waking hour demanded the organisation of endless practical arrangements. Even when night came, her mind queried, then queried again whether she forgot to do something. But when she did fall asleep, it was only a fitful slumber until the first dawn light appeared, and the race began again.

Moses and Emma continued to stay with Tom and Bessie, but when they heard the tenants had left their smallholding, they began to plan their return.

John kept away from the whirlwind of rushed conversations and frantic packing. Instead, he played with Val and his brothers until he was called to the kitchen for meals or told to go to bed. He breathed every minute of every hour as the clock on the mantlepiece ticked its slow, inexorable rhythm and pushed through another day.

The day before they were due to leave, he went into the garden for the last time. The sun was shining, the clouds raced across the sky and a fresh breeze chilled the air. The cherry tree blossomed full and pink, the crisp, brown petals of faded spring flowers lay scattered beneath its boughs, whilst the fresh buds of the nearby lilac bush poised ready to take their place. As he walked down the path to the wooden bird table, the sparrows and blackbirds took off and settled in nearby trees. He sprinkled breadcrumbs on the table, stepped back, and let the chirruping chorus swoop down. His stomach wobbled like a jelly.

They were going home. Back to the island. Back to the farm.

When the day of their return arrived, they said goodbye to kind neighbours and friends, left the house and crossed the road bridge onto the island.

Annie's mouth felt dry, and her breathing came in short, disconnected, puffs. George had warned her about the state of the farmhouse, and she tried to imagine what she would find. Would the lower rooms be habitable? What would be the state of the children's bedrooms? Would their personal possessions and keepsakes be where they left them? Such questions, along with many others, buzzed around in her head.

She was not surprised at the state of the yard. George had often spoken about the quagmire of mud, the destruction of many of the cattle stalls and the misplaced vegetation. But when she walked inside the farmhouse, she staggered and almost sank to her knees. The walls were marked with chalky, horizontal salt lines and emitted a strong smell of damp, and the floors were caked in mud. She walked through each room.

Oh, no.

The family photographs had gone, the cabinet George's parents had given them for their wedding lay in splinters, and its contents of small porcelain dishes and silver pots smashed to the floor. Random, soggy, grey clumps were all that remained of a collection of the children's' books, her cookery books, and magazines. Even the clothesline had gone from the garden except for the two end pieces attached to the fence posts.

We should have moved things upstairs.

She scolded herself as she walked through the farmhouse. Then she remembered how the flood had swept across their land and almost drowned her husband, and her tears turned to stifled sobs.

28

Annie began to clear and clean the farmhouse. She flung open every door and window, took the rugs outside and beat out the dried mud and dust. She swept and scrubbed the downstairs rooms from top to bottom and cleaned the windows. Their oak kitchen table had survived the ingress of water, and with the addition of a few coats of linseed oil and some old wooden chairs from the attic, a central point for the family was established. George managed to purchase two second-hand armchairs. He pushed the exposed springs back into their stuffing and she repaired the covers. The children's seating was less luxurious, wooden pallets with old cushions on top.

She considered they were fortunate; other than dust, the bedrooms were the same as the day they left. The beds, bedlinen and blankets were untouched. Clothes still hung in the wardrobes and the same box of toys which George brought to the mainland, returned with them.

Annie walked through the house and surveyed her efforts.

The walls need time to dry out and the rugs still contain mud, but it's a start.

'Mummy, Mummy! Olive is outside.'

Douglas pulled at Annie's skirt and jumped up and down. She placed down the mixing bowl and joined the children at the kitchen window. Olive was thinner than before, and her clothes hung about her as she moved. Annie opened the door and the children surged forward like released, coiled springs.

'John! Val! Douglas! Dennis!'

Olive kissed and hugged the children.

Annie kissed her on the cheek.

'We have all missed you, my dear, especially the children.'

The girl's eyes welled up with tears as the children hung onto her hands and pulled her into the kitchen. She looked around and gasped.

'Yes, the flood hit us bad and there is still so much to do. Are your family safe, Olive? Was there much damage?'

'We all survived thank the Lord. We had some flood damage, like everyone did, but father saved the livestock and we managed to get some of our furniture upstairs.'

'It's good to know you are all safe.'

Annie was relieved the girl and her family survived the flood, but she did not want to talk about livestock and family possessions.

'Olive, can we play?'

'I have got my tractors.'

'They are my tractors.'

'Children, no squabbles please. I'm sure Olive would like a cup of tea first. Then, if you ask her nicely, I am sure she will play.'

The children raced upstairs.

'I am so glad you came over. The children have been asking after you every day.'

Olive sipped her tea.

'I wanted to come over earlier, Mrs Hadley, but since we returned to the island...I felt strange, not been myself.'

She sniffed and fumbled for her handkerchief.

'When we were evacuated, it was the first time I left the island. And then when we returned, I could not leave the cottage. I don't know why, I did try and go out, but I felt so anxious and stayed indoors.'

She shrugged her shoulders and blew her nose.

Annie remembered how Olive was before the flood. Then, she had been a happy, smiling girl, but now her brow was furrowed, and her movements contained an intermittent nervous twitch.

'When can I come back, Mrs Hadley? I miss the children so much, and you, and Mr Hadley.'

Annie's cheeks coloured.

'I don't know, Olive. I mean...sorry...we would love to have you back. But I must be honest with you, we don't have the money to pay you. I am so sorry, Olive, but that's the way it is, and I do not know when it will change.'

It was Annie's turn to find her handkerchief.

'I am not worried about the money, Mrs Hadley, not whilst you are in such a state here.'

'Well, that's a kind gesture, dear, but I should pay you.'

'As long as I can have my meals here, Mrs Hadley, it will be fine. Mother and father will have one less mouth to feed and they get plenty of help from the others.'

She laughed.

'They won't miss me. I have been moping so much, my brothers and sisters will be glad to see the back of me.'

'Thank you my dear, thank you so much.'

'Oh, Val is shouting at the boys.'

Olive rose.

'I'll go, Mrs Hadley.'

Annie placed a plate of ham and eggs in front of George. She scraped the remaining tea leaves together at the bottom of the tea caddy and reminded herself to buy some more.

'I've just seen Eric.'

She stopped scraping and shut the lid.

'He has been one of the lucky ones. His farm is close to the access routes across the sands, and some of his livestock was saved and ferried across to the mainland. They are being transported back to the island today. He has a fine herd of cattle and a good breed of sheep.'

George gulped his tea. The hot liquid burnt his mouth and caused his eyes to smart.

'His pastures are higher up from the sea and may contain less salt. He might even be able to put his cattle out to graze.'

His hand tremored as he placed down the cup.

'I'd better get back to it. The meeting takes place this morning.

29

George collected the keys from the church warden, unlocked the main door, and went inside. Attempts had been made to clean the village hall, but the unmistakable smell of salt water prevailed. The farmers began to arrive. They sat in small groups, rolled their cigarettes, and lit their pipes. For some, it was their first contact with other farmers since their return to the island.

'Why, it's good to see you, Ed.'

'And you, Rob. So pleased to know you're all safe.'

'Old Riley's farm, they found his dog alive. He was floating on the dining room table.'

'Best use of that table I reckon...'

'Well, his neighbour, their cat was found up the chimney!'

'My chickens survived. Their legs were swollen for days, but they're "right as rain" now and are laying again.'

'Jack, did you know old Smithy lost all his livestock. I saw them; they were all laid out in the back lane.'

'Well, Martin managed to drive his cows along the remains of the sea wall. He got them loaded onto army trucks and across to the mainland.'

'He was lucky. We only managed to get the suckling pigs out. All the others were too heavy to carry...'

'Well, I had the same problem as George. They killed my pigs with a .22 rifle, but it wasn't man enough for the job, and I found them still alive. I can't forgive them for that.'

'My corn stacks were dry, but full of wildlife, rabbits, and the like. I reckon they sought refuge until the water went.'

'The same happened to me with my corn stacks. We saved some potatoes, hay, and straw too, but I lost all my barley and wheat.'

'Well, you know the funniest thing was when I started to clear up, we found all sorts, dead gulls, Brent geese, all inland, about a dozen of them. And I had to kill twenty rabbits I found huddled on some high ground. They were starving and had no chance.'

'Well, that bit o' high land near my cow sheds, I found dead foxes and rabbits together on there. Who would have thought they would be on the same bit of land without any killing goin' on!'

George checked his watch.

The farmers lived by their routines. He knew he had three hours to get through the agenda and if he went beyond half past twelve, the farmers would leave and go home for their lunch.

The island farmers were creatures of cultural expectations too. They owned and worked their farms down through each generation. The farms were handed down to the eldest son, whilst the daughters married into another local farming family or remained at home as spinsters. The pace of life was slow on the island and change only happened over years, either when the next generation arrived, or when necessity forced change.

George brought the mallet down on the table.

'Good morning, gentlemen, can I have your attention please.'

One farmer ignored George and continued to talk.

'Yep, Eddy lost some of his livestock. We carried a lot

of his sheep onto boats. Those born in April before the flood, they had less weight to them. Mind you...'

George crashed the mallet down on the table.

'Gentlemen!'

The men ceased their conversation and scraped back their chairs.

'Thank you. Good morning to all of you. I am glad to see so many familiar faces.'

Agreement murmured around the room.

'Commiserations to the Barber family on the loss of Joe. He was a fine farmer, and we will ensure his widow and children get all the assistance they need.'

The men nodded in assent.

'For the rest of us, we must continue to deal with the effects of the flood. As you all know, the temporary repairs to the sea wall held against the February spring tide and permanent repairs to the sea wall are now under way. We can be optimistic we will not experience another flood like this one, certainly not in our lifetime anyway.'

He cleared his throat.

'You may be aware there has been communication from the government, from the Ministry of Agriculture and Fisheries. There are notices up on the mainland and at the checkpoint about it. Two representatives from that department are coming to the island next Monday which is why I called this meeting.'

Voices buzzed around the hall.

'Gentlemen!'

He raised his hand.

'The two representatives from the Ministry will provide information and advice on how we treat our land. Also, how we claim compensation for our losses.'

'Aye, we'll need compensation all right. It will take years to get the soil back to what it was.'

Heads nodded in a domino effect and several farmers folded their arms.

'Yes, we've all been hit by the flood,' said George. 'But we need to see what help the government will give us. It's our best chance to get things back to normal.'

'How're we goin' to restore the land? We know gypsum can neutralise salt but where do we get it from and how much will it cost?'

'Aye, we're broke after the flood.'

'I have not used gypsum in large amounts before. How much gypsum should be spread per acre?'

'Why can't we just wait for the rain to wash the salt out of the soil? We don't want to go mixing chemicals into the earth without knowing the impact on future crop yields.'

'Yes, but remember, it's not just the salt content we have to worry about. We have silty soil in some parts of the island; down in the south the water has gouged out large areas of soil.'

'The other problem we have got is marsh weed. It is everywhere; its growing in our fields and it is a bugger to remove. What with that and the salt, we are up against it.'

George raised both hands.

'All valid points, gentlemen, but I think the best way forward would be for us to appoint a spokesman for the meeting and that person can voice all our concerns to the government officials. Another issue is timescale; the ministry men must be informed it will take some years before we get a decent crop yield and, in the meantime, we will need financial assistance. Gentlemen, we need to have a vote.'

He looked around the room for potential candidates.

'Why, you're our best bet, George.'

George muttered under his breath, ignored the

suggestion, and introduced formality.

'We need nominations and a seconder for each nomination.'

George turned to the only woman in the hall. She sat to his left and scribbled in a notebook.

'Daphne, are you taking this down?'

The room hushed quiet as a mouse.

'Of course, I am!'

She flashed her eyes at him. It had the same effect as a stray bullet close to his ear. Daphne Ditchin had been pursued by several farmers in her youth, but in her middling years she developed an acerbic tongue, and a burgeoning figure which defied all corsetry. George gave her his best appreciative smile and turned back to the meeting.

'Nominations, please.'

He waited. A voice came from the back of the hall.

'I nominate George Hadley.'

George quietly groaned.

'Seconded,' said another.

There were no further nominations.

George did not thank his nominee and seconder. Already, he had tasted officialdom with the slaughter of his livestock and had no desire to encounter it again. But the deed was done, and he consoled himself with the fact he would be the first to know what the ministry men wanted and how they were prepared to help.

'Right, gentlemen. Let's get down to business.'

The discussions continued all morning and Daphne noted down ten agreed questions.

George was ready to face the ministry men.

30

A mist of rain hung in the morning air. Rain so fine it could not be seen or felt, but which caught one by surprise when it permeated and saturated the skin.

Annie rummaged amongst the coat hooks and pulled out her Macintosh. She slipped it on and patted the pocket which contained her shopping list. She collected the car keys, picked up her basket and left the farmhouse.

As she walked towards Tom's car, she stopped and looked back at the farmhouse; it had lost some of its damp, forlornness and regained some of its former homeliness and charm.

She smiled.

Our beautiful farmhouse has been waiting for us to return.

As she drove towards the village, she saw a woman ahead of her walking along the side of the road. Phoebe was a dot of a woman and had the brightest eyes, a large hook nose and ruddy cheeks. She wore a white cap, and her stooped figure gave her a curious gait. Her black coat was pulled tight around her body and the bottom of her white pinafore shifted in the breeze.

Annie recalled Moses telling her about Phoebe and her nine siblings. They were all born on the island and the whole family lived in a tiny labourer's cottage. The cottage only had two bedrooms. One for Phoebe's parents and the two youngest children, and the other for Phoebe and the other seven siblings where they slept in one bed top-to tail. When Phoebe's parents died, her siblings left the island, but she remained a spinster and continued to live in the cottage.

Annie stopped the car and wound down the window.

'Hello, Phoebe.'

'Well, hello, Mrs Hadley. It's a warm owd day.'

'Yes, it is, Phoebe. Would you like a lift?'

Phoebe smiled and her face crinkled into a thousand lines.

'No, I be fine, thank you, Mrs Hadley. It's good to have a spot of sun.'

Annie drove on and parked the car by the village green. She was pleased to see some of the shops open. It was another sign the island was returning to its old community.

Mr Brewer owned the saddlery shop which was adjacent to the butcher's shop. She recalled his bygone leatherwork skills; his ability to repair all forms of leather ware, including working horse harnesses. She wondered if he still made the bever bags used by the farm workers to carry their beverage or food and cold tea when they worked out in the field. She knew he still sold hemp fishing lines and hooks, because George mentioned he wanted to make a purchase.

The post office was open.

The new post mistress must have arrived on the island.

A short way from the Post Office was the Gatherers' Arms. It was owned and ran by Eddy Turner and was the only public house on the island. A few steps past the public house, stood the village hall and the church.

She smiled to herself when she thought about the proximity of the public house to the church. One could drown one's sorrows first and then go to the church for salvation. Or attend church first, sing hymns, say prayers, and seek liquid lubrication afterwards.

Reverend Peak did not seem to mind whether his parishioners went to the Gatherer's Arms before or after they attended his service, provided they did attend and heard the word of God. In fact, Reverend Peak rather liked a tipple of brown ale himself and was often seen in the Gatherer's Arms drinking with his flock.

She peered over the wall of the village school.

The playground will be full of children in a few weeks' time when the school reopens. Val is so excited. John liked Miss Brown. I wonder if she will return to the school.

The grocer's shop was situated on the north side of the village green next door to the butcher's shop. There was a long queue for the grocery shop. She knew most of the women in the queue, but there was a small number she did not recognise.

How lovely, we have some new families on the island.

As she approached, she heard snippets of conversation.

'Our walls are still damp.'

'Well, at least you can live in your cottage. We are still staying with the in-laws.'

'Have you got your grant from the Lord Mayor's Fund yet?'

'My boy is looking forward to going back to school.'

The drizzle dissipated. The sun shone in short bursts and broke through the remaining clouds. Annie placed her basket on the ground and folded down her collar. She straightened up and looked across the fields. The landscape still showed grey from the saturated salt. However, there was a slight variation in the field colours which were a little brighter than a few weeks before. She watched Eric's herd of angus cattle, their heads down as they pulled at the grass.

He must think the grass is safe for them.

'Ooh, first thing I need is a new ration book.'

Annie delved into her basket.

'I have one coupon left.'

Dickie Byers placed a new ration book on the counter. He had been the greengrocer on the island for many years. He was a large man, with an outrageously red complexion, and eyes that reduced to pencil lines when he laughed. Most of the islanders were registered with him for their food ration books and relied on him for flexibility with credit.

'There you are, Mrs Hadley.'

'Well, thank you.'

She checked her list.

'Now, I need half a pound of cheese, same of flour, oh, and a loaf of bread please.'

He weighed the cheese, followed by the flour, and placed the items in brown paper bags. When it came to the bread he paused, and in a flamboyant gesture, placed a second loaf on the counter.

'Here, this will help.'

He winked at Annie.

'I would appreciate some of that flood damaged wheat from George for my new hens.'

She nodded and read out her list.

'I need some cooking fat, two tins of peaches, a tin of evaporated milk and one of spam please.'

She paused whilst he located the items and placed them on the counter.

'Some tomato ketchup, oh, and a tin of corned beef and sardines. She picked up the second loaf and gestured with it.

'Thank you, I will ask George about the wheat.'

She placed the remaining items in her basket and opened her purse.

'Just three shillings, Mrs Hadley. Three shillings are ample.'

'Well, thank you, Mr Byers, but there's no need to do that. I really should pay the full price like everybody else. I don't know how much wheat George can spare.'

'Never you mind about that, Mrs Hadley. It is my pleasure.'

The grocer towered over the counter and beamed at her.

'Well, it's most kind of you. Thank you.'

She closed her purse and left.

Ah yes. Sausages.

'I need some of your best pork sausages please, Frank. The ones we had before went down very well with George.'

She pulled out a meat coupon and placed it on the counter. Frank Thomson was a dark, slim man. His black rimmed glasses gave him an air of austerity and his butcher's apron swamped his small, angular frame. He disappeared to the back of the shop.

'They look lovely.'

He wrapped the sausages in greaseproof paper and handed them to her.

'I'll be re starting deliveries next week, my old van is up and running again.'

'Well, that is good news, Frank. A delivery would be very convenient.'

She placed the coins on the counter and pushed the sausages into her basket.

'How is your wife, Frank? I heard she had a bout of nerves. Is she any better?'

Frank peered over the top of his glasses.

'Oh, she's a little better, thank you. Yes, a little better'

'Would it help if I popped in and had a cup of tea with her? What do you think? I don't want to intrude, only...'

'I don't think she's up to anything like that. I mean...well, thank you, it's very kind of you but she has not been herself since the flood. You know how it is, it affected people in different ways. She's been bad with it, bad with her nerves.'

'Oh dear. Well, if there's anything I can do, anything at all, please do let me know.'

He nodded, looked down at the counter and picked at an imaginary piece of meat.

'Well, I had better get back.'

She drove home under a canopy of clear blue sky, just in time to prepare George's lunch.

31

John placed his toy tractor back in its box. He glanced over at his brothers. They were playing their own noisy game and did not bother him. Val sat by the window with Olive. He could tell his sister was enjoying the attention because she swung her legs back and forth when she spoke.

He was bored. He wanted to go out in the fields with his father like he used to before the flood came. He recalled when his father let him take over the wheel of his tractor, the smell of the earth and the paraffin as they bumped across the fields. How they looked for the birds and talked about their nesting habits. Or when they spotted a hare with her leverets, and tried to guess where she would place them, to protect them from predators. But since their return to the island, he had never been alone with his father. And if he sidled up to him and listened to the adult conversations, they spoke about the same things; the drainage problems, the ditches, and culverts, how the salt and weeds had invaded the land and the mending of fence posts.

He knew the salt had destroyed the soil and killed all the insects and small animals. He had seen it with his own eyes; their tiny, complicated bodies rigid on the ground, the earthworms, like a string blanket of white threads spread across the grey earth. And when he looked for the plants and weeds, they appeared in strange places on the island where he had never seen them before. He knew the ditches and culverts had to be cleared but he could not see the point of mending fence posts if there were no cattle. His father had promised him he would buy some cattle and pigs when they returned to the island, but the pigsties and remaining cattle stalls stood empty. And when he asked his father, he got the same answer.

'Oh, I don't know, son. One thing at a time.'

John wiped away a tear and screwed up his eyes. He heard voices in the yard. He saw his father and Jake talking together, whilst Reggie and two other farm workers stood further away. He wanted to go outside and stand by his father, give him a nudge, and ask him if they could go out on the tractor. But he knew what would happen.

'Not now, son. Go and see Mum or Olive.'

'How are you getting on with the work on the wall. Do they still want you?'

George and Jake walked a few steps together and stopped.

'We are doing two days a week, guv'nor. What with clearing the ditches with the dragline diggers and shoring up the permanent repairs, there is plenty of earth to shift.'

Jake glanced across to Reggie and the other men.

'However, we just wondered, guv'nor, can you afford to have us back, or do we need to look for another job?'

George wanted his workers back on the farm, but the secondment payment he received helped feed his family. He scratched his head as if he was thinking about the matter for the first time.

'What about...if you all do a day a week for me here on the farm. We can see how we go, until we can get the land right.'

Jake pondered the idea for a few seconds.

'Let me speak to the others.'

The men formed a huddle and drew on their cigarettes. They watched Jake as he returned to George.

'The men say yes, guv'nor. When do you want us to start?'

'Well, thank you, Jake. Please pass my thanks on to all of them. Tomorrow if you can. The bever hut is still flooded so we will meet in the first pigsty. Usual time.'

'That was fun!'

Olive's cheeks were flushed from the cold air, and her eyes darted clear and bright. The children made a circle around her as she placed a basket on the kitchen table.

'Val, can you count the eggs please.'

The child peered over the top of the basket and surveyed the eggs. As she picked up each egg, she counted out loud, and placed it in a bowl.

'Twelve eggs.'

She folded her arms and gave a triumphant smile. The boys feigned disinterest. Annie glanced at Val and winked at Olive. George wondered how they would survive.

32

Eloise turned to face Barrett.

'What do you mean, Jim?'

'All I'm saying is I won't be coming here for a while.'

'But why? I don't understand.'

She tried to control the wobble in her voice. Barrett swept his fingers through his hair and inhaled through closed teeth.

'Things have changed, girl.'

'What things?'

An uneasy sensation invaded her gut.

'All I'm saying is, let's cool it down for a while, maybe a month or so...'

She blinked back tears.

'Oh, so you want to finish with me.'

Suddenly, Barrett kissed her full on the lips. She felt her body start to yield but pushed him away. He got out of bed and pulled on his trousers. Her face crinkled and her mouth shaped into an 'O'.

'Don't go, Jim. Please...'

Her hot tears fell, and she began to sob.

His eyes glittered with disdain.

'There's no need to cry.'

He pulled his shirt from the back of a chair.

'But Jim? I thought you...'

She gasped. She couldn't bring herself to say the word.

'I like you a lot, Eloise, you know I do, but this sneaking around behind your husband's back, it just doesn't feel right anymore.'

She turned like a whippet.

'Well, it was your suggestion.'

He slipped on his jacket and picked up his boots.

'I have to go.'

She flung back the covers and pulled a robe over her naked body.

'Jim, no! Wait! Please! We can't leave it like this!'

She tied the belt of her robe and followed him down the stairs.

They danced to a strange tune as he tried to reach the front door.

'Can't we talk?'

She grabbed his arm, but he dislodged her and pulled on the latch.

'Sorry, girl.'

He ran out the house, his bare feet silent on the path. The gate slammed shut. Gone.

Eloise clung to the coat stand but her knees gave way and she slithered to the floor. She flung back her head and emitted a silent scream.

Barrett stopped to get his breath.

That was tricky.

He stepped into his boots and pulled the laces tight. He exhaled slow and straightened his jacket. He hated to see women cry. Only his mother's tear-stained face invoked feelings of pity and he remembered how, as a child, he wanted to comfort her. But tears in other women did not have the same effect. Instead, they caused his emotions to harden and created an inaccessibility within him that no woman could penetrate.

Maybe I am like my father after all. I hope she is safe. But I can't go home. It is too dangerous. Too dangerous for all of us.

'But we have not seen them for months, Derek.'

Dorothy glared at her husband.

'There is no reason to visit them.'

He glanced down at the book on his lap.

'But he's your brother, Derek. We don't need a reason.'

Her tone was tight, exasperated.

'I can always go over and see them after work, just check everything is okay.'

'That's not what I meant. Why don't we ask them over for tea.'

He frowned.

'Well, as I said the other day, I am very busy at work. Do you remember me talking about the permanent repairs to the sea wall on the island? You probably don't...'

'Of course, I do! You have mentioned them several times. In fact, you talk about little else.'

He did not respond. He recalled the tension between Dorothy and his brother. A palpable, pulsating discomfort that throbbed between them every time they met.

He sighed and picked up his book.

33

When the army withdrew from the island Barrett returned to his daily routine of drill practice, kit inspection and other barrack-based duties. He felt stifled. He thought about Eloise from time to time and bragged to his friends about an affair with a married woman, but she was confined to history, a pleasurable distraction from the chaos of the flood. Barrett needed female company, not that of seductive giggles and yielding flesh, but helpful conversation, even advice. He decided to pay Mrs Stirling a visit.

He stepped inside the pet shop. A rabbit in a hutch nibbled at some cabbage leaves and a solitary budgerigar hopped across a perch in its cage. After a few moments, Mrs Stirling appeared from the back of the shop. She was a graceful, slim woman in her mid-fifties. She wiped her hands on her apron and tucked a stray hair behind one ear.

'Why, Sergeant Barrett! How nice to see you!'

'Good day to you, Ma'am.'

He returned her smile and looked around the shop.

'Have you managed to return all the animals to their owners?'

'Yes, I have. Well, apart from one dog. He was returned to the owner, but unfortunately, she passed away. Her neighbour brought the dog back to be rehomed. I asked that lady if she would keep him, but I have not seen or heard from her since.'

She removed her glasses and placed them on the counter. Despite her elegant appearance, her complexion lacked colour. She had worked non-stop since the flood and taken in and cared for dozens of traumatised animals. At one point, she struggled to feed and look after them, but a local newspaper reported on her efforts, and volunteers and generous benefactors came forward and eased the strain.

'Is the dog here?'

'Yes, he's out the back.'

They went to the back of the shop and entered a lean to; it looked different to his last visit. The cats and dogs had gone, and the pens and kennels stood empty. There was a small amount of dog food in a box together with two blankets.

'Here we are.'

She pointed to the only occupied kennel. The dog was lying down with his head on his front paws, but when he saw his benefactor, he stood, panted, and wiggled his tail and body. She bent down and stroked his head and neck.

'Good boy, good boy.'

Barrett crouched down in front of the dog.

'Hello, old friend.'

He patted the soft, curly fur and let the dog's busy nose travel across his hands and up and down his legs.

'Here.'

She handed the sergeant some bacon fat scraps. He laid them out in the flat of his hand in front of the dog's mouth. The dog swept his tongue across the sergeant's hand, gulped down the scraps and licked the rim of his mouth. Barrett laughed.

'That didn't last long! I've nothing more for you!'

He displayed empty hands and stood up. The dog

slumped down and placed his head back on his front paws.

'He's a dear little dog. It's a shame he doesn't have a home. He's very good with children, so gentle.'

Barrett nodded towards the animal.

'I have met Buster before. I saw him with Daisy and Jennifer when they collected him from your shop. The child told me they were taking him home to his owner who lived next door.'

'Yes, that's right. Well, that was the neighbour who passed away. Whether her death was due to the flood in some way I don't know, but it left Buster without a home.'

The dog lifted his head and thumped his tail on the floor.

'Jennifer was keen to have him. Daisy said she might take Buster and that she would let me know, but that was almost three weeks ago, and she has not returned. I presume she's changed her mind...I...'

'I could take Buster to Daisy and see what she wants to do, Mrs Stirling. If she doesn't want to keep him, I will bring him back. At least you will know where you stand.'

He turned to the dog.

'And this little fella needs a home.'

'Well, thank you, sergeant. That's so kind of you.'

She wrote Daisy's address on a scrap of paper and passed it to the sergeant.

They walked back through the shop with Buster on his lead. She opened the door.

'Off you go. And good luck!'

Mrs Stirling watched the sergeant and Buster until they disappeared.

Well, you aren't the first and you won't be the last. But everyone deserves a chance of love.

Barrett walked along the main street. He remembered every detail when he rescued Daisy and thought about her every day. But when he saw her outside the pet shop, he had been distracted by her beauty and disappointed by her cool response.

This time it is going to be different.

He gave an affirmative nod.

Buster stopped and cocked his leg. He rechecked the address. It was the same road Daisy took with Jennifer when she declined his offer to accompany them. He turned into the road. Buster pricked up his ears and scurried along the pavement. When they stopped outside Daisy's house, Buster pulled at his lead and tried to walk up the neighbouring path. He shortened the dog's lead and steered him towards Daisy's front door.

He straightened his uniform, took a deep breath, and knocked on the door. There was no answer. Buster whined and pawed at the door. He was about to leave when he heard an indoor bolt slide back.

Barrett had rehearsed what he planned to say, but when Daisy opened the front door, her loveliness threw him into a state of joyful agitation. She appeared even more beautiful than he remembered. He wondered if she was Irish, but her features carried a hint of exotic shores which he could not place. He saw the colour of her eyes for the first time, they were green with flecks of grey. But he also noticed the dark shadows beneath her eyes; dark, bruised pouches, against her pale, translucent skin.

Daisy looked at the sergeant, down at Buster and back at the sergeant. Her ruby red lips were slightly parted, and her eyes bore the curious, unflinching expression of a child's gaze.

'Good morning, Ma'am.'

She clasped the collar of her housecoat.

'Good morning.'

She looked at the dog as he wagged his tail and pulled on his lead.

'You have Buster!'

She laughed. Barrett smiled.

'Yes, here he is.'

He handed the lead to Daisy.

'Well thank you for bringing him home, Sergeant. My daughter had whooping cough these past few weeks and I have not been able to get out.'

'That is my pleasure, Ma'am. I'm sorry to hear that. I hope she's made a full recovery.'

'Yes, she is fine now, thank you.'

'Oh, Ma'am, my name is Jim – Jim Barrett.'

Daisy smiled and closed the door.

34

George surveyed the sky.

That's good. We'll have time before breakfast to finish those fence repairs down by the north field.

He whistled for Sam and set off at a brisk pace.

A quarter of a mile later, the black Labrador appeared alongside him. The dog's legs and underbelly were streaked with mud, and his black fur stood in stubborn wet ridges. He patted the top of the dog's head.

'You saved all of us from the flood, Sam. You were our only warning system.'

The dog looked up at his master with loyal eyes and wagged his tail in soft sweeps. Suddenly, the dog was distracted by a sudden scurry in a hedgerow and disappeared. A few moments later, he reappeared with burrs stuck to his ears. George clicked his fingers; the dog came to heel and let his master remove the spiny seed heads. Then he was gone, busy with his nose, eyes, and ears.

George reached the outbuilding. The door was swollen from the flood. He kicked it open and went inside. He collected a pair of leather gauntlet gloves, two wooden stakes, a pair of wire cutters, a fourteen-pound hammer and a large mallet. He placed the hammer and large mallet outside. Then, he slung the bag of tools over his shoulder, picked up a roll of barbed wire and a bucket of staples.

'Morrr-ning!'

Josh jumped down from the tractor.

'Morning to you, Josh, and a fine one at that.'

George placed the barbed wire and bucket of staples on the ground and fastened the door. He turned and nodded towards the gap in the fence.

'I reckon we'll get that finished before breakfast if we crack on with it.'

He pointed at the gap.

'We need one stake that end, next to the hedge, and another one in the middle of the gap.'

The two men walked down to the fence. They were used to each other's way of working and settled down to the task in hand. George pulled on the gauntlet gloves. He took one end of the broken barbed wire, turned it through, and twisted it into a loop. Josh positioned a stake and hit its top with the hammer.

'You will split it with that. Use the mallet to bed it in.'

Josh changed tools.

'Them tides are back to normal ain't they, guv'nor?'

He swung the mallet over his shoulder and brought it down hard on top of the stake.

'Yes, they are. I have checked them every day since our return.'

George picked up the other broken end of the barbed wire, turned it into a loop and twisted it.

'I am glad I released Jake and Reggie from the farm. Quite a few of us released our farm workers to work with the engineering corps. Those boys made a grand job.'

Josh tugged at the stake.

'They liked the rum ration. They got that every day. Warmed 'em up in that freezing weather, kept their spirits up too. Would you be introducing a rum ration on the farm in the winter, guv'nor?'

'Not bloody likely!'

Josh laughed and gave the stake a final tap. He stood the second stake up and positioned it ready for the mallet. George inserted a new piece of barbed wire between the two barbed wire loops, took a claw hammer from his pocket and pulled and twisted the wire tight.

'I saw the blacksmith's widow, Alice Wright, yesterday,' said Josh.

He secured the second stake.

'She's had a hard time of it, what with those boys and no husband. She's trying to get help with the cottage. The flood knocked out part of the back wall and the rain comes in.'

They measured and cut three fresh lengths of barbed wire.

'I didn't know about David.'

George measured knee high from the ground.

'It will be difficult for her without him, there's no doubt about that. Who is repairing the cottage wall for her?'

He attached the first length to each of the new stakes.

'I don't know. I only found out about it yesterday, but she needs help sooner rather than later.'

'I agree. I will pay her a visit and bring some of the men with me. You and I, we have our families and our health. It is difficult for those who haven't, especially the women who must struggle on their own.'

The men fell silent in their work. They measured the height of a hammer handle up from the first length of barbed wire, attached the second length to the stakes and did the same with the third length. They stapled the new wire and the repaired wire to the posts.

'That will do for now,' said George.

The fence stood chest high and was strong enough

to contain cattle within the field. He stood back, repositioned his cap and surveyed their work.

'Now, let's go and have breakfast.'

The men from the Ministry arrived at ten minutes to ten.

George wiped his mouth and rose from his chair. He pulled on his boots and jerkin and stepped out into the yard. The men shook hands.

'Do you want to see the land now? I can take you around the island if that would help.'

'Yes, we will do that, Mr Hadley. Do you have transport? Or, if you prefer, we can take our vehicle.'

'I will come in your vehicle if I may.'

The men gathered around the car.

Mr Browning opened the driver's door.

'Please, Mr Hadley, do sit in the front.'

George slid onto the passenger seat. Mr Cuthbertson sat in the back with his case on his lap.

'We can go to my fields first, then drive to the arable areas nearest the sea wall and do a circular route back. That should cover the main areas, but if you need to see more, just let me know.'

'Sounds fine. Let's do that.'

Mr Browning drove the vehicle out of the yard and onto the back lane.

'Now, these fields all around here, they were all submerged,' said George.

He pointed in front, from right to left.

'My wife and children were rowed across from here to the sea wall.'

'I need to take some samples of the soil,' said Mr Cuthbertson.

Mr Browning stopped the car.

The scientist alighted from the car and walked into the middle of the field. He placed his case on the ground, opened the lid, and began to scoop quantities of soil into different containers.

Mr Browning turned towards George.

'This island is an interesting place, Mr Hadley. What's the soil like here?'

George relaxed, happy to talk.

'It's a good quality soil, suitable for growing barley and wheat.'

'But I thought it was marshland.'

'Aye, it is.'

'Doesn't it crack and dry out in the summer?'

'Well, yes it does, but underneath the topsoil is a peaty mass, caused by wet, winter weather and rainfall throughout the year. In the summer, when it dries out, the topsoil draws up and absorbs the water retained by the marsh below.'

'Ah, yes, natural hydration.'

'Aye. Even when we get a dry, hot summer the crops grow, and we get a good harvest.'

'And the same system for many hundreds of years, Mr Hadley.'

George nodded.

'The Dutch came here in the 17th century. It was their engineering expertise which resulted in erection of the sea wall, and the system of culverts and ditches you see right across the island.'

'I was brought up by an aunt and uncle not far from here.'

Mr Browning nodded towards the mainland.

'The house next to the Post Office, just along from the army barracks. It is still in our family. I often take the train from London and spend weekends down here, more so since my wife passed away.'

As he spoke about his personal circumstances, his voice inflected a hint of Scottish accent.

'Well, I'll be damned. I have driven past that house many times. You know the area well then if you spent your childhood here.'

'Yes, well I suppose I do and there has been little change, which is not a bad thing. It is a shame this flood happened, Mr Hadley. It has had such a terrible impact on the land.'

'Aye, it has. This flood has been like no other. It has upset the natural hydration system and disrupted our normal farming methods. We have got to find a way of repairing and rejuvenating the soil and we need to do it soon. We are running out of money and won't be able to sustain our farms for much longer.'

'Okay.'

Mr Cuthbertson slid onto the backseat.

The men continued their journey and stopped by the sea wall.

'That's a fine piece of civil engineering,' said Mr Cuthbertson. 'Back-breaking work has gone into that.'

'Yes,' replied George. 'The army coordinated the earlier work on the wall, helped by hundreds of Essex volunteers, including our farm workers here on the island. The wall will protect our families and future generations. We must never have another flood like this one.'

They sat in silence and studied the structure. As far as they could see, from left to right, the sea wall stood in all its glory, as strong as a fortress and ready to face the elements.

The men continued their journey around the island. Whenever Mr Cuthbertson made a request, they stopped the car, and he took further soil samples. Two hours later, they returned to the farmhouse.

'Cup of tea, gentlemen?'

George slammed the car door shut.

'Yes, thank you,' said Mr Cuthbertson. 'We are ready for that.'

'The land is drying out,' said Mr Browning.

He sipped his tea and brushed cake crumbs from his coat.

'Aye, it wasn't that long ago it was under water,' said George. 'The problem we have now is the salt level in the soil, tons of it, and we need to get rid of it.'

'Once Mr Cuthbertson has analysed the samples, we will be able to advise you.'

'And how long will that take?'

Mr Browning turned to Mr Cuthbertson.

'Oh, two to four weeks, do you think?'

The scientist nodded, his mouth full of cake.

'And then what? I have a list of questions here, from my neighbouring farmers. They know you are here today. They are expecting answers.'

'Mr Hadley, the starting point must be the salt content of the soil. There is no point in discussing anything else until we have the test results in front of us.'

'Well then, can I arrange another meeting with you? We need to get things moving and sorted out as soon as we can. Why Farmer...'

'Mr Hadley, you must be patient. You must let matters take their course. Some of the tests on the soil may take longer than expected and some may require further testing. We hope it will only take a few weeks, but it could take longer. And in the meantime, both you and your fellow farmers must wait and do nothing to the soil. That is very important. Do you understand? Do nothing to the soil until we come back with the test results. Otherwise, you will compromise your compensation claims. Please tell that to all the farmers.'

George swirled the remains of the tea in his cup.

'Can I get you gentlemen any more tea?'

'No thank you, Mrs Hadley. Thank you for your kind hospitality.'

Mr Browning stood followed by Mr Cuthbertson.

'We will be in touch, Mr Hadley.'

35

One afternoon, when Annie was darning a pair of George's socks, there was a knock at the scullery door. A knock at the scullery door was a common occurrence, but on this occasion, it was different. The knock was soft, timid in its delivery, and with no extraneous sound of shuffling feet or movement.

Annie recognised the woman; she had seen her in the village accompanied by three small children. The woman was young, barely out of girlhood, but lines etched her fine, pale skin and deeper, furrowed lines ran across her brow. Her hair was matted with dirt and scraped back under a filthy head scarf, and her eyes bore a world weariness which took her beyond her years.

'Can I help you?'

The woman opened her mouth, but no sound came out. She stooped under the weight of a large canvas bag slung over her shoulder.

'Afternoon, Ma'am.'

Her voice was a whisper.

'Ma'am, I have items for sale.'

The woman dropped the canvas bag to the ground and knelt beside it. She pulled out bundles of rag, unwrapped each one and placed pieces of cracked and chipped crockery on the ground.

'I'm sorry, my dear. But I do not need any crockery.'

The woman looked up at Annie and nodded. She

rewrapped each piece of crockery, placed them back in her bag and stood up. She hauled the bag back onto her shoulder.

'I am sorry to have bothered you.'

Her voice was just audible, and a slight tremor appeared on her lower lip.

Annie smiled.

'Can I help in any other way?'

The woman remained still.

'Would you like a cup of tea? I've just made a fresh pot.'

The woman hesitated, then nodded. She dropped her bag by the backdoor and followed Annie into the kitchen. Annie poured a cup of tea, cut a slice of fruitcake, and placed them in front of the woman. The woman stared at the piece of cake and the tremor in her lower lip increased.

'Are you all right, my dear?'

The woman nodded, then shook her head. She continued to look at the cake but did not touch it. Eventually, she spoke.

'May I take the piece of cake home for my children?'

'Why of course! But please, do have a piece yourself and I will wrap some up for your children. How many children have you got?'

'Three; two boys and a girl.'

She bit into the cake and shovelled the loose crumbs into her mouth.

'What is your name, dear?'

'Molly. I live with my children, in the village. It is the last cottage on the left as you go towards the sea.'

'With your husband?'

'No...'

She started to cry

Annie held Molly's hands and after a while, she told

her story. When the flood arrived, her husband removed part of a ceiling and she climbed up into the eaves. He managed to lift each child out of their bed, through the gap and into her arms. But by the time he lifted the third child through the gap, he had no strength to save himself and was swept away by the flood.

'My brother helped us across to the mainland, but he died in hospital a few weeks later.'

'I'm so sorry, my dear. So sorry for all of you.'

She took the handkerchief offered by Annie.

'When we returned to the island, I cleaned up our cottage as best I could, but I had no furniture and no money for food.'

'It must have been awful for you. How did you manage?'

'Well, I got a voucher for coal to help dry out the cottage, and a coupon from the committee on the mainland.'

She wiped her eyes and blew her nose.

'I managed to buy some second-hand beds, and a table and chairs, but that's all. There was talk about everyone getting a new carpet, but I have not heard anymore.'

'Have you claimed national assistance for yourself and the children?'

'What is national assistance? I have not heard of that?'

'It is help from the government, money you get on a regular basis. But you need to apply for it. The post office on the mainland should be able to help you. I will be going to the mainland on Friday, I can give you a lift.'

'Thank you. I have got my ration book but...'

'Well, you shouldn't have a problem with your ration book. Mr Byers, the grocer in the village deals with those. Have you registered with him?'

'Yes, and I do use my ration book in his shop. Only the trouble is...well, to be honest he is a problem.'

Annie frowned.

'What do you mean? Can you tell me?'

'When I go in, I tell him what I want and hand over my coupons. I pay for what I can, and he gives me credit on the other items until the end of the month. But when he gives me the chit of what I owe him, he has added in extra things I haven't had or charged me twice for the same item. The last time he did it was last week when I had a loaf of bread. He wrote down what I owed him, but when he gave me the chit a few days later, the cost of the loaf had doubled, and he expected the extra payment.'

'Oh, did he really.'

Annie's jaw set hard, and a twitch pulsed down the side of her face.

'I can't go anywhere else because I am registered with him. He has one customer in at a time, so there is no one who can back me up.'

She started to cry again.

'Well now, when you have finished your tea, we will pay Mr Byers a visit. Don't forget the cake for your children.'

Annie placed Molly's ration book on the counter.

'Now, my dear, tell Mr Byers exactly what you told me.'

She placed her arm around Molly's shoulders and stared at Dickie Byers. As Molly spoke his complexion began to deepen. He looked away from Annie. He glanced back. His complexion turned a glorious purple.

'Of course, there must be some mistake.'

He unfolded his arms and rubbed his temples and the sides of his face.

'I see, Mr Byers, a mistake. Well, that is one way of putting it. What I want to know is how you are going to put it right. Of course, it would be unfortunate if word got out that you were defrauding your customers.'

'Are you accusing me of theft, Mrs Hadley.'

'Yes, I think I probably am.'

'Why, that is preposterous.'

'Is it Mr Byers? We could get the police involved and see what they think.'

'Now hold on a moment, there is no need to go that far. I maintain it was a mistake. I will put it right. Yes, I will.'

'Now, that is much better, Mr Byers. Molly, would you be content with some groceries equal to those you have paid for but not received? I am sure Mr Byers will be generous when he works that out for you.'

'Yes, Mrs Hadley. But would you mind making sure for me?'

'Of course, I will.'

The women waited while the grocer checked the invoice chits and completed some figurework.

'The boxes can go in the back, Mr Byers.'

Annie changed gear and pulled away.

'You won't have any more trouble from Dickie Byers.'

'Thank you, Mrs Hadley. You are so kind. And thank you for the cake, the children will love it.'

36

Over the next few days Annie's thoughts returned to Molly and those widowed from the flood, and when she saw Anita after the Sunday morning church service, her mind was made up.

She spoke in low tones and told Anita about Molly and Dickie Byers.

'But that is disgraceful! That man presents himself as a pillar of the community! Come to think of it, he does always have one customer in his shop at a time and I suppose that is why.'

'Well, he got short shrift from me I can tell you. He won't be cheating Molly anymore, but that doesn't mean he won't continue with others. We need to form a welfare committee and let him know we are helping them. It might make him think about what he is doing, even stop him.'

'Who can we ask to join us?

'What about Lavinia Everitt, the good doctor's wife? I'm sure she would want to be involved. Also, Margaret Barling. She has excellent connections with people of influence on the mainland.'

'What a good idea.'

'I will leave now, Mrs Hadley, and bring the children back by half past four in time for their tea.'

'Thank you, Olive.'

'Are you at home, Annie?'

A female voice boomed through the farmhouse and beyond. Margaret Barling's stentorian voice matched her physique; large, jolly unmissable. She was married to Donald Barling who came from the oldest farming family on the island and was well known amongst the islanders.

'Why, hello, Margaret. Let me take that for you.'

Annie took the voluminous tweed cape and hung it up.

'Thank you. Good to see you, my dear. This meeting, what a super idea!'

She winked at Annie.

'I wish I thought of it myself.'

She patted her hat and stepped into the kitchen. She wore sturdy, sensible shoes and a tweed suit which covered her masculine frame. Her strong, no-nonsense legs were the result of daily walks with her Labrador dogs 'whatever the weather,' and her large, pendulous breasts a testament to her fecundity and production of four boys in quick succession.

Anita and Lavinia arrived at the same time.

When Annie married George, she knew no one on the island, only her parents-in-law. However, within weeks of her arrival, Anita had introduced herself and they became firm friends.

Anita hung her cardigan over the back of a chair. She placed the teapot on a tray, together with the sugar bowl, crockery, scones, butter, and jam and took it through to the lounge. However, when she saw there were only two armchairs and the children's wooden pallets for seating, she returned to the kitchen and laid the items on the table.

'Hello, Mrs Everitt, it's so good of you to come.'

Annie smiled.

'Oh, do call me Lavinia.'

Lavinia Everitt was a beautiful woman. She was slim and petite with a fair complexion and clear blue eyes. She had the tiniest of feet which pattered rather than strode, and her hands were fine and delicate. She wore a floral-patterned dress; it reminded Annie of a doll's dress with its lace collar and dainty buttons. Although Lavinia had been married to Dr Everitt for many years and was a mother to their three girls and a boy, Annie recalled that whenever she saw Lavinia and her husband together, they looked like father and daughter, rather than husband and wife.

'Come and sit down,'

Lavinia put a dainty foot forward and picked her way across the flagstones to the kitchen table. Anita poured tea and offered the scones.

'It's lovely to see you all,' said Annie.

'I think this is a marvellous idea,' said Margaret. 'We must do something for these women who have lost their menfolk.'

Margaret Barling sat back from the table on the edge of her chair and sipped her tea. Although her feet were together, her knees were apart and exposed the tops of her thick, nylon stockings.

'I know where these women live,' said Lavinia. 'They all live in abject poverty and, of course, their children suffer too. I have on occasion provided them with food, but a coordinated approach would be much better for them. They need something they can rely on.'

The women continued their discussions and by the time they had drank their tea, they agreed a plan and were ready to start.

37

Eloise curled and stretched her body. She was still in bed. Although she had finished her voluntary work some months ago, her tiredness had not abated, and she needed to rest.

She often thought about the flood and how it touched her life. Different people had passed through the reception centre, some of them wealthy, whilst others were already ground down by poverty. Men, women, children, grandparents, all were plunged into chaos by the flood. But when the flood victims first arrived at the centre, she and her volunteers were ready to help. They gave words of comfort and hugs to terrified children, provided practical support to their distraught parents and bewildered elderly folk, and cups of tea to exhausted rescue teams and medics.

The smallest gesture made a difference. A warm smile, a sympathetic ear, a hot meal, and dry clothes. All helped soothe the angst of destroyed homes, lost toys, and missing pets. She would never forget their tears and smiles of gratitude when they said their farewells. She felt appreciated, even loved. It was an extraordinary experience for her.

She felt nauseous.

A cup of tea might help.

As she pulled back the covers, a surge of bile hit the back of her throat. She ran to the bathroom, fell to her knees, and vomited into the toilet bowl. She gulped in air and waited for the retches to subside. After a few moments, she clutched the side of the bath and heaved herself up. When she looked in the mirror, she saw a grey, perspiring reflection. She splashed her face with cold water and licked the droplets of liquid from her lips. Her legs began to wobble. She forced herself to sit on the edge of the bath.

Oh God. I feel dreadful. I can't be...

She shuffled through to the kitchen, and with trembling hands, poured herself a glass of water. Later, she could not recollect entering the lounge or laying on the sofa, and when she awoke two hours later, her face felt cold and clammy.

Must get dressed. Will feel better.

However, when she started to dress, she could not close the button on her skirt. She breathed in and tried again, but it was no good, the skirt no longer fitted.

Oh no! I must be....

She gasped and raised her hand to her mouth. She checked the dates in her head; she was late. She sat down hard and stared at the floor.

She had always wanted a child, but whenever she raised the subject with Fred, his mouth snapped shut like a clam, and he went to the room with his train set and stayed there for hours. And later when she retired to bed, she found him already there, fast asleep. She wished he had told her before they married, he did not want children, and as the years passed, her attempts to speak about it lessened until she ceased altogether.

She sat for several minutes, then said his name out loud.

'Sergeant Jim Barrett.'

38

Jake and Reggie climbed into the back of the truck. They sat amongst spades, shovels, and trowels, and leant against a pile of sand and cement covered with old cornsacks.

'Righto,' said Josh.

He slid onto the front seat. George turned the truck around and drove out the yard.

The cottage stood in a mire of mud, its path delineated by two parallel railway sleepers. George remembered the cottage before the flood, with its garden full of flowers and well-tended vegetable patch. He raised the knocker but before he could bring it down, a woman opened the door.

Alice Wright was the widow of David Wright, the island blacksmith. George had ignored the rumours and stories as to how David died, he only knew the flood took him, and left Alice and the five boys to fend for themselves. David's family had owned and run the forge for over fifty years, but now its doors were shut, the anvil silent and its furnace cold.

George removed his cap.

'Mrs Wright?'

'Yes, that's right.'

Her eyes flickered towards the men in the truck. A boy of about fourteen years old appeared beside her and glared at George. He wore ill-fitting clothes, and his discoloured, scuffed boots were split around the toe section.

George nodded to the boy.

'Hello, lad.'

'Ronnie is my eldest boy.'

She touched her son's arm, but he did not speak.

'And a fine-looking lad too. I heard part of your back wall collapsed in the flood. We can repair it for you, rebuild it, make it sound.'

The woman raised her eyebrows. She opened her mouth, as if to speak, then closed it.

'May I come in and have a look at the wall?'

She stood to one side, but her son did not move. George slipped through the gap between the boy and the door frame. The cottage was one of the smallest on the island. Four young boys sat on the floor in a circle around a collection of stones and pebbles. He nodded to the boys and walked through to the kitchen. The room was sparse with little sign of food and an old boat sail covered the back wall. He knelt and pulled it back to reveal a large hole.

'Well, the flood took a big, old lump out of that.'

He looked around.

'The bricks must be here somewhere.'

'There's a pile of 'em out the back,' said Ronnie.

The boy stood in front of his mother, his arms folded. George ran his hands over the surface of the wall. He pointed to the hole and the surrounding fractured bricks.

'We can re-cement those, then rebuild and fill the hole.'

He looked up and across the ceiling.

'Roof looks all right from the inside. Let's go and have a look outside.'

The trio climbed through the hole in the wall and

turned to face the back of the cottage. The boy pointed to a pile of bricks stacked by the wall.

'We got those up after the flood. They were everywhere.'

'Well done, lad. We can re-use those.'

He surveyed the roof.

'Well, the roof looks sound to me. We will repair the wall first. I will come back in a few weeks and check the roof, but if, it leaks in the meantime, just let me know. I live at Butterwood Farm. It is...'

'We know where you live, Mr Hadley.'

Her gaze was steady, less suspicious. She cast her eyes over the damaged wall.

'We thank you for your kind offer, Mr Hadley, but we have no money to pay for this work.'

The boy kept his arms folded.

'Don't worry,' replied George. 'We came here to help, Mrs Wright, not to be paid. My men will repair the wall for you. It won't take long. We should be finished today if we can get on.'

She nodded and the muscles in her face relaxed. She ushered Ronnie back through the hole in the wall.

'Thank you.'

Alice Wright stood stiff and angular, and a tension returned to her face. It was as if the statement took a physical toll on her body.

'It's no trouble,' replied George. 'None of us can survive on our own. We all need help.'

She gave a shy smile. Since David had gone, she found it hard to accept help, and her eldest boy provided an additional layer of resistance whenever a man entered the cottage.

George changed the subject.

'What do you plan to do with the forge?'

He wanted to add 'now your husband has gone' but

shut his mouth and waited.

'I don't know. Several island men have knocked on the door and asked about it.'

She gave a wry smile and put her arm around Ronnie's shoulders.

'Men who never gave me the time of day before, when David was alive, but who now have a desire to speak with me. Anyhow, I can't have a stranger working in there; I'm here on my own with the boys. My brother, Willy, he is interested in taking on the forge, but I am not so sure.'

She gave no further explanation and looked at her son.

'Ronnie is too young to work the forge, although goodness knows he'd try. It hurts both of us to see it idle. David began to teach him, but he's not ready yet and now...'

'Why don't you rent out the forge on condition they take Ronnie on as their apprentice? I'm sure we can find the right tenant for you.'

She stood quiet and still. Despite the offer, her face was devoid of expression.

'Well, I had better get my men back to the farm. I will call by again and check the wall.'

He replaced his cap and raised his hand. As he walked towards the truck and the waiting men, one continuous thought ran through his mind.

Annie, my love. I am so glad I have got you.

39

The sun shone bright and warm.

Barrett was not due to report for duty until the afternoon. He decided to go to the beach. He drove his truck along the high street.

The town was busy. Children skipped along the pavement and tugged at their mother when they saw a sweet shop. Men, young and old, stood in groups and discussed the follies of government, the cost of tobacco and whether they had time to place a bet. Housewives scurried along, their ration books and empty shopping bags ready as they peered in shop windows to check the queues. They walked, talked, laughed, and foraged. First the war and then the flood, but at last, they had a chance.

Why, that's Mrs Stirling.

Barrett recognised the tall, elegant figure of the pet shop owner as she strode along the pavement ahead of him. Her hair was piled up in its usual elegant jumble and a sleeveless blouse exposed her bare arms to the heat of the sun. He wound down the window of his truck, lowered his elbow over the edge, and steered the vehicle alongside the kerb.

'Good morning, Mrs Stirling.'

She stopped mid stride; her skirt swung out in a half circle and her basket bumped into her hip.

'Good morning, Sergeant Barrett.'

She looked at the sky.

'And what a beautiful morning too!'

'Yes, it certainly is.'

He had not seen Mrs Stirling since he returned Buster to Daisy and Jennifer. She looked fresh and well. Her complexion had a healthy colour and her shoulders no longer hunched into her neck.

He nodded towards her basket.

'That looks heavy. Can I give you a lift somewhere?'

'Well, that is very kind of you, Sergeant, thank you. I am going to the church. It is my turn to clean today. Oh, and there are a couple of heavy boxes in the vestry that must be moved. Would you mind...'

'Not at all!'

He stopped the truck, got out and walked around to the passenger door. She climbed in and placed her basket on her lap.

'Thank you, Sergeant.'

'It's busy today, must be the weather.'

'Yes. It's good to see people out in the town again.'

Barrett drove to the end of the high street, turned into the lane alongside the church and parked his truck in front of the graveyard. He nodded towards the gravestones.

'There will be some new residents in there now.'

'Yes, I'm afraid there will, and quite a few too.'

They alighted from the truck.

She smoothed down her skirt and collected her basket. She raised her eyebrows, looked at the sergeant, and nodded beyond him.

Barrett followed her gaze to the furthest corner of the graveyard. His eyes widened, and his breath became shallow. Daisy stood in poignant isolation next to a new headstone. She finished her prayer and dabbed at her face with a handkerchief. As she crossed the graveyard, her black dress swayed stark against the static headstones, and her flat, black shoes disappeared into the long grass.

When she saw Barrett and Mr Stirling, she gasped and took a sideways step, like a startled animal about to be trapped.

Barrett raised his cap and gave a small bow.

'Good morning, Ma'am.'

She gave a stifled cry. Her eyes shone bright with tears and the pink, wet patches on her skin glistened in the sunlight. She hovered a handkerchief near her face, hesitated and tucked it into a sleeve. She opened her mouth, then paused for a few seconds before she spoke.

'Oh, good...good morning, Mrs Stirling...Sergeant.'

She pressed her ruby red lips together and fresh tears sprung from her eyes. She quickened her pace and disappeared around the corner of the church. Barrett exhaled long and slow and shook his head. Mrs Stirling turned towards him.

'She is beautiful isn't she.'

Barrett nodded, groaned, and closed his eyes.

'She is widowed. Poor chap, he drowned during the flood, after he got Daisy and Jennifer to safety.'

'Yes, I know. I rescued Daisy and Jennifer from the top of their Nissan hut. It was a dangerous business.'

He drew a tin of tobacco from his pocket, opened the lid and removed a slither of paper. Mrs Stirling moved close to the sergeant and spoke sotto voce.

'I wouldn't leave it too long if I were you, sergeant. You won't be the first, although he got nowhere.'

A surge of envy rose within him. He had not considered the possibility that another man would pursue Daisy so soon after her husband's death. And before him too!

Mrs Stirling reverted to her usual volume.

'Daisy is a lovely girl. I have known her a few years

now and her husband too. She struggles without him and continues to suffer, as does the child.'

'I have tried to speak to Daisy a few times, but she doesn't seem interested.'

Barrett's face contorted.

'She's cool towards me. A man needs some encouragement even if it's only a little encouragement.'

He lit his cigarette and inhaled. He held the smoke in his mouth and exhaled in one long plume.

'If it is meant to be, if she is the one for you, Sergeant, it will happen. I always think affairs of the heart are interlinked with fate. As for how long it will take, well I don't know the answer to that.'

What else could she say? She knew Sergeant Barrett was in love with Daisy. She could see it in his eyes when he looked at her, his restlessness, his agitation, when he spoke about her.

She looked at her basket full of polish and dusters.

'I must go now. Nice to talk to you, Sergeant, and thank you for the lift. Oh, would you mind helping me with the boxes before you go? The ones I mentioned, they are in the vestry.'

Barrett nodded, extinguished his cigarette, and followed her into the church.

40

'Annie! We have a visitor!

The pad of her feet fell on the stairs.

'Now, about the samples we took the other week. I have the results here.'

Mr Browning took a thick report from his briefcase, placed it on the table and pushed it towards George.

George eyed the report and scratched the top of his head.

'I haven't got time to read that lot, Mr Browning. Just tell me what it says and when we can cultivate the soil again. That is what I want to know, that is what we all want to know. When can we start to grow our crops?'

'I'm afraid it's not that straightforward, Mr Hadley.'

He pointed towards the report.

'The samples we took from the soil here, well, there is a high salt content in all of them. Of course, that's no surprise, but the soil samples that were taken near the sea wall, those samples have an increased level of salt content. For example, the sample we took from your land, Mr Hadley, had approximately forty tons of salt per acre. Whereas the samples we took from land nearest the sea wall, the salt content went up to eighty tons an acre. And between those two land points, there is a variation in the other soil samples. As we expected, it is bad right across the island.'

George cursed and drummed his fingers on the table.

Mr Browning continued.

'The other issue is the impact of the flood on the National Food Production Programme. Do you know anything about the National Food Production Programme, Mr Hadley?'

'Well yes, I am aware of it, of course, but...'

'Over two hundred and fifty farmers in Essex have been affected by the flood, and like yourself, they all want to start growing crops again as soon as they can. The sheer number of farmers, and the likely impact your collective success or failure will have on the national food programme cannot be overlooked by the government. We cannot have our national food programme stalling, not after what we have been through since the end of the war. The country is recovering from food shortages, but it's still a fine line. The government understands you and your fellow farmers are keen to get your livelihoods back, and that you need scientific advice which will work alongside your traditional farming methods. It also understands you need financial support. But I can't stress enough, Mr Hadley, the scientific advice must be followed, and the relevant procedures adopted.'

He nodded towards the report.

'Section three of the report sets out the sample results. There is also information about which crops can tolerate various levels of salt and there is a section on how to make a compensation claim. Remember, to be able to make a successful claim, you must follow the government guidelines. All the requirements are in there.'

He tapped his index finger on the cover of the report.

'You must read this report, Mr Hadley and do what it says. Tell your fellow farmers to do the same. I have brought extra copies with me.'

He delved into his briefcase, took out several copies of the report and placed them on the table.

George sighed.

'It is a lot to take in. Of course, we will have to do what is required. We have a small pot of savings, but they are almost gone. All of us here on the island are concerned about our livelihoods. We can't hold out much longer. We must get our farms working again.'

Suddenly, George stood up and held out his hand.

'Well, Mr Browning, thank you for your visit. And good day to you.'

'Oh, right. Righto.'

Mr Browning hastily pushed back his chair, grasped the proffered hand, and shook it with vigour.

'As I said, it's all in there.'

He donned his hat and picked up his briefcase.

'Nice doing business with you, Mr Hadley.'

He turned towards Annie.

'Sorry I couldn't stop for tea, Mrs Hadley.'

Being told what to do is hardly conducting business.

George moved towards the door.

George settled into his chair. He picked up the report and held it at eye level. He sighed, placed the report on a small table and closed his eyes. When he awoke an hour later, the report was still in the same place. He picked it up and looked at it under the lamplight but was not encouraged to read it. He placed it back on the table and closed his eyes. This time he did not sleep. Instead, his mind buzzed and whirred. He knew he must read the report and its content had to be conveyed to his fellow farmers. He opened his eyes.

Better get on with it.

He reached for his glasses and turned the first page, but his eyes refused to focus, and the words appeared jumbled.

'Is that the report the gentleman gave you this morning?'

Annie stood behind George's chair and looked over his shoulder.

'Aye, and it's bloody huge. Such a lot to read.'

He reached out for her hand.

'Come and help me.'

She pulled a chair alongside him.

The first part of the report was dedicated to the government's aims for the National Food Production Programme. The next section referred to the various stages, to be carried out by farmers, to ensure rehabilitation of the land.

George pointed to a page.

'It states ditches must be cleared and water channels opened to ensure drainage of the land. Well, that's common sense that is, and we have done that already.'

George sat up in his chair and adjusted his spectacles.

'They mention here, the need to take samples of the soil and for nothing to be done until the results come back. Well, we complied with that as well.'

He flicked through the pages of graphs and figures until he came to the section about the impact of salt on the soil. He read what he already knew; salt destroys the structure of the soil, and the sodium in the salt clings to clay particles in the soil and displaces the calcium.

'Such a disaster for the farming community,' murmured George. 'But we must follow these procedures through and make sure we get it right. It will affect our crops and livelihoods for years to come.'

He pointed to a paragraph in the report.

'They recommend gypsum is spread on the soil which will be provided by the government free of cost.'

He removed his glasses. The final section of the report detailed the requirements for a claim for acreage payments.

'Provided the scientific government advice is followed,' said Annie as she read further along the paragraph.

'The "so called" Acreage Payment Scheme.'

He spoke with an exaggerated lilt in his voice. She pointed towards the bottom of the page.

'It says you must apply to the Lord Mayor's fund if you seek compensation for loss of livestock.'

'Aye, we will be doing that all right, but we need to get this one right when we make a claim.'

She tapped at the last page of the report.

'George, look at this.'

He replaced his glasses and read out the final paragraph.

'It is imperative the farmer follows all procedures set out in this report. Once the results of the salt samples have been provided, the farmer must do nothing to his soil until the results are given and the gypsum is delivered. The gypsum must be spread on the soil according to the instructions. Once the gypsum has been spread, the farmer must do nothing and wait for further advice. The "Do Nothing Policy" is based on scientific advice and is an integral part of the soil restoration programme. There must be strict compliance with each stage of the process. If any advice or procedure is not followed, a claim for compensation will be unsuccessful.'

George handed the report to Annie.

'Well, that is bloody marvellous, it will take months to do what they say. Also, it doesn't say how long we must wait after we spread the gypsum, so we still don't know when we can plant crops again.'

He took off his glasses and rubbed his eyes. Annie left the room and returned with a glass and a bottle of brandy.

'Thank you, my darling.'

He poured the golden liquid into the glass.

'I must call another meeting. Best get it over and done with. I will call it for Friday.'

When George attended the meeting and informed the farmers of the contents of the report, their reaction mirrored his own.

'Bloody shambles...clueless lot sitting in offices...we must comply, our livelihoods are at stake.'

A week later they each received a letter from the Ministry. The gypsum would be delivered within the fortnight.

41

George busied himself with jobs on the farm while they waited for the gypsum to arrive. He checked the previously drained ditches and water channels and made sure his tractor and trailed spinner were ready to spread the gypsum. But whatever he did, whether he worked in the yard, ate a ham sandwich, or lay in bed at night, the fragile state of the family finances returned again and again, like an irritating itch in his side.

He knew all the islanders were suffering a similar plight and, in some cases, much worse. The beleaguered, widowed wives and their hungry children, and his own farm workers whom he could only afford to employ for one day a week, all struggled to provide for their families. Even the young, single men were sick of being idle, and after bouts of heavy drinking they could ill afford, Saturday night brawls at the Gatherers' Arms were commonplace. Eddy Turner, the publican had managed to contain the ugly scenes and fights without involving the police, but it was a worrying sign that frustrations were spilling over into the islanders' everyday lives.

And for George and Annie? Well, their savings were almost depleted, but he wanted to be his own man. George, like all farmers was resourceful, and could barter as good as the next man; a side of bacon for a bottle of whisky, a dozen rabbits for some sliced brisket, or a dozen eggs for flour and butter. However, food was still rationed with no sign of when that would change. Rabbits and hares were still scarce, and wildfowling only came in the winter months. The main resource was the sea with its plentiful supply of fish. He smiled to himself. The flood from the sea had caused devastation and now provided the island with its only substantial food source.

He pondered whether he should ask Annie to cut back within the household, but she kept the budget tight, and Olive worked for nothing. The small government, secondment payment he received for his farm workers when they worked on the sea wall, barely kept them in food.

We need our crops to grow again. There's no other way. They are the life blood of the island.

The temperature was cool for May. The fine rain continued for days, and the unwelcome wet season saturated the soil. However, despite the volume of rain, an acrid smell of salt hung in the air; it was a smell reminiscent of the early days after the flood.

George stood with Joe in his field as a blanket of drizzle enveloped them.

'They are everywhere and more,' said Joe.

He stuck his stick into the sodden ground.

'Don't matter whose field it is, it is the same for all of us. This rain is causing havoc. And we don't need more havoc.'

He raised his stick and pointed to the swathes of fresh, green growth.

'Just look at them bloody weeds. Weeds are growing everywhere, helped by this wretched rain. I have seen creeping thistle, ox tongue and there is barley grass over there. And on other fields I saw twitch grass. All of them have deep roots and will be a bastard to remove. And in the meantime, nature is giving them a grand water.'

'It is even worse for those poor buggers farming near the sea wall. Yep, it is.'

Joe swirled his stick around him.

'They have all these weeds plus the sea plants which have been swept inland and misplaced by the flood. Why, when I was down that way yesterday, I saw samphire right across the fields, and no doubt there will be sea asparagus, sea asters and sea beet in the coming months, all growing on the land when the soil should be growing our wheat and barley. Tis' a terrible mix up all round.'

'Aye, my fields are the same. It is so wet I can't get my tractor and disc harrow onto the land to uproot the weeds and chop them up. This wet weather will cause the machinery to sink, which will compact and ruin the soil. And even if I could get on and got rid of the weeds, if this rain continues, I won't be able to get my trailed spinner onto the land to spread the gypsum for the same reason. I don't suppose the men in suits thought of that.'

George looked up and let the rain wash over his face.

'This fine rain, if we had crops sown it would be welcome, but not this year. This year is going to be like no other.'

42

June 1953

Queen Elizabeth held a special place in the hearts of the Essex people. She travelled to the Essex coastline after the great flood, visited some of the devastated areas and spoke with the survivors and their families.

As the 2nd of June approached, anticipation and excitement grew across the country. The national conscience had buzzed with expectation for weeks, and millions of people looked forward to a day they would never forget. For the islanders, there was no community event to celebrate the coronation. It was too soon after the flood. Instead, families organised their own celebrations to commemorate the day.

'We have been invited over by Eric and Anita to celebrate the coronation.'

George finished his toast and held out his cup.

'What about Mum and Dad?'

'They are invited too. We will be able to watch the coronation on Eric's new television and Anita is going to organise a party for the children.'

Annie beamed.

'How lovely! A TV party!'

Annie listened to Marjorie Anderson on 'Woman's Hour'. The coronation had been the main topic for weeks and members of the public were interviewed about their plans for the special day. Some intended to travel to London and hoped to see the Queen go by in her golden coach, whilst others organised concerts, street parties, pageants or bonfire displays. But many people were content to stay in their own homes and celebrate the event with BBC radio and a special tea with family and friends.

The big day dawned cold, grey, and wet. However, the weather did not dampen the children's enthusiasm. The thought of being able to watch a television and have special party food, was almost too much to bear.

Annie and the children sat in the car ready to leave.

George handed her a bottle of whisky.

'A little something for Eric and Anita.'

He reversed the car and drove out the yard.

The sky was dull, and heavy drizzle hung in the air. However, the Hadley family were in high spirits; it was their first family outing that year.

'Look!' said Val.

She pointed to a bunting of small union jacks strung across the front porch of the farmhouse. As the car slowed, Anita appeared in the doorway. She wiped her hands on her apron and waved.

George alighted from the car.

'Morning!'

He looked at the sky and pulled a face.

'Weather could be better.'

'Careful, walk nicely now.'

Annie helped the children out of the car and handed each of them a party hat.

'Lovely to see you, Anita. It is so kind of you to invite us over and the children are so excited!'

Annie kissed Anita on the cheek and handed her the homemade, special celebration cake.

'So glad you could come. Yes, mine are the same, they hardly slept last night! Such a beautiful cake and thank you for making the party hats.'

'You are very welcome. That extra ration of sugar and margarine we were allowed was a godsend.'

'Yes, and the government lifted the ration on sweets too!'

Annie gave Anita three party hats.

'Here you are.'

'Thank you, the children will love them. I have forbidden mine to go near the party food until later.'

'Good idea. We had a good breakfast this morning.'

They ushered the children through the house and into the kitchen. The smell of freshly cooked pastry lingered in the air, the homemade cinnamon biscuits, with their knobbles of dried fruit, were laid out on plates on the table and the bacon joint whistled and hissed in the pressure cooker. Annie felt cocooned in warmth and friendship.

The two women sat with the children around the kitchen table.

'Ooh, lovely, thank you.'

Annie took the cup of tea from Anita and stirred in two teaspoonfuls of sugar.

Anita smiled.

'It's nice to have a treat.'

Annie sipped the sweet tea. The children drank their lemonade and ate their biscuits.

'We watched the Coronation Music Hall on the television on Saturday evening,' said Anita. 'It was wonderful.'

She pushed a second plate of biscuits towards the children.

'How marvellous to be able to watch such things.'

Anita nodded towards Val and John.

'Did they get a commemoration booklet from the school?'

'Yes, they did, and a nice gesture it was too.'

'Yes, mine got the same. I think they are a lovely thing for the children to keep.'

'Looks like Moses and Emma have arrived.'

John rose from the table.

'Mum, can I go outside and see the cows?'

Anita nodded to Annie.

'Yes, you can,' replied Annie. 'But don't get in the way.'

He ran across the yard.

'Steady, lad.'

Moses held Emma's arm and guided her towards the kitchen door. Her pace was hesitant and every few steps she stopped and put her hand to her chest.

'What are you after, young John?'

Eric gave the boy a playful punch to the top of his arm.

'He wants to see your cattle, Eric.'

George laughed.

'I can read him like a book.'

Eric made a sweeping gesture.

'Ah, well, lad, you are in luck. Come this way. We have got the heifers back and the bull is here too.'

'Em is inside now,' said Moses.

The old man looked around the yard.

'I have not been over this way for a while, George. Seems like Eric is getting things back together.'

'Aye, he is.'

'Listen, son, I meant to tell you, I have some heifers you can have. I have a dozen. What with keeping them fed, I only want six. I will drive the other six across to you in the next few days.'

'I have no money to pay for heifers, Dad.'

George kicked the ground.

'Don't matter, son. We will sort that out another time.'

Before George could answer, Anita appeared in the kitchen doorway.

'Gentlemen, the show starts in five minutes!'

She laughed and disappeared.

The television stood on the best table in the lounge, its screen just nine inches across, and even less in height. The screen and dials below, were encased in Bakelite with a wood surround and gave the appearance of a large radio. Framed family photographs interspersed the antenna on top of its case, whilst the aspidistra sat demoted on the windowsill. Two rows of chairs were positioned in front of the television and the curtains pulled across for a true cinema effect. A separate table contained Anita's best glasses, a bottle of sherry, bottles of brown ale, and a bowl of sweets.

The children stood in a huddle in the corner of the room and whispered to each other. They stared at the television, as if fearful something would happen if they looked away. After a few moments they became emboldened and moved towards it.

'Don't touch! Just look.'

The two women suppressed laughter at their synchronised comment; they bowed their heads and repositioned the chairs.

Eric turned on the television. Rows of jagged, black, and white horizontal lines appeared across the screen accompanied by a loud crackling sound. Everyone watched as he twiddled with the knobs and fiddled with the antenna. Then a man's voice came from the screen. It was distorted by the buzzing which increased and decreased as Eric tuned the television.

'I think that is Richard Dimbleby speaking,' said Annie.

She took a glass of sherry offered by Anita and passed it to Emma.

'They mentioned his name on the radio the other day. He is the commentator for the BBC.'

Suddenly, a picture appeared on the screen and a gasp encircled the room. It showed the Mall in London. The pavements were crowded with people. Some sat on the kerb, whilst others stood and jostled for position. The rain was heavy, and many of the spectators wore long Macintoshes. The less fortunate wrapped themselves in layers of newspaper.

'Well, I never.'

Moses adjusted his glasses. Emma looked at her glass of sherry as if it was the culprit.

'It's a pity,' said George. 'But it looks like there will be no let-up in the weather.'

He drained the dregs of his brown ale and placed the empty glass on the table.

The camera switched to other roads in the city.

'Those flags are like yours, Auntie Anita.'

Val pointed to bunting strewn from the top windows of houses.

'Here in the Mall people have made the most of the public holiday and camped out overnight to get a good view...Queen Elizabeth is the 39th sovereign to be crowned at Westminster Abbey...she will travel to and from Westminster Abbey in her golden coach...all eyes of the world are upon her...people want to see their queen, to acclaim her, show their loyalty, pay their respects...the roar of the crowd and adoration for their queen...the pomp and solemnity of the occasion...there is a hushed reverence as she enters the annexe to Westminster Abbey.'

Moses and Emma watched with their mouths open.

'Doesn't he look handsome,' whispered Anita to Annie.

HRH Duke of Edinburgh was dressed in his full naval uniform.

'And the Queen looks beautiful in her white satin dress. Look! She's got six ladies in waiting.'

Val turned and glared at Annie and Anita. The two women smiled at each other like naughty children.

When the Archbishop of Canterbury conducted the six-part service, the room fell silent. Then at last, the Queen came out of the Abbey and a thunderous roar came from the crowds. She wore the imperial state crown and stepped into her golden coach.

'A new era, a new beginning for the people of the Commonwealth.'

The commentators voice, previously hushed and reverential, boomed out joyous over the shouting crowds. George started to clap. Moses stood and raised his glass.

'To our Queen. To her good health. May she have a long and prosperous reign.'

Glasses were raised and chinked. Wet eyes were dabbed.

'Ooh, weather is still bad,' said Annie as the golden coach entered the grounds of Buckingham Palace.

'And much the same here.'

Anita nodded towards the window and rose from her chair.

'We will have something to eat now. Eric, can you turn off the television please. We can watch it again later.'

'I wonder if the Queen will come out on the balcony at Buckingham Palace,' said Annie.

'She did when she got married,' said Anita. 'And if

she does, we will be able to see her.'

Anita served a lunch of boiled bacon, mashed potatoes, and peas, whilst the children ate spam sandwiches, jelly, and ice cream.

'We should get your cattle fed, Eric.'

George stood and winked at the women.

'Lovely lunch Anita, thank you. And the celebration cake, Annie, it was splendid.'

John appeared beside his father. Annie looked at George and spoke to her son.

'Just half an hour, John.'

The torrential rain prevented the children from playing outside. However, Anita and Annie ran with them through the thunderous downpour, across the yard and into the barn. For two hours the children played hide and seek, blind man's bluff, hopscotch, and ring-a-ring-o-roses. They ran, skipped, and jumped until steam came off their clothes, their legs wobbled, and their voices became hoarse.

Later, they huddled around the television and got a final glimpse of the Queen as she emerged on the balcony at Buckingham Palace. And finally, a toffee apple for each child, followed by hugs, kisses, thanks, goodbyes, and home.

43

The bull pen stood at the end of the cattle sheds. It was built of brick and its interior walls were finished with smooth concrete. It had an air slit at one end and a closed window at the other end. It had a stable door, and each half of the door was lined with flat tin and painted in red oxide. A restraining iron bar was positioned mid-way across the area of the top door. The top door was shut at night or during adverse weather conditions. When the top door was open, it provided ventilation, and the iron bar prevented escape.

The bull pen had a dual purpose for the farmer and his bull. Firstly, the pen had to be capable of housing a bull. Secondly, the bull would seek out a heifer in season, and sometimes she was put in the pen with the bull so he could serve her.

A bellowing, bad tempered bull was a dangerous animal. But even when a bull was in a good temper, his sheer strength, tonnage, and curiosity made him dangerous. The farmer led the bull with a rope fed through a ring in its nose, a painful reminder to the bull the farmer was master and could take control.

Farmers swapped stories about their prize bull. George's favourite story was about his Hereford bull, Winston. When the mood took him, Winston positioned his horns under a five-bar gate and lifted it off its hinges, dropped it to the ground and walked over it. If a bull was not in residence, the bull pen was used for other cattle.

Annie glanced at the clock.

'You are late this morning.'

John pulled on his rubber boots.

'Make sure you're back for the school bus.'

He stepped out into the morning light and walked towards the bull pen. As he approached the pen, a young heifer's head appeared over the stable door, her eyes wide and curious. She chewed with an even rhythm and her nostrils puffed out spirals of breath in the cool morning air.

Panda was beautiful; she had a white face, black body, and white socks. Her mother was a Friesian cow and her father a Hereford bull.

John looked after Panda. He visited her twice a day, before and after school. He refilled her manger with fresh hay, changed her straw bedding, and kept the cattle drinker clean. Panda was eighteen months old. She stood a little taller than the bottom half of the stable door and weighed heavier than any human being.

John unbolted the stable door and slipped inside. The summer sunshine beamed into the pen and enveloped Panda in a haze of light.

'My Panda.'

He stroked her velvet forehead and tugged at her ears.

'Now I'm gonna get you some straw.'

He bolted the stable door. Panda put her head over its edge and watched him walk to the haystack. He positioned a pitchfork under the strings of a bale and heaved it onto his shoulder. When he arrived in the pen, he dropped it to the ground, cut the bale strings with his pen knife and separated out the bale. Panda watched as he littered the new straw on top of her existing bedding. She twitched her nostrils and nuzzled the honey sweet straw. Suddenly, she picked up a large mouthful of the new straw and threw it into the air.

'Panda, you want to play!'

The boy laughed and continued to litter the straw. The heifer tossed her head and moved from side to side in a gentle lumbering dance. He finished her bed and moved towards the stable door; Panda moved at the same time. She snorted with delight, twitched her tail, and danced sideways.

'Come on, Panda.'

He reached out to pat her nose, but she tossed her head away.

'Come on, Panda, come on girl. Out the way.'

The heifer made a soft rumbling noise and took a step towards him. He made a sudden movement towards the stable door, but she blocked his path. The animal advanced towards him and only stopped when her hooves touched the front of his rubber boots.

He recalled his father's words.

'That's sixty stone of heifer you have there, son and don't you forget it.'

His stomach leapt into his mouth. They continued their slow synchronised dance, but each time he made a move towards the stable door Panda blocked him.

He began to tire. His breathing became laboured, and his legs felt heavy. He leant against the wall and tried to think what his father would do. The manger was positioned further along the wall. He picked up a handful of fresh bedding and inched towards it.

'Here, Panda, over here.'

He waved the barley straw at the animal. She hesitated, walked towards him, and pulled the straw out of his hand. When he reached the manger, he lifted some of the hay and trickled it through his fingers. Panda leant over its rim and began to eat.

He slid along the wall, out of the bull pen and into the yard.

44

Barrett knocked on Daisy's front door. There was no answer. It was his second visit in two weeks. He bent down and pushed open the letter box. Letters lay strewn down the hallway. He stepped back and looked up. The bedroom windows were closed.

'She's gone away.'

A man of about fifty years leant over the neighbouring fence. He wore a grubby, open necked shirt and the stub of a cigarette hung from his mouth.

'Do you know where she's gone?'

The man's eyes travelled over the sergeant's uniform.

'To London. She's been gone a few weeks.'

As he spoke, the stub of the cigarette stuck to his lip and moved up and down.

'Do you know when she's coming back?'

Barrett's tone was casual, an encouragement to talk.

'No. She took the child and dog with her.'

Barrett glanced up at the bedroom window.

'Thanks.'

He touched his cap and closed the gate.

Barrett entered the pet shop. It was cool and quiet. Mrs Stirling stood in the far corner with a customer. He could hear their conversation and her soothing tone washed over him. She walked towards him, her elegant figure weaving like a quiet willow on a shady bank. The customer left and they were alone.

'Hello, Sergeant, how nice to see you.'

She beamed and pulled at her cardigan slung around her shoulders.

Barrett stepped forward and removed his cap.

'Good day to you, Mrs Stirling.'

She moved towards the front of the shop.

'I'm about to shut the shop for lunch. Would you like to come and sit in the garden and have some tea?'

'Well, that's very kind of you, Mrs Stirling, thank you.'

'You are welcome, sergeant.'

She slid the bolts across the shop door and turned the sign to 'Closed for Lunch.' He followed her through to the back of the shop, past the familiar lean to and into the garden. She gestured towards a chestnut tree which canopied a small table and two wrought iron chairs. The weather was fine, and patches of warm sunlight broke through the leaves of the tree. He sat and placed his cap on the table. The garden was long and narrow, and the first part was laid to a neat lawn with flower beds on either side. Gladioli, standard roses, groups of delphiniums, and lupins, all stood tall and fresh in a scattered, elegant display. It contrasted with the end section of the garden which bore the remains of a neglected and unused allotment.

A movement caught his eye; it came from the sunniest spot in the garden. The undergrowth rustled and a tortoise appeared. He jutted out his neck and looked around with bright, beady eyes. Then, with purposeful, juddering steps he advanced across the lawn. When he reached a dandelion, he stopped and began to pull at the weed with his hard, rimless mouth.

'Here we are.'

Mrs Stirling placed a tray on the table.

'Now, Sergeant, can I pour you some tea?'

'Thank you, Mrs Stirling.'

She sat, pushed a plate towards him and picked up the tea pot.

'I have made some fish paste sandwiches. Please, do help yourself.'

He took a sandwich.

'How long have you had the tortoise?'

The tortoise had devoured the dandelion and basked in the sun.

'Oh, about a year now. He came from Greece.'

She placed a cup of tea in front of him.

'During the winter months he must go into hibernation. I put him in a box of straw and keep him in the lean to. It seems to suit him.'

She laughed.

'He keeps the dandelion population down.'

Barrett gulped his tea and carefully placed the cup back on the saucer. He was not used to the delicacy of porcelain.

'I paid Daisy a visit this morning.'

'Oh?'

Her hand hovered above the plate of sandwiches.

'Well, what I mean is I went to her house but there was no one at home. It was my second visit. I went last week but she was not there.'

'Ah, yes.'

'I saw her neighbour. He told me she's gone to London.'

'Yes, that's right. She came to see me just before she left. Poor girl, she was in a terrible state. Her mother was ill last year. She did recover, but then suddenly she deteriorated, and Daisy had to make a quick decision.'

A silence hung in the air. Barrett placed his elbows

on his knees. He blinked as the sun reflected the shine of his boots. Mrs Stirling poured a second cup of tea. She glanced at the fish paste sandwiches but did not touch the plate.

'Do you know if she is coming back?'

'Yes, she is. Despite what she's been through she intends to settle here. Jennifer likes her school. They need stability.'

'She could be in London for months.'

'Yes, that is possible. She will stay with her mother until things are clearer.'

He scuffed the ground with his boot.

'Maybe I should visit her, in London I mean.'

'No. No, Sergeant, I wouldn't do that. That could be difficult for her. I will let you know when I see her.'

She proffered the fish paste sandwiches but he declined.

'Love is never easy sergeant.'

'It is impossible! I have met this beautiful woman and then she disappears and who knows for how long!'

'But she is going to return. That is what you need to remember, Sergeant.'

'Well, I suppose so.'

She pushed back her chair.

'Now, I must go and open the shop.'

'Here, let me take that for you.'

He picked up the tray.

45

'The cinder whistler is coming this morning to sweep the chimney and clean the fire grates. He's a new lad and I will need to keep an eye on him.'

Annie cracked eggs into a pan.

'He is only fourteen and won't be around for long. Once he is strong enough, he will work on the farms alongside his older brothers.'

The eggs hissed and spat.

'While he is here, Olive, can you take the children for a picnic please.'

'Of course, Mrs Hadley. I will take them to the beach, they will enjoy that.'

She picked up a knife from the floor dropped by Douglas and brought it to the sink.

'I will give you a lift in the car. Oh, and if you can find any samphire, can you bring some back please. George likes a spot of fresh samphire with his boiled bacon.'

She smiled to herself.

The children love going to the beach.

Olive prepared fish paste sandwiches, fruit cake and squash, and placed the hamper in the car together with buckets and spades for the children. After breakfast, Annie drove them to the sea wall. The seagulls screeched their welcome and dipped around in the sky, but the cawing clamour of the nesting seabirds had gone, their young already on the wing, hatched and flown from their nests.

The children collected their buckets and spades and followed Olive up the steps to the top of the sea wall. The wind cut cool across their faces, but once they had clambered down onto the beach, they were sheltered, and a warm breeze embraced them.

'There are lots of bumps this morning.'

Val pointed at the worm casts made by the lugworms.

'Your father would like those when he goes band line fishing and puts his hooks in the sand.'

Olive turned to the children.

'Here's a nice spot.'

She spread an old army blanket on the ground and set down the hamper. The children placed their buckets and spades on the warm sand. A cluster of small rocks curved to their left and rivulets of water shimmered like glass and filled the furrows in the sand. The tide was out, and the sea drew a distant blue line on the horizon.

The children surrounded Olive.

'Can we run out on the sands?'

'Yes, but we will all go together.'

They ran across the yellow flatness, their bodies mere dots in the vast seascape. The sky was clear, clouds were forgotten, and their faces flushed red from the heat of the sun. The children returned to their buckets and spades. They turned rocks, caught crabs, whelks, and mussels, and built sandcastles in the soft sand. By mid-day the heavier wet sand signalled the returning flow of the tidal waters. Olive called the children back to the picnic hamper. They sat on the blanket and ate their sandwiches.

Val pointed to two men further down the beach.

'What are those men doing?'

The men walked at a slow pace; their eyes fixed on the ground around them.

'They are shoring,' replied Olive. 'They are looking for wood that has been washed up on the shore. They take it home for firewood.'

'I saw a man with a piece of wood tied to his bicycle the other day. He had to push his bike.'

'Yes, well, that's what happens when they find a big piece of wood. They walk it home.'

Olive repacked the hamper.

'My brother will be along soon to take us home. But first, we must get some samphire.'

They left the beach and walked further along the sea wall to the edge of the marsh land, to an area the islanders called the 'saltings'.

Olive turned to the children.

'Careful, it is muddy down there.'

They filled the hamper with samphire and turned onto the track. Within minutes Jason arrived with his tractor and trailer. He steered the machinery onto a patch of sand and gravel, stopped the engine and jumped down. He took a bale of hay out of the trailer and positioned it on the ground.

'Up you go!'

The children and Olive climbed onto the bale and into the trailer.

The movement of the tractor created a pleasant breeze. Olive closed her eyes and turned her face to the sun. As the tractor travelled through the village, a woman waved whilst she picked wildflowers and an elderly man leant on his spade as he stood in his allotment. They arrived at the farmhouse just before one o'clock. Olive removed the samphire from the hamper.

'Here it is, Mrs Hadley. There was still some on the saltings. I will give it a wash for you.'

'Thank you. Did the children enjoy themselves?'

'Yes, they had a lovely time. They are outside near the sandpit.'

'Those boys! They must play with their toy tractors. It's in their blood.'

46

Fred shut the front door. Eloise ran a film in her head. Fred returns an hour later at exactly half past nine in the morning. He takes off his coat and hooks it over the coat stand. He changes into his slippers, picks up the newspaper from the hall table and goes through to the lounge. She provides him with a cup of coffee. He rustles the newspaper in acknowledgment. She returns to the kitchen and prepares Sunday lunch.

Eloise sighed and pulled the bed covers up to her chin. Within the last week, her morning sickness had ceased, and her hormones settled, but the physical signs of her pregnancy were beginning to show. A few weeks back, loose clothing had been sufficient to disguise her hardly discernible bump. But since then, she had developed a pronounced curve at the front and sides and increased in size each day. She got out of bed and went to the window. June had brought beautiful weather and warmth and light enveloped the garden.

Fred loves his garden.

She looked out onto the neat lawn. His beloved roses were in full bloom, and the border flowers looked healthy and strong.

He spends a lot of time out there. Maybe he goes into the garden to get away from me.

She stroked her stomach. Her hands trembled.

Fred returned at half past nine and completed his

Sunday ritual. The temperature increased throughout the morning, and by the time lunchtime arrived, the warm, dry heat had become a cloying humidity. They ate their lunch of roast chicken in silence but when it came to dessert, he barely touched the apple pie and pushed the dish away.

He picked up his cup of tea and went through to the lounge. Eloise was surprised at his decision to stay indoors on such a warm day, but she followed him and sat opposite.

The air hung heavy, oppressive, and the clock ticked loud in the silence. He picked up a section of the newspaper and disappeared behind the opened pages. She used the remaining section as a fan. After a few minutes, she placed it down and shifted in her chair.

'Fred, darling, I have something to tell you.'

She coughed and tapped her chest.

'Fred, I...'

He lowered the newspaper and peered over the top.

'Yes?'

He didn't wait for a reply. He folded the newspaper into perfect parallel lines and placed it down the side of his chair.

'What did you want to tell me?'

His eyes bore a strange glint and despite the strong sunlight, his face appeared half in shadow.

'I, we...we are expecting a baby!'

She emphasised the word 'baby' and smiled.

He took off his glasses and stared at her belly.

'I know you are expecting a baby, Eloise. Your condition...well, it's obvious.'

'No, darling, *we* are expecting a baby. Isn't that wonderful? I never thought, I...'

'Eloise! Stop this nonsense. Stop it at once!'

His tone was patronising, calm, and the glint in his

eyes bore into her soul. A coldness crept over her. She shivered and cradled the curve of her stomach.

'I don't know what you mean. It is not nonsense...'

'Your pregnancy is nothing to do with me, Eloise. It is not my child.'

He held up his hand.

'You need to speak with the father of your child and decide what you are going to do.'

'But I don't understand, Fred. We are married, darling. This baby is yours... *ours.* How can you say anything different?'

He pointed a trembling finger at her.

'This baby, that baby is your lover's baby not mine, and don't you ever dare suggest otherwise.'

He sprung up and paced the room, his face white, furious. Then he came to an abrupt halt, as if a giant hand hit his chest, and dropped back into his chair.

Her forehead creased into lines of perplexity. She had not expected an outright denial from her husband, and such a confident denial too, so solid, so sure.

'You see, Eloise, your baby is not my child. I know that because I...I cannot father a child. It is just not possible.'

She felt a sharp slap to the side of her face, but there was no assailant.

'I don't understand. What the hell do you mean?'

'I say it because it is true.'

The lines on her forehead deepened and her stomach rode a sea of anxiety.

'But we've been married for years. You have never said anything. Why didn't you say? You had no right to withhold that from me!'

He stood, steadied himself, and turned to face her.

'I couldn't...I mean, you might not have married me if I told you. And I would never have coped with that,

Eloise, you not marrying me...not becoming my wife.'

Her mind struggled with a jumble of fast-moving images; all the scenes over the years, when he avoided her questions about starting a family, flooded her mind like a burst dam. She walked towards him. Then she punched him, her fists hammered his chest, and she knocked his glasses from his face.

'I hate you! You are a lying bastard! You are spineless! You're no husband of mine!'

Her voice rose in a crescendo of hysteria as he braced himself against the blows. But when his glasses fell to the floor, he crumpled like a tent that lost its pole and fell back into his chair. He covered his face with his hands. His body heaved and shuddered, and great sobs ripped from within him. When he spoke, his voice was a whisper.

'But I couldn't tell you, Eloise, I was too afraid of losing you and I couldn't bear that. I couldn't cope without you. I am so sorry.'

She stared at her husband. Steady, predictable Fred. The man she thought she knew so well, she didn't know at all.

47

The islanders relied on fresh fish and several species were available throughout the year including eel, bass, flounder, and plaice. They practised the traditional 'band line' method of fishing and used lug worms, or log worms as the islanders called them, for bait.

The tide was due at midnight. George usually set his band lines after six o'clock in the evening. However, he had promised John he would take him fishing, and decided to start an hour earlier.

There is always a good supply of fish and God knows we need it.

'He is ready to learn,' said George as he pulled on his thigh boots.

Annie plunged her arms into soapy water.

'He will enjoy himself, George. He has talked of nothing else these past few days.'

He picked up his kedger bag, bait pail and fork.

'Where is he?'

'By the farm truck waiting for you.'

She smiled and swirled the water with her hands.

As he approached the truck, John jumped up and down. He gestured to the boy to get into the vehicle and placed the kedger bag, bait pail and fork in the back of the truck.

They stopped by the sea wall.

George slung the kedger bag over his shoulder.

'Right, son, bring that bait pail and fork. We need to dig the log worm.'

John turned to his father.

'Why is Sam at home?'

'He will get tangled in the lines, son, there's no job for him here.'

They climbed over the sea wall. The tide had ebbed, and an expanse of sand lay before them. George made a cam in the sand, lifted the wet clods, and built a moat around the edge.

'Here.'

He handed John the bait pail.

'Bail that water out, son.'

As he dug deeper, streaks of perspiration lined his face.

'Ah, here we are.'

He turned over a clod of sand. John picked out the worms and placed them in the bait pail.

'There are several here today, makes life easier.'

He turned over more clods and held them out for his son.

'That should do it.'

About sixty log worms lay in the bucket. The seagulls sensed a source of food and hovered above them. George stood up and wiped his brow. He slung the kedger bag over his shoulder and picked up the bait pail.

'Let's go and set the bands.'

They strode towards the distant white lines of foam; the sand, wet and burnished, softened beneath their boots.

'We won't go too far down. Not as far as that kiddle.'

He nodded to his left.

'That net belongs to Harry and Joe. They will get a big commercial catch with that.'

He took the band line out of his kedger bag, unwound the first peg, and kicked it into the sand with his heel.

'When I have put the middle peg in, you can start baiting.'

John held up a large worm.

'Dad, look at this one. It's huge!'

'Aye, it is. I reckon that one will do three hooks.'

He kicked the second peg into the sand.

'Right, you can start baiting now.'

John baited the hooks with the log worms.

George kicked the third peg into the sand. When he had finished the second band, he helped his son bait the remaining hooks.

'We'd best cover them up, otherwise the gulls will get them. It won't be dark for a few hours yet.'

They covered the hooks with sand.

'That's a good job done, son. We will come back after high tide has gone in the morning and see what we've caught.'

That night John dreamt about the fish and the sea; his father set line after line, and he followed with the log worms. It was light and warm, and the sun shimmered on the water. Great shoals of plaice and flounder swam with the flow of the tide towards the island. Then suddenly the water turned rough, huge waves crashed onto the shore, and the sun and the fish disappeared.

Darkness.

He awoke startled, his face wet with tears. He got out of bed and went into his parents' bedroom. It was quiet and calm. His parents were asleep, and a soft breeze rustled in through the open window. He climbed into bed beside his father.

'Ah, my alarm clock.'

After a few minutes, George lifted the covers and got

out of bed. He put a finger to his lips and crept across the room; John tiptoed after him. They got dressed, drank their tea, and left the farmhouse. When they crossed the beach, the first rays of light appeared over the horizon.

George lifted the first line.

'There are a few flounders here, son.

They approached the second line.

'Dad! Dad! Look at this one!'

'He's a bass,' said George. 'He must be five pounds. Mum will be pleased. Now, we don't need all these fish. They will go off in a few days. These small flounders, we will put them in the pan holes, and they will muddy themselves.'

He picked up the band line whilst John placed the smaller fish in the pan holes. As the fish touched the water, they wriggled and disturbed the sand until their orange spotted bodies became camouflaged in the murky water. When the water had settled the fish were gone, safely submerged until the tide took them back to the sea. John looked up at the circling sea birds.

'They can't eat them now.'

George flung the bigger fish into a sandbag and picked up the kedger bag.

'Next time we go fishing we will get some rods and go to the river.'

'Here you are, Annie.'

George tipped the sandbag into the sink. The fish tumbled out: silver scales, glassy eyes, open rimless mouths, some round, some flat, all fresh from the sea.

Annie filleted the fish and placed the big bass in the pan ready to cook for their breakfast.

48

Annie stood in the doorway and watched John and Val as they crossed the yard and disappeared down the back lane to catch the school bus.

It's so good to see them back at school, even if it is only for a few weeks.

She returned to the kitchen. She hummed to herself and placed a rasher of bacon in the pan.

'Good morning to you, Annie. Is George around?'

'Why Bob! How lovely to see you! Do come in. Have you had breakfast? I can put an extra rasher in for you.'

'Thank you, but I won't stop, I'm on my way to meet Eric. I have brought your boys a present.'

He held a large box in his arms. It was tied with string and had makeshift airholes in the lid.

'What have you got there?'

Before he could answer, George arrived.

'Good morning, Bob! It's good to see you!'

Bob balanced the box on his left arm and shook George's hand.

'Bob has brought the boys a present,' said Annie.

She turned the bacon in the pan.

'Ah, a present,' said George. 'The boys like a present.'

Bob placed the box on the table, untied the string and lifted the lid. Inside the box was a young, but full-grown crow. The bird was docile from its containment and blinked at the rush of light.

'He's an interesting one,' said Bob.

He took the bird out of the box and held him with both hands. The bird's beady dark eyes darted around the room.

'He was originally a family pet. You can see that by the way he lets me handle him.'

He stroked the back of the bird's body. His dark quilled feathers were smooth and black as jet and his claws lay inert against Bob's fingers.

'Mind you, he has got a history. The family that reared him, well, he became vicious, and they didn't want him.'

Bob pointed to himself.

'So, they called in Bob the pest controller to take him away.'

'Ah,' said George.

Bob stroked the bird.

'Look at him. He is as docile as a new-born lamb.'

'Aye, but he will be a different bird when he predates for his food or defends himself. However, a crow is a rare sight around here. The boys will be able to handle him, and it will do them good.'

George moved his hand towards the crow and stroked its feathers. The bird turned at the new touch, looked at him and relaxed back into Bob's hand.

'Leave him with us. We will look after him.'

'Good on you. He might like a few titbits and some water.'

'Aye, we will do that. I will keep him in an old meat cage in the scullery, until John gets home from school.'

'Here he is, boys.'

Three pairs of eyes watched as George placed the meat cage in the centre of the table.

'Crows belong to the carrion species. They are scavengers. That means they will eat dead animals. Do you remember the dead mouse we saw in the yard yesterday?'

The boys nodded.

'Well, that would have been a tasty breakfast for him.'

George smiled. He could tell by the look on the boys' faces they were trying to understand how a dead mouse would make a tasty meal.

'Crows like insects and live animals too,' continued George. 'But they also eat plants, nuts, and seeds. Crows are one of the smartest birds around. They are powerful too. Those claws help him balance and grip, but he also uses them to carry off small prey. Remember, boys, crows can be vicious. A crow pecked the eyes out of two of Eric's lambs last spring, one of them whilst it was being born.'

John spoke first.

'How do we know he won't be nasty to us, Dad?'

'This bird is from old Bob, he won't do you, boy. But don't tease the bird and be aware of his beak and claws when you handle him.'

He picked up the bird and handed him to John.

No one could remember when or how Charlie acquired his name, but when he was called the bird appeared, his gaze fixed, his head cocked. The bird adapted to his new life at Butterwood Farm. He took up residence in the pear tree outside the scullery door and appeared on the windowsill each morning to receive leftover food scraps. Charlie had an audacious and curious personality and stories emerged of his propensity to bury items, sit atop a surprised bullock, or terrorise children in the school playground by landing on their heads and scratching at their hair.

John and Val alighted from the school bus. Their large satchels banged against their legs, and they walked with an awkward gait. John knelt and retied his shoelaces. He stood, pulled up his socks and humped his satchel back into position.

They took the short cut across the fields.

After several minutes, Val stopped. She turned towards John and placed her hand on her hip.

'Come on.'

John ignored his sister. He liked to dawdle across the fields after a day at school. He loved the feel of the earth beneath his feet and the salt, sweet smell of the island air.

Val shouted at John again. He knew her patience was coming to an end. Then, she would walk back, grab him, and propel him forward. However, before she could do so, Charlie appeared in the sky. The bird flapped his wings in slow motion and hovered above them.

'Charlie!'

John shaded his eyes and looked up at the bird.

Charlie glided in circles like a plane without an engine. Suddenly, he unfurled his wings and swooped downwards. He landed on Val's head, pecked her ear, and flew up a few feet above her.

'Raaah! Raaah!'

Val did not hesitate. She removed her satchel from across her shoulders, held the strap like a lasso, and swung the satchel in circles above her head.

'Get off, Charlie.'

Thwack, thwack. The satchel hit its target.

'Raaah! Raaah!'

Charlie took off into the sky.

After a few moments he swooped for a second time and came to rest on the familiar landing pad of Val's head. The bird triumphantly displayed the full span of his wings. Then he scrabbled with his claws, and turned Val's thick, curly hair into an electrified nest.

She tried to push the bird away.

'Get off, Charlie! Get off! Dad should ring your neck.' She made one further attempt with her satchel, but Charlie was ready. He took off and soared in the sky, until all that remained was a small black speck.

Charlie lived for a few more months. Then one morning they found him dead by the pear tree.

'That's a shame, boys. But nature takes her course and there is nothing we can do about it.'

49

A sharp downpour fell from the sky.

Dorothy stepped inside the butcher's shop. It was busier than usual, and she looked around for a space. She squeezed behind three women; their heads were drawn together, and they spoke in loud, conspiratorial whispers. It was a hopeless attempt at privacy. She looked away, but their proximity made her a silent participant.

"Well, I only know because Mrs Purdy at number forty-five told me. The girl's parents are very angry about the whole thing and attempted to contact the boy's parents.'

The woman who spoke folded her arms, gave a knowing nod, and looked around her. The second woman gave a sly smile.

'They won't see him for a while. He's had his fun and gone.'

The third woman spoke.

'She's a silly girl. She will pay the price now.'

The sly smiler spoke again.

'They will take the baby from her. She won't be allowed to keep it and her parents will never live it down.'

At first, Dorothy listened with interest, but after a while she felt trapped by the women's wagging tongues. She cleared her throat in a loud, exaggerated way, and flashed a look towards them. As the women turned and faced her, they received the full force of her disapproving eyes. The three women looked at each other. Then the sly smiler glared at Dorothy and giggled, whilst the other women watched. Dorothy returned the glare and jammed her lips together; thin and unforgiving, unable to escape the judgmental rut.

She looked away and focused on a large string of pork sausages. When she reached the front of the queue, her face felt so hot she thought she might explode.

'Are you all right, Madam?'

Dorothy turned and looked over her shoulder.

'Madam, I'm asking you. Are you all right?'

She turned back.

'Me? Why... yes! Yes, of course I am!'

Stupid man!

She raised her eyes to the ceiling and shook her head.

'Two slices of ham please'

She rummaged in her basket.

'Of course, Madam.'

The butcher wrapped up the ham and placed it on the counter with a heavy thud.

'Nice ham.'

Derek gave Dorothy an approving look.

She breathed. He wiped the corners of his mouth with his napkin, in a neat, detailed movement.

'Are you well, Dorothy? You look a little pale.'

She jumped in her seat and twitched like a frightened rabbit.

'Yes, I think so. I mean, yes, I am.'

She tried to smile.

'You don't sound very sure.'

She placed her knife and fork on the edge of her plate.

'Well, it's awful really.'

She hesitated and continued.

'When I was in the butcher's shop today, there were three women in the queue. They were gossiping about Kathy Sanderson.'

She gave her mouth a genteel dab.

'She is expecting a baby, but she's not married. She is only eighteen.'

Derek shrugged his shoulders.

'Oh, I see.'

'Don't you think it's disgraceful, Derek?'

She placed her glass down a little too hard. Droplets of water travelled down from its rim.

'I mean it's terrible for her parents. Apparently, the boy in question has disappeared. It's outrageous. Why, if I was Kathy's parents, I would...'

'But you're not, are you.'

'What do you mean?'

'You are not Kathy's parents and really, it is nothing to do with us.'

'Well, I am not so sure about that!'

Her voice had lost its hesitant quiver and became firm and robust.

'That kind of immoral behaviour affects all of us. I don't know how Mrs Sanderson will be able to walk down the street if...if her daughter keeps the baby. The whole thing is quite disgraceful!'

She pursued her lips and puckered her cheeks.

'Mrs Sanderson will walk down the street pretty much as she does now, I imagine. Is there any pudding?'

'Derek! Don't you care?'

'Care about what? She is not our daughter, Dorothy, and even if she was, we would sort it out.'

'Derek, I can't believe you have just said that!'

Her eyes sent darts of anger. She collected the plates

and pushed back her chair. When she returned to the table, Derek was resetting his watch. She placed a dish of semolina pudding in front of him, untied her apron and dropped it on the chair.

'I have got one of my headaches coming on. I am going to have a lie down.'

50

It was that time of year again. Uncle Tim was due to visit the farm. He had been a captain in the army, and his officer's haircut and wonderful handlebar moustache gave him a strong military bearing. He walked with a limp and if anyone asked, he always gave the same answer.

'A souvenir from the Japs.'

'Tim will notice the difference since last summer.'

George got into bed and pulled up the covers. He did not add the farm looked run down, only had half a dozen cattle and no pigs, or how the farmhouse still lacked basic furniture.

'We won't be shooting any birds. There are so few of them on the island, it wouldn't be right, even though it would help us feed everyone. The rabbits are regenerating quite well though, so we might get a chance to shoot one or two of those.'

His mouth salivated at the thought of rabbit stew.

'The children get more excited each day,' said Annie.

'Aye, his visit will be good for all of us.'

The children played all morning, alternating between sun and shade as they ran across the yard and around the outbuildings. Just before one o'clock they arrived at the scullery door, their faces flushed from the heat of the sun.

'Why, you are all back! And on time!'

Annie smiled. Most days she resorted to an old police whistle to round them up.

The children formed an obedient queue in the scullery, washed their hands, and seated themselves at the kitchen table. They had voracious appetites and ate chicken pie, mashed potato, and carrots, followed by rice pudding. As they waited for permission to leave, they exchanged furtive glances and tapped their feet against each other under the table. Annie collected the empty plates and dishes.

'Off you go then.'

They scraped back their chairs, ran out of the house and across the yard, their legs spinning like wheels through the dry summer dust.

Annie changed into her favourite summer dress. Its fabric was redolent of summer flowers. She descended the stairs, looked around the kitchen and picked up the car keys.

'I'm going now, George. Keep an eye on the children please. I won't be long.'

A grunted response came from the living room.

As she drove away, four pairs of eyes watched her leave the yard. The children gathered around the pear tree. The tree stood adjacent to the scullery door. It had survived the flood and managed to produce a small crop of fruit. As they climbed the pear tree, they picked the small, hard fruit and stuffed it into their pockets. They reached the top and positioned themselves under the canopy of foliage. A short while later, the car turned into the yard. The children peered through the leaves. Uncle Tim alighted from the vehicle, put on his hat, and picked up his case. He looked across the fields.

'Super afternoon.'

The leaves of the pear tree rustled.

Annie and Uncle Tim walked across the yard towards the farmhouse. Suddenly, a small, fruity missile hit his arm. Stifled giggles came from the tree as more pears were thrown.

'You scoundrels! You will be on extra duties! All of you!'

Uncle Tim passed his suitcase and hat to Annie, picked up the lid of a large metal dustbin and held it upside down over his head.

Boing! Boing! Boing!

The pears rained down and bounced off the lid. Uncle Tim peered out from underneath and looked up at the tree.

'I'll get you! All of you! Get out of there and come down!'

The children scrambled down from the tree and ran towards him. He placed the dustbin lid in front of his body and stepped backwards and forwards as if in a jousting match.

'Back off, Val! And you boys! You fantastical enemy! Back off the lot of you!'

He thrust the dustbin lid towards them a few more times and dropped it to the ground. He held his arms above his head and pretended to wave an imaginary white flag.

'I surrender to the enemy!'

'Uncle Tim! Uncle Tim!'

The children surrounded him.

'Let Uncle Tim get into the house.'

Annie nudged at the children.

'Come in, Tim, and have some tea.'

She ushered the children through the doorway and into the kitchen. She made a pot of tea and gave the children lemonade and cake. But the children could not settle, and their chatter was full of the stories they wanted Uncle Tim to tell, and the games they wanted him to play.

She shooed them outside.

'You will see him in a while. Go and play until I call you in.'

After tea, when Uncle Tim had finished a bedtime story, Annie turned to the children and pointed at their beds.

'Come on, you've had a long day'

Uncle Tim and Annie said goodnight to the children and went downstairs. For the rest of the evening, they sat with George and caught up with family news. And when Annie retired to bed, the men's voices softly buzzed as they chinked their glasses and spoke on into the night.

One afternoon just before dusk, Uncle Tim borrowed George's .22 rifle. As he sat in George's office and polished the wood of the gun, the boys appeared in the doorway.

'Quick, Uncle Tim! There's a rabbit in the shrubbery!'

John pointed towards the garden and beckoned Uncle Tim to follow. He gave the gun a final wipe and followed the boys into the sitting room. John eased open a window as Uncle Tim placed a chair in front of it and straddled the seat. The boys clustered around him and pointed through the window. In the middle of the shrubbery was a rabbit. Its top half was exposed, and its face turned towards the farmhouse. Uncle Tim kept his eye on the target and waved at the boys to stand back. He placed the gun on the back of the chair and slid the barrel through the open window. He aimed and fired. The bullet hit its target and the rabbit wobbled. He shot again. The bullet hit the centre of the rabbit's body. It remained upright.

Uncle Tim turned to the boys, but they were nowhere to be seen. He looked at the rabbit again. It had a bore hole right through its upper body but remained in the same position.

'What the....?'

He called out the boys' names, but there was no answer. Then he heard adult laughter interspersed with laughter from the children. He looked out through the window.

'The bloody thing is stuffed!'

George's head appeared through an adjacent window.

'Looks like you failed to bag that one, Tim!'

George roared with laughter.

'You boys! You absolute terrors!'

Uncle Tim brandished the gun.

'Why, it took me in. I had to fire a second shot before I realised!'

51

'Three sickles, good for cutting weeds down, where are we with these?'

The auctioneer spotted a bidder.

'I'm bid two shillings...at the back there...two shillings and thru'pence, thank you, Sir. Anymore?'

The mallet hit the table and the buyer stepped forward. The next lot was two mustard forks.

'Those old forks have seen better days.'

George turned to see who bid for them.

'A few were using them before the flood,' said Eric. 'But I'm not sure whether they will use them again once the soil gets sorted out.'

The men stood near the back of the crowd, half listening as the auctioneer worked through the smaller lots.

Eric nodded to his right.

'I had a look at the two-wheel tumble carts in that field. There are some good ones there.'

'Aye. It's a shame they must go. Some would say it's progress, but I'm not so sure.'

'Mechanisation is gathering pace, but some farmers still use cart horses. Those Suffolk Punches, Clydesdales, Shires, and Percheron, they are wonderful horses, although most of the ones I have seen in recent years were cross bred with cobs.'

'I'm not sure if our young farmers would be

interested in ploughing with a cart horse. Some would say hitching those horses to a plough and walking eleven miles to plough one acre, is too much like hard work.'

'But they will still be useful for transporting mangels, beet, sacks of corn and the like.'

'Their swung axle makes it easier for the horses to pull a greater weight. During harvest time when I have hitched horses to those carts, they can pull two or three tons of corn sheaves back to the stack yard.'

'I am not sure how many of the horses are left on the island now.'

'Old Dick has still got his two; Daisy and Dixie...?'

'Yes, come to think of it, I have seen them since we've been back on the island.'

'Now, gentlemen, next lot is a set of duck foot harrows. They will make a good seed bed. Who will start the bidding on this lot?

'Thank you, sir. You won't regret it.'

The auctioneer brought down his mallet.

'Those harrows could be pulled by a cart horse,' said Eric.

'Aye, or adapted and pulled by a tractor,' replied George.

There was a break in the bids whilst the auctioneer spoke to one of the farmers.

'How are you getting on with that gypsum? You finished spreading it yet?'

Eric tutted and raised his eyes.

'We have two fields left to do, but the weather's been so wet we can't get on. Not much point in spreading gypsum, to neutralise the salt, if you ruin your bloody topsoil with the weight of heavy farm machinery.'

'Aye, we've had the same, but we will be finished this week. And then what? Nothing! The government's "Do Nothing Policy" says we must do nothing for months until they say so. And after all that, they will return to take further samples. I wish now I had offered to provide the Ministry with a field for experimental grass or crop growing. At least I could have sown some crops, but we will have a wretched wait and that's the worst of it.'

'Did you hear about Frank up at North Farm? He sowed a crop of barley when he first got back on the island. The inspectors saw it when they were last here and they told him, he won't get his compensation.'

'He will face financial ruin. Those compensation payments will save all of us, although I wish they would hurry them along.'

The auctioneer picked up his mallet.

'It's the tumble carts next,' said George.

'I recall learning how to use one of those when I was a boy,' said Eric.

'Dung chrome, shooting stick, greasing jack, and hammer. We had to learn how to do all those things so we could maintain them.'

'I have not brought my tumble cart today. I am going to keep mine in case I need it at harvest time.'

Whenever that will be. If this government ever allows me to be a farmer again.

'I have kept ours too. The ones for sale here today, the farm workers will buy those for firewood.'

'Right, gentlemen, it's a sign of the times these carts are up for sale. Some are still good for work, but I can see by the interest amongst you, most of them will go up in smoke.'

The crowd laughed and moved forward.

'Right, come on, who will start me?'

The bidding was fierce and fast, and the sale of the tumble carts was soon over.

George left the field and walked towards his tractor.

As he got closer, he noticed a crowd gathered further down the lane.

'Excuse me, please. Excuse me, thank you.'

He reached the centre of the throng. A young farm worker leant against his pushbike. His clothes were spattered with blood. As he gasped for breath, George gestured to the crowd to quieten down.

'What's happened, lad?'

'It's Jake's son, Billy, he's had an accident! I have been to his house, but they're not at home!'

An anxious murmur arose from the crowd.

'Where is Billy now?'

'Over at Frank's farm.'

The young man gulped in air.

'You follow me back to my yard, lad. We'll pick up my car and get Billy to hospital. Quick now! You can tell me what happened when we're on our way!'

The young man nodded, mounted his bike, and followed George through the crowd to his tractor. Within minutes they were back at Butterwood Farm. As George swerved the car out onto the lane, they caught hold of the open car doors and slammed them shut. George repositioned himself and straightened the car.

'Now, lad, tell me what happened.'

'Billy was hitching the gypsum spreader to the tractor when the draw bar pin slipped. He screamed out terrible. I think he's lost a finger.'

The farm worker shook his head and turned his face towards the window.

'We will be there soon. We'll get him sorted.'

They swept into the farmyard. George yanked up the handbrake and flung open his door. He recognised Billy; he was large like Jake. The boy sat on the adjacent wall, his body hunched forward, a bloodied rag wrapped around his right hand.

'Hello, Billy. We're going to get you to the hospital. Have you got your finger there?'

The boy looked up. His ashen face was streaked with tears and perspiration spotted his forehead. George unwrapped the rag, the injured hand juddered and seeped blood.

'Yes, that is bad, lad. But the finger is still there! Only just, mind.'

He rewrapped the wound.

'Right, let's get going.'

They helped the boy off the wall and into the back of the car. George nodded to the farm worker and the boy's half-closed eyes.

'Keep him awake!'

He skidded the car out of the yard, veered to the left and stamped his foot on the accelerator. Within minutes, they were off the island.

The car sped towards the hospital.

'Thank the lord for the National Health Service.'

He pulled up outside the main entrance as a young nurse appeared.

'Billy had an accident. His finger is almost off.'

The nurse glanced at the boy.

'I'll get a wheelchair.'

She disappeared. A few minutes later she returned with a wheelchair and two blankets. She lifted the bloodied rag and peered into the boy's face.

'Hello Billy. I'm nurse Stanton. We are going to try and save your finger.'

The boy opened, then closed his eyes.

'How old are you, Billy?'

His voice was just audible.

'Fi...fteen.'

'I will speak to matron. We need to get him straight through for surgery.'

She turned to George.

'Can you let his parents know as soon as you can please, and ask them to come to the hospital.'

'Yes, of course.'

'Thank you, gentlemen.'

She waved them to one side and took hold of the handles of the wheelchair.

'Now, if you please.'

She turned the wheelchair around and disappeared through the main doors.

'Hmm...she's a bossy one,' said George.

He scratched his head.

'Yeah, bossy but pretty,' replied the farm worker. 'I wouldn't mind her telling me what to do.'

The men laughed and made their way back to the car.

52

John lay awake. He could hear his mother as she moved around in the kitchen.

It was a school day, but he was in no hurry to go.

He wished the birds would return. Although there were seagulls and some larger birds on the island, the small birds were still sparse in number. Many of the inland birds died during the flood, but those who had survived, the salt water destroyed their food sources and nesting habitats.

The dawn chorus still greeted him each day, but it was different. Last year, the first chirrup and warble of nature's alarm clock awoke him at four o'clock in the morning. But this year the dawn chorus was a thin, reedy affair and the surviving birds had dissipated and struggled to find food.

He knelt on his bed and rested his elbows on the windowsill. He could see Sam by the scullery door watching the new chickens as they pecked at the ground in the yard.

A moment later a house wren appeared on the window ledge.

For a second, the bird's buff white barring was displayed, but when it folded its wings, the markings disappeared. John could see the black and white spots on the bird's small, round body as he darted along the windowsill. The bird cocked his head and turned his inquisitive eyes towards him.

'There were lots of you last year, especially during the spring.'

He spoke to the bird through the half-opened window. It was so close, he could have touched the tip of its tail. He always recognised the wren's song; its shrill trill barely ceased in the early hours and its cackle and chatter continued throughout the day. The wren danced sideways along the ledge. His long, grey upper bill was still, and his lower, yellow mandible closed.

'You had moss in your beak last spring.'

He knew the house wren did not migrate and recalled how their tiny, dynamic bodies flitted around the garden and collected pieces of moss, dried twigs, and grass. When their nests were complete, they were a perfect construction, a small round ball with a circular entrance. The female laid one egg every day from early May through to August, until she had a clutch. The adults fed their young on insects, but the flood decimated their food source.

'You will find it hard to feed your nestlings this year, but you have survived the flood, so you will find a way.'

He remembered when he first started school and how his stomach churned fear and anxiety.

'You can't not go to school, lad.'

Annie had propelled him towards the school gates and watched him whilst he walked into the building. Nowadays, his stomach no longer performed somersaults, and when Val gave him a nudge onto the school bus, all he felt was a sense of resignation.

Once in the classroom, John watched the black metal hands of the school clock move around its enamel face. For him, the tick of the clock was the loudest thing in the room. If he was asked a question, all eyes turned towards him, and he froze. Sometimes, he provided the right answer, but other times he got caught in the full glare of his own inattention, and his eyes widened like the frightened rabbits that lived on the farm.

When the bell rang, chairs scraped back from desks, and coats and hats were collected. John was free to go home.

Back to the farm, the fields, and the sea.

53

'We need to talk.'

Eloise glanced at Fred.

'What about?'

She placed her plate in the sink. She had developed breathlessness in the later stages of her pregnancy and wanted to lie down.

'I want to give you an explanation.'

His tone was impatient.

'Very well. When do you suggest?'

'Now, right now.'

She stroked her bump.

'It won't take long.'

She sighed and followed him through to the lounge. He sat opposite. Her stomach rode a sea of anxiety and the baby kicked, but the rest of her body felt numb.

He drew in a deep, long breath.

'It happened during the war when I worked in the meat factory in London before we married. There were six of us on a night shift. We had been there for about an hour when a doodle bug bomb hit the factory.'

Why are you telling me this now?

She wanted to leave the room and go to her own bedroom. Get back to their routine of separate mealtimes and polite but distant conversation.

'I have no memory of what happened after the bomb, but I was told by the rescue services the factory received a direct hit and the building collapsed. I was the only survivor although my spine was injured, and well, as you know, even now I have problems with my back. But the worst thing was my mind...it went completely.'

A visible tremor ran through his body.

'I...I ended up in a mental institution.'

He looked at her.

'There! I've said it.'

A little while longer and he will be finished.

'When I was in the mental institution, I managed to avoid having electric shock therapy and a lobotomy. Then, both forms of treatment were used, even though many medical men considered them barbaric. However, I was lucky; my psychiatrist was a pioneer in the new idea of talking therapies. We discussed the impact of my spinal injury, and he suggested I get tested for infertility. That's how I found out.'

Her voice was calm.

'You should have told me before...should have let me know before we got married. I was bound to find out. Anyway, it is too late now.'

An ocean of silence followed.

He nodded towards her stomach.

'Who is the father?'

'A local man.'

'What's his name?'

He held up his hand.

'Don't worry, I won't contact him.'

'Sergeant Barrett. Jim Barrett. Are you going to divorce me?'

He removed his glasses and ran his finger along a crack in the lens.

'Fred, I am going to keep my baby. If you want to divorce me, go ahead. I will take the consequences, but don't try and persuade me to get rid of my baby.'

54

'It is so nice to be able to do this again.'

Anita pushed the sugar bowl towards Annie.

'Yes, it is.'

Annie looked around the kitchen.

'Your walls have dried out well. Ours are taking ages. I don't know why, maybe the salt content is higher where we are.'

'Yes, we were lucky. The flood level was not so high around here. We had plywood laid onto battens and attached them to the walls to create a gap, so the walls could dry out. The damp, salty smell has almost gone thank goodness, but we must wait until next year before we can paint and decorate.'

They finished their tea.

'Are you ready for a demonstration?'

Anita giggled.

'I sound like a salesman! Mind you, he was here for an hour when we bought it.'

They pushed back their chairs and entered the scullery.

Annie watched as Anita filled the top-loading washing machine with hot water and soap flakes. After the machine had agitated the clothes, she lifted them out of the soapy water with a pair of wooden tongs and began to feed them through the mangle on the top of the machine.

Annie peered at the clothes.

'They are so clean!'

Anita stepped aside and let Annie turn the handle on the mangle.

'Yes, it is wonderful. I don't have to stand over the sink with a washboard anymore, and beat and scrub the clothes by hand, or wring each item out one by one before they are hung out to dry!'

They fed the clothes through the mangle for a second time.

'With this machine your clothes will be washed and out on the line by mid-day. It will save you so much time!'

Annie returned to Butterwood Farm. The September sunshine covered the land in a mellow, golden glow. But despite the beautiful weather, the visit to her best friend had triggered a deep emotion within her and her eyes pricked with tears.

Whatever is the matter with me? Oh...

She stopped the car and dabbed her eyes.

Every time I go there, I find it difficult.

She recalled the look on George's face when he told her how most of Eric's cattle and sheep had been saved from the flood and transported to the mainland by the army. And when the salt test results showed less damage to his soil compared to any other part of the island, which enabled him to use his pastures for grazing his animals. She remembered their coronation party, the new television and the plentiful food and drink. And now, Anita was the proud owner of a new washing machine!

And they have not received their compensation yet.

Suddenly, she felt ashamed of her thoughts. She dried her face and started the car.

'Is Mr Hadley in, Ma'am?'

The young boy blushed and took off his cap.

'No, he's out on the farm,' said Annie. 'Although he did say he would be back early. He is expecting a lorry. Ah, you are Jake's boy.'

The boy nodded and shuffled his feet.

'And how is your hand? George told me all about it.'

'Fine, thank you.'

He looked around willing George to appear.

'Come on, boys. Don't dawdle.'

Olive stood by the back door, waiting for the twins.

'Shall I give them their tea, Mrs Hadley?'

'Yes please, dear. John and Val should be back soon. Oh, there's the lorry.'

The vehicle turned in the yard followed by George and Josh in the truck.

George conversed with the driver of the lorry and pointed to one of the outbuildings. He crossed the yard and entered the kitchen.

'George, you have a visitor.'

Billy stepped forward.

'Ah, hello, lad.'

George nodded towards the boy's hand.

'Looks like they've done a good job there.'

The boy held up his hand. It showed a deep, healing scar across the base of his index finger.

'You were lucky there, lad. You nearly lost it.'

'Yes. Sorry to turn up like this, Mr Hadley, but I wanted to come over and thank you for getting me to the hospital so quick. They said if it had been left any longer, I would have lost my finger.'

'I am glad I was able to help, boy. It is good to see you looking so well.'

He ruffled the boy's hair.

'Off you go and keep yourself safe.'

55

George jumped down from his tractor. Eric's truck had gone from his yard and the farm was quiet. He waited for a few minutes and decided to go home. As he turned to climb onto his tractor, he heard male voices and laughter. The sound was light and jocular, one of camaraderie, as if they were in a public house on a Saturday evening.

'Excuse me, Sir!'

George was surprised; the voice was female. He looked around the yard but could not see anyone.

'Sir!'

A young woman appeared from the direction of the cattle sheds. She wore fawn breeches and rubber boots with thick woollen socks rolled over the tops. Her green wool cardigan was cropped above the waistband of her breeches and her headscarf styled like a turban. George guessed her age as late twenties. The woman was tall and her stride quick and long. She tugged at George's arm.

'Please, Sir, please come and help! Our farmer has gone to market, and they have locked Maisie in with the bull!'

They ran towards the bull pen. Five farm workers stood by the pen. Two of the men leant on the lower half of the stable door and peered into the pen, whilst the remaining three men stood behind them, and tried to get a view. George and the young woman approached, and the three men stood aside. However, the two men nearest the stable door did not move.

'I need to get in there! Step aside, please!'

The men ignored George. He didn't ask again. He grabbed hold of the men's shirt collars and pulled them to one side. He leant over the stable door, squinted, and blinked. The pen was dark, and a lack of ventilation enhanced the strong smell of dung.

At the back of the pen stood Eric's pure-bred Hereford bull. The bull's distinctive red body and white face matched the colouring of the pure-bred heifer who stood in the opposite corner. Behind the heifer, with her back against the wall, stood a young woman.

George grabbed a pitchfork and turned to the men.

'Has that heifer calved? Is she on heat?'

He didn't wait for an answer and unbolted the stable door. The bull glanced at him but turned back to the heifer. He shut the stable door, kept his eyes on the bull and spoke to the girl, soft and slow.

'Keep still. Don't move.'

The bull twitched his tail and stepped towards the heifer. George kept his back close to the wall and edged sideways along the length of the pen. When he stood next to the woman, he whispered in her ear.

'Are you all right, lass?'

The woman nodded. Her body was rigid, and her breathing came in uneven gasps. She was small and slim and wore similar clothes to her friend. He whispered instructions. She nodded and shifted her position.

'Let's go now.'

They moved sideways along the wall towards the stable door. He gripped the pitchfork and kept his eyes glued to the bull.

Suddenly, the bull surged forward and attempted to

mount the heifer. The woman opened her mouth, but before she could scream, George pulled her in front of him and out of the pen. When she reached the arms of her friend, her legs gave way and she burst into tears.

George threw the pitchfork to the ground and turned to the men.

'You bloody idiots! What the hell d'you think you're doing!'

'Was only a bi' of fun, guv'nor. No 'arm done.'

But the man's face held a sneer and he placed his hands on his hips. A snigger arose from the group.

George did not hesitate. His punch struck hard and fast, clean across the man's jaw. The man stumbled backwards and hit the ground with a spectacular thud. His eyes remained closed, and blood trickled from the corner of his mouth.

The farm workers huddled in a group. They whispered to each other and eyed the unconscious man.

'Any more of you idiots think it's a joke?'

He glared at each of the men in turn.

'If any of you do, I will break your bloody neck.'

The men's eyes flickered towards the supine figure.

George pointed to the farmworker on the ground.

'Get that fool up to the farmhouse and get back to work. And mark my words, you haven't heard the last of this.'

He turned to the two women.

'Get your things. You are staying at my farm for a few days, until this is all sorted out.'

By the time George and the women arrived at Butterwood Farm the sun was up. Annie showed the women to a bedroom and offered horse oil ointment for cuts and bruises. Ten minutes later, they came downstairs for breakfast.

George sat at the head of the table.

'I reckon you have learnt a few things since you've been in the land army.'

'We certainly have, Mr Hadley.'

Margaret was the taller of the two women and her accent was clipped and precise. She pulled her chair towards the kitchen table and accepted a cup of tea from Annie.

'I cleaned out many stalls and byres,' said Margaret.

'Also, I carted and spread lime. One farm where I worked, a land girl drove a caterpillar tractor, and we worked with the timber teams. I helped carry the chains to the trees and put them around the trunks before the tractor got to work and pulled them down. The men just stood and watched us. Always, they refused to help.'

'I helped one farmer catch his sheep for maggoting and dipping,' said Maisie.

'We increased milk production on that farm by over 100%; the farm workers hated us for it.'

'Whereabouts did you work?' asked Annie.

She placed her own plate on the table.

'Lots of places, Mrs Hadley,' responded Maisie.

'We worked on farms in Wiltshire and Somerset,' said Margaret.

Annie moved a plate of bread and butter along the table.

'Did you go together?'

'I went to Wiltshire first,' said Margaret. 'And after six months, Maisie joined me from a farm in Somerset.'

Margaret sipped her tea and bit into a piece of buttered bread.

'I was on that farm in Somerset in 1944,' said Maisie. 'And I was so glad to leave it.'

A slight tremor entered her voice.

'The farm workers were all right, but the Italian

prisoner of war workers, they were terrible. They wouldn't keep their hands to themselves. However, the worst thing was the food, well, lack of it. I worked from six o'clock in the morning every day, and when it was harvest time until ten o'clock at night. We were meant to get extra rations for that work, but the farmer's wife was mean, and all we got for breakfast was bread and dripping on one slice of bread and just scraps of meat with our big meal.'

She blushed and diverted her eyes to the label on the marmalade jar.

'But the farm in Wiltshire was wonderful,' said Margaret.

'We both enjoyed our time there. The farmer and his wife were lovely. She was so kind, and the food was good too. Her pies and puddings were superb, and she helped us wash and repair our clothes.'

'I thought the land army was disbanded,' said George.

'Yes, it is,' replied Margaret. 'It disbanded in 1950, but some of us decided to stay on.'

Maisie nodded.

'Didn't you have families to go home to?' asked Annie.

'Yes, of course we did.'

Margaret placed her knife and fork together and pushed her plate to one side.

'Before the war I worked in a big department store. My parents found it difficult. They wanted me to meet an eligible bachelor, get married and have children. That was fine for later, but I wanted to enjoy myself first. So, I joined the Women's Land Army. I had lived away from home before when I went to boarding school, but living on a farm is so much more fun. The countryside, well it's just wonderful with its fresh air and open spaces.

There is nothing quite like walking down a lane first thing in the morning. I love the crunch underfoot from the winter frost, and the cool summer mornings before the heat gets up. I wouldn't go back now.'

'It is all of that and more for me,' said Maisie.

'I worked in a factory before I joined, but I wouldn't go back to it. Here on the island before the flood came, why you could go down to the beach and have a swim and a picnic. One of my favourite things though is when we have planted the fields with crops, it's backbreaking work but I like the way you can see what you've done. When the last cartload of corn has gone from the fields after harvest, I love to see the golden stubble and brown earth. But best of all, I love the animals; the soft noses of the horses, they're like velvet and they have such trusting eyes. I wouldn't go back, not even if you paid me.'

Margaret and Maisie spent the rest of the day with Annie, Olive, and the children.

George visited Eric who told him he had sacked the farm worker and wanted Margaret and Maisie to return. George took them back the following day.

56

'What are you doing over Christmas, Jim? Are you going home, or do you have a nice little number around here to snuggle up to?'

The men winked and laughed as they drunk their beer. When they were off duty the lines of authority dissipated.

'Neither.' replied Barrett. 'I don't care about Christmas. It has no meaning for me.'

He drained his glass and placed it on the counter.

'I'm off.'

He stepped into the silent flurries of snow. Shadows of figures hurried ahead of him. When he reached the corner of the road to Daisy's house he stopped. He wondered whether it was worth going to the front door and knocking again. Then, he recalled his last visit a few weeks ago. Her neighbour had given a derisory snort and offered his advice.

'I should give up if I were you, mate.'

The sergeant turned away and crossed the road.

The snow came thick and fast, a bright whiteness under the streetlamp. He took an envelope from his pocket and opened it. His finger followed his mother's elegant, slanting handwriting. The ink cantered across the page as if written in secretive haste.

Dear Jim,

Hope all is well. We all miss you. He is still here.

I have sent you a parcel. You should get it Christmas Eve.

Love and kisses.

Mum.

The snow began to blur the ink. He slipped the card in its envelope and placed it in his pocket. He felt a swathe of depression wash over him.

Dorothy was so excited she could barely breathe. They had been invited to a drinks party by Mr and Mrs Bates.

'What do you think it means, Derek? Are you in line for promotion?'

She gave her bouffant hairdo a final pat and picked up her string of pearls.

'The whole department is invited, Dorothy. It is a festive gesture of thanks, nothing more.'

Derek pulled his bow tie into place. He felt exasperated. He found his wife's attempts at small-time social climbing tedious. However, the arrival of the invite had provided a well-timed distraction. She seemed to have forgotten about a visit to his brother and sister-in-law.

'Ready?'

He held out her coat.

57

The Hadley household began preparations for Christmas early that year.

Annie ordered a hock of ham and extra sausages from the butcher. Apples and pears, salvaged from the sporadic autumn harvest, were bottled, or made into mincemeat for pies and tarts. The children made yards of paper chains and wrote their letters to Father Christmas, and a space was chosen in the lounge for the Christmas tree. Annie and George scrimped and saved for months for the children's presents: some books for Val, a toy tractor each for Douglas and Dennis and a second-hand pushbike for John.

'John is not well. I am going to call on Dr Everitt.'

George and Olive watched in silence as Annie swept through the kitchen and into the scullery.

During the night, Annie awoke to the sound of John's peculiar and persistent cough. By morning his complexion was effusive, his eyes unnaturally bright and his temperature high. She pondered whether to wait another twenty-four hours, but when he told her he wanted to stay in bed, she made her decision.

Dr Everitt was an empathic man. He combined a kind bedside manner with a swift and precise diagnosis. His surgery was situated at the back of his house and was open each weekday morning. Each afternoon, he undertook home visits.

Annie relayed John's symptoms to the nurse.

'Wait here, Mrs Hadley, while I speak to the doctor.'

She reappeared a few minutes later.

'Two o'clock this afternoon, Mrs Hadley. Until then, Dr Everitt said to keep John in bed and give him plenty of water.'

'It's whooping cough.'

Dr Everitt removed his stethoscope and placed it back in his bag.

'I will give him a course of penicillin. After five days he will cease to be contagious, but while he recovers, he will continue to have coughing fits, especially at night when he lays down. You have probably already heard your boy make that "whoop" sound at the end of a coughing fit.'

Annie nodded.

'In the meantime, keep everyone in the household away from John and ensure your other children sleep in a different room. Keep him in bed, give him plenty of fluids and try and get him to eat. He must remain indoors for the next two weeks. After that, he can go outside for short spells, but keep him in your sight. We don't want him catching anything else on top of this disease.'

'Yes, doctor.'

Dr Everitt turned and smiled at John.

'Don't worry, lad. You will start to feel better soon. Best behaviour now and do as your mother tells you.'

He handed Anne a prescription, snapped shut his black bag and followed her downstairs.

'You might want to think about getting your other children vaccinated, Mrs Hadley. Whooping cough can be a nasty disease. It's been prevalent on the island this year along with other respiratory diseases, probably due to the flood and its aftereffects.'

'Thank you, doctor.'

That evening she read the 'Cock Robin' story to John first and repeated the story to the other children. When they were settled she returned to the kitchen, made a ham sandwich and handed it to George.

'John might not be well in time for Christmas.'

She wiped her hands on her apron.

'He's a strong lad. He will be up and about in no time.'

John stayed in bed for five days. His only visitor was his mother who brought him bowls of broth and jugs of water.

The dark mornings displayed a small, high moon, and beamed silver hatched lines into his room. As the stars extinguished and daylight appeared in the hoary sky, he heard the thud and stamp of boots on the frost-bitten ground. He pulled back the covers, stood on his bed and watched the shadowy figure of his father cross the yard and walk towards the cattle sheds.

'Panda. My Panda.'

He knew his father would feed Panda, but he wanted to go to the bull pen and see her himself. He tried to visualise how she would welcome his father. Would she let him stroke her nose? Would she step back, when his father entered the pen, and nuzzle him for food?

He placed his arms on the window ledge and slumped his chin into his cupped hands. Then he heard footsteps on the stairs, but by the time his mother had opened the door, he was back in bed, his eyes closed, the covers drawn to his chin.

George checked the barometer; it forecast freezing

temperatures through to Boxing Day.

Good. The poultry birds can be killed and hung without them going bad. They will keep fresh in this freezing weather.

However, he didn't instruct the girls to kill the birds. Instead, he drove his tractor to a neighbouring field. When he had parked, he shouted out loud across the landscape.

'Tis a sight to behold!'

He watched two cattle as they grazed. Grazing cattle in winter was never done. They came inside in November and were fed winter fodder. But a handful of farmers had obtained government approval to grow experimental grass mixtures on previously flooded land. He recalled an article he read. If the grass showed a good mat of turf, then the soil beneath was less damaged and cattle could graze.

He felt joyous and hopeful. Even his money worries did not seem so bad.

He returned to the yard and approached the poultry shed. He could smell the droppings of the birds, and when he pushed open the shed door, their cacophonous squawks invaded his ears.

'These birds are ready.'

'Righto, Mr Hadley.'

Molly and the other women tied their aprons.

'I will collect the boxes later and take them to Frank Turner. Remember to keep some back so that Annie and Anita can distribute them.'

He reminded himself to make sure Molly and Alice Wright each received a bird.

'Now, where is he.'

George looked for the large red comb of the cockerel and moved towards him. He caught it in one silent swoop, pulled, and twisted its neck and laid it on a wooden table. It was a nice, plump bird and would make a fine centre piece for their Christmas lunch. He plucked it, and hung it by its neck in the scullery, ready for Annie to clean on Christmas morning.

Christmas Eve arrived.

Annie herded the children into their beds and read the story of 'Rudolph the Red Nosed Reindeer.' Afterwards, she went downstairs and filled their Christmas stockings with jelly babies, spangles, fruit sherbet fountains and bars of chocolate.

Two hours later she crept back into the children's bedrooms and hung the filled stockings on the end of their beds. She went to John's room last. She hung up his stocking and smoothed his covers. He was in a deep sleep, his face peaceful and content. She kissed his forehead and crept out of the room.

As the silent night made its journey, the temperature dipped, and snow fell. And by the early hours of Christmas morning nature's overnight transformation was complete. The snow covered the island in a cape of soft, white goose feathers.

The children awoke early and squealed with delight as they emptied their Christmas stockings and unwrapped their presents. But when Annie went into John's bedroom, she found his stocking untouched and his bed cold. She ran through the house and called out his name. George appeared from the scullery, the dead cockerel in his hands.

'George! Have you seen John? He's gone from his bed!'

George flung the bird on the table and turned on his heels.

A quietness struck the yard, disturbed only by the

scurry of an animal as it sought refuge from the cold. He turned one way, then the other, took off his cap and scratched his head. He knelt and checked the ground. Then, he sprung up and ran towards the bull pen. The tracks of the boy's footsteps in the snow stopped at the stable door of the pen, but John was nowhere to be seen and Panda stood alone. George circled the cattle stalls and ran out into the lane.

'John! John! Where are you son?'

After a few moments, he saw him in the distance. He slowed and quietened his pace. Then he saw what John saw, a robin on a snow laden branch of a tree. The bird hopped one way, then the other, his orange, red breast visible like a fresh berry against the white of winter.

He approached and put his arm around his son's shoulders.

They watched the bird in silence.

'Come on, lad. Your mother is worried about you. Grandpa and grandma will be here soon. Let's get you home.'

As they pressed their boots into the powdered snow, the smell of woodsmoke curled through the still air, and the windows of the farmhouse twinkled like a dozen lit candles between the bare trees. When they got closer, they heard the murmur of voices, the chink of crockery, the hiss and bubble of pans. Their mouths watered from the smell of the roasting cockerel and their nostrils tingled from the rich, sweet smell of cinnamon and spices. They saw holly-berry red, evergreen, and gold, the palette of Christmas.

Annie glanced at John, but she did not scold him.

'There you are, John. Come and get warm.'

'Merry Christmas!'
Nanny Em gave a loud hiccup and raised her glass of

sherry.

George smiled at his mother, glad to see her better.

'Here, let me help you with that.'

Moses took the plate of roast cockerel from Annie and placed it on the table. The old man held up the carving knife and fork.

'Are you going to carve, George? Or shall I?'

'I will do it, Pa. You sit down.'

'Grandpa, the seat has come off my tractor.'

Dennis clambered onto his grandfather's lap.

'I will read with you later, Val.'

Grandma Em leant back in her chair and enjoyed the effects of the alcohol.

George smiled at Annie.

'Lovely lunch.'

The children left the table and played with their toys, whilst their grandparents fell asleep by the fire.

'Queen's speech in ten minutes,' said George.

'It will be different this year. She is still on her tour of the Commonwealth so her Christmas broadcast will come from New Zealand.'

He followed Annie through to the kitchen. As she stood at the sink, he put his arms around her waist, kissed the back of her head and pressed his face into her soft, brown hair.

'You give me hope, my darling.'

She turned and embraced him.

Their love, their luck, their survival.

PART THREE

58

January 1954

The bever hut was opposite the cart lodge and was twice the size of a horse's stable. It had wooden sides and floor, and a roof of wood and corrugated metal. The chimney was made of cast iron and travelled up through a hole in the roof. In the middle of one wall stood an Atlantic fire stove, on top of which sat a small wire tray which was used to melt cheese on bread. Positioned in a half circle around the stove were discarded chairs, interspersed with small, homemade tables.

George lifted the latch and entered the bever hut. The farm workers had already arrived and stood huddled around the cascading heat of the stove. They had ruddy complexions and even the younger ones wore a weathered look. But the warmth and glow of the stove relaxed their bodies and cast a softer hue across their faces.

'Morning.'

George replaced the latch and took off his cap.

The men chorused a reply.

'Morning, guv'nor.'

They stamped their feet and warmed their outstretched hands.

'Bloody cold out there.'

George took off his oilskin and threw it over the back

of a chair. The men moved away from the stove and took their seats. Their reddened faces looked hopeful of indoor jobs. Even the workshops and outbuildings held no attraction in such inclement weather.

'Right, first up. Annie and I were pleased to see all of you at the commemorative service yesterday.'

The men murmured in response. Each had their own tragic memories to bear, and the service gave them and their families an opportunity to pay their respects.

'Now, some good news. I have been informed by the Ministry we can grow some barley this year.'

The men cheered.

George paused and cleared his throat.

'It has been a long wait,' said Jake. 'It will be nice to get back to it.'

The men murmured in agreement. They leant forward and fixed their eyes on George.

'As far as today goes, we will start by sorting out the sugar bags. God willing, we will need them this summer.'

'The sugar bags are stored above the old stable,' said Reggie.

'Yes, they are,' replied Jake. 'But it's been over a year since we checked them, the mice might have got them.'

'Aye,' said George. 'But not the flood water. We can make a start on them today. We will use the sugar bags for the barley crop. The corn sacks weigh eighteen stone when full and are too big and heavy.'

'The crop might yield a ton an acre and we have permission to sow a field of twenty-five acres. So...'

The men waited whilst George did some calculations in his head.

'Let's say three hundred bags to be on the safe side.'

He slapped his thigh.

'Right then, men, let's get started.'

He replaced his cap and picked up his oilskin.

The men ran across to the old stable, collected the sugar bags and tools and returned to the bever hut. The bags varied in quality. Some required repairs and could be used again, whilst others were only fit to be used as repair material. The men shook out the bags and separated them into two piles.

The sugar bags were made of hessian and required certain tools to repair them. Some of the men turned pieces of kindling wood into pasting sticks, whilst others found small boards of wood, strong glue, and hammers.

'Terrible weather outside,' said the oldest farm worker.

He fixed his eyes on Jake and Reggie.

'Not much chance of a "sea waller" today.'

The men sniggered.

'Why mate, you're past all that,' said Jake.

'Just wishful thinking,' replied the old man. 'There's no 'arm in that.'

The men laughed.

The old man removed half a cigarette from his pocket and lit the end.

'Who's gonna do patches?'

'Reggie,' said another. 'He'll be good at that.'

Reggie took the scissors and gathered up the torn sugar bags. The rest of the men each took a bag that required repairs, returned to their chairs, and placed a board of wood inside the sugar bag to provide a back to the hole.

'Coconut... orange... apple... egg.'

Reggie cut an appropriately shaped patch from the old sugar bag and threw it in the direction of the request. The men pasted one side of the patch and placed it over the hole in their sack. They tapped the edges into place with the hammer and peeled away the board.

'Another patch, Reggie.'

The men smoked and talked their way through the work. By bever time twenty repaired bags lay in a pile.

Jake pointed to the remaining bags.

'They will keep us busy for a few days yet.'

Bever took place around the stove. The farmworkers rolled and lit fresh cigarettes, topped their bread with cheese and placed it on the wire tray on top of the stove. After their bever, the men resumed work and completed thirty more bags.

'I reckon fifty sacks is a fair morning's work.'

The men agreed with Jake and stopped for a break. For a while, they played cards, followed by rounds of 'Ringing the Bull'. At half past twelve they left the hut and went home for lunch.

59

Eloise lay in bed. She had not seen or heard from Sergeant Barrett. However, the thought of meeting him replayed in her head. What would she say to him? Would she express frustration, even hatred? Or forgiveness and expressions of love? Would there be commitment to her and the unborn child? Or continued abandonment? She had endless questions but no answers.

She got dressed, padded downstairs and pulled shut the front door with a quiet click. Despite being in the last stages of her pregnancy, she decided to walk rather than take the bus. However, when she reached the high street, she felt nauseous. She stepped inside a café, chose a table by the window, and ordered a pot of tea. A man sat at a table and ate bacon and eggs, whilst at another table a mother tried to soothe her fractious child.

Eloise saw the young woman first. Her dark hair fell in waves and her ruby red lips smiled and laughed. Although she noticed the woman's hair dye and heavy makeup, what struck her most was the woman's sheer joyousness of the moment as she sashayed along the street with her companion.

Eloise jolted in her seat and gripped the edge of the table. Sergeant Barrett wore civilian clothes. His pinstripe suit and fashionable moustache gave him the air of a post war salesman. She watched them cross the street arm in arm and walk towards the café. Then, in a jaunty, stripe-ridden blur, they were gone.

The nauseous feeling returned. She stroked her stomach, but the sensation did not subside.

'Are you all right, madam?'

The waitress looked at Eloise's stomach.

'Yes, thank you. Just a little dizzy, nothing more.'

The waitress hovered by the table.

'Oh yes, sorry. Can I have the bill please.'

The waitress bobbed and disappeared.

Eloise did not return home. Instead, she walked to the school and stood outside. The flood victims had gone, and the classrooms were full of children, their arms upstretched as they waited to be picked by their teacher. Her memories of Sergeant Barrett lingered. She recalled their first meeting when he walked across the hall, when they made love between exhausting shifts and when he left her house for the last time.

She felt alone, scared, unloved.

When she returned home, she was surprised to see Fred.

'My back has been bad. I did not go to work today.'

His face contorted with pain as he tried to stand straight.

'Would you like some food?'

She shook her head and climbed the stairs to her bedroom. She sat on the bed, tripped off her shoes and stretched her legs.

What a mess we are in.

She had expected their days living in the same house to be difficult until their divorce, but they settled into an uneasy pattern. Fred left for work each day before she got out of bed and returned late in the evening. The late returns had made her wonder if he had a lady friend and she remembered how her eyes filled with tears. Then she discovered he met Derek in the local public house. That was a surprise.

They were never close. Maybe things changed between them. Perhaps Fred has told Derek about the pregnancy and our divorce.

She had always liked Derek. He was a kind, tolerant man, but he was married to Dorothy and her superior, sneering personality prevented any close ties.

Well, it is too late now. I doubt whether I will see them at all.

The next day Eloise stayed in her room. Later, when she heard Fred open the front gate, she peeped through the net curtains and watched him walk to the front door. His bad back caused his right foot to scrape on the ground.

She found him trying to prepare vegetables, his gait awkward as he leant over the sink. He moved across to the cooker, picked up a pork chop, but dropped it on the floor. He clutched the back of a chair. His body was stooped and low, and his glasses dangled from his nose.

'Why don't you sit down. I will cook you something.'

He dragged a chair to the table.

She picked up the chop and washed it under the tap. 'Here.'

She gave him a glass of squash.

When she placed the plate of cooked food on the table, he curled his fingers over her hand.

She nodded to his meal.

'That'll get cold, Fred.'

'I have never stopped loving you, Eloise. I have always loved you. Just didn't know how to tell you.'

He lifted his head. His glasses were steamed up from the heat of the food. He wiped his index finger across each lens, like a mechanised wiper blade.

'We could keep the baby. Look after him together. Bring him up as our own.'

60

The second week of March brought fine, settled weather, perfect for sowing barley. George stepped into the field which had been worked by Josh and checked the soil. The field had been 'pulled down' by the harrow. It had levelled the soil and killed the weeds resulting in a finer seed bed. George grabbed a handful of soil and broke it up with his fingers.

Ah, yes, the sun and wind have dried the surface. Nature's done her job, it's nicely hazled, and ready.

The Ministry scientists had run final tests on the soil and were content with the results. But George remained cautious. The soil's ability to yield a marketable crop was still unknown and his final compensation payments were yet to be paid.

On the surface, the field contained good quality, oxygenated soil, a mixture of large and small clumps, rather than a salt ridden mass. But he knew the proof would come after the seed was sown and recalled crops grown by farmers without permission from the government. At first, the seeds had shown promise, but once their roots penetrated the topsoil, the seedlings died, poisoned by the salt still hidden below the surface. However, a year had passed, and time improved the land. Worms were plentiful, some cattle had grazed in the pastures and the islanders talked of starting to grow vegetables again. He had seen birds return to the island too. At first, he saw one or two lapwings only, but in more recent weeks the numbers increased ready for the mating season.

He checked his watch and whistled a favourite tune, its provenance an unknown folk song. The seed merchant was due in an hour with the first delivery of barley seed. He raised his arms in celebration and set off for the farmhouse.

Just before seven o'clock the following morning George met Josh and the farm workers in the bever hut. He tasked some men to check and finish the sugar sacks, whilst others started new jobs.

'Josh, I need you on the back of the drill.'

He turned to the men.

'The weather is set to be good for at least a week, if not two, so let's get on.'

The men picked up their caps. They did not linger for casual banter; they wanted to work.

George and Josh stood outside and watched the men scatter across the yard.

'Did you dress that seed with copper sulphate yesterday? We don't want insect infestation to ruin our first crop.'

'Yep. All done, guv'nor.'

They attached the Suffolk Coulter drill to the tractor and loaded it with bags of seed.

'That's it.'

George slapped the side of the tractor and climbed onto the seat. Josh stepped onto the running board at the back of the drill. They trundled along the lane, swung wide of the hedgerows, and entered the field. George turned the tractor in line with the edge of the field and started to drill. The drill coulters pulled and dropped the seed into the soil. Within minutes the seagulls arrived.

Whether it was cultivating, drilling, or ploughing the soil, the tractor was a welcome sight for the bird population. The gulls followed the vehicle secure in the knowledge there would be rich pickings in the exposed soil.

As George drove towards the top end of the field, he spotted a solitary bird take off from the ground. He stopped the tractor and climbed down.

'There is a lapwing's nest right in the middle of our next row.'

He indicated the spot to Josh. Josh disengaged the coulters unsure whether George intended to drive across already sown land. George walked towards the nest.

'Ah, there you are.'

The lapwing's nest lay hidden in a dip in the ground and contained four freshly laid eggs. They were slightly pointed in shape which gave them protection and prevented the eggs from rolling away. He knelt and made a pyramid of clods next to the nest. Then he carefully removed the eggs from the nest, put them in his cap and placed them on the recently drilled soil.

He returned to his tractor.

After he had drilled across the original nest area, he returned to the pyramid of clods. He made a fresh indentation in the earth with his knuckle, lined it with pieces of straw and dried grass, and placed the eggs in the new nest. By the time he climbed onto his tractor, the female lapwing had landed and returned to her eggs.

The weather remained fine, and two days later the drilling was complete. They left the field for a few days and waited for the earth to 'hazle'. When it was dry enough, Josh prepared the Field Marshall tractor. He attached the non-mechanised roller and returned to the field. As he drove up and down, the rolls pressed the soil against the seeds which retained the moisture for good germination.

George and Josh surveyed the completed field.

'There is no telling what weeds we will get now.'

'Hopefully just some broadleaf to spray off in a few months,' said Josh.

'Aye. A few days of warm humid weather will give us good germination. We are in God's hands; we must wait and see.'

That night George prayed. He prayed nature would provide his seeds with fine, steady rainfall, hours of warm sunshine, and cloud cover at night to keep the hoary frosts away.

In previous years, once he had sown the crop, he left it for a week before digging down to see if it had started to 'chit' and put out a root. Then, two to three weeks later, he would check again to ensure the fresh, green shoots had burst through the soil. And by the time he spread the fertilizer on the soil a few months later, he would be confident his crop was on its well-trodden path to full growth and eventual harvest.

But this time things were uncertain. Apart from the seasonal vagaries of the weather, there was the added concern of whether the salt levels further down in the soil, would poison, and kill the roots of his crop as they grew and reached down for hydration. And another worry was the issue of his compensation claim and payment by the government. When he received the forms, he had completed and posted them the same day, but since then he heard nothing. It was one big waiting game.

At first, he told himself to let nature take its course, but after five days and nights he could wait no longer, and on the sixth day he entered the field. He hovered at its edge, then paced up and down and looked for signs of growth. Of course, there were none. The weather had not been exceptionally hot to cause early germination and he knew it was pointless to dig up some seeds to check their progress.

He forced himself to leave the field and kept company with Josh and his farm workers throughout the day. But on the seventh day he rose at first light and went straight to the field. He knelt, took a deep breath, and parted the soil with his hands. Within the crumbled earth lay several barley seeds each with its own tiny straggle of tentative roots.

Thank the Lord.

He sat back on his heels and took several deep breaths. After a few minutes he covered the seeds up and left the field. However, he continued to worry about the impact of the remaining salt in the soil. He had no money to buy fertilizer, and any sign of the shoots turning yellow would confirm the existence of salt and the death of his crop. And even when he did see the fresh, green shoots of life as they burst through the soil some weeks later, he could not relax. His mind remained in a perpetual state of anxiety.

He did not discuss his concerns with anyone. Josh and his farm workers had enough to worry about and he heard snippets of conversations of their own hardships; their lack of food, how difficult it was to carry out repairs to their homes when money was scarce, and their turbulent emotions when a child was born and whether they could manage. The men had endured loss and hardship, and although they remained loyal, George knew every man had his limit. But they never complained about their pitiful and sporadic pay or told him how their wives tried to persuade them to get a job on the mainland. He never forgot their loyalty. They stayed with him on the land and what it had to offer.

61

April brought several thunderstorms. Hailstones fell from the sky and frozen droplets pummelled the ground in short, furious bursts. By late afternoon each day, the temperature had cooled further, and the last traces of winter chilled the air.

'Ready?'

Josh held the bike in the middle of the handlebars and on the back of the seat. John nodded, his face flushed with excitement. He gripped the handlebars and looked ahead at the track that ran around the duck pond.

'One...two...three!'

John began to pedal. Josh ran alongside for several seconds and gave the bike a push. The ducks unfurled their wings, flacked across the water, and disappeared into the reed bed on the far side of the pond. The boy pushed hard on the pedals as the bike wobbled and bounced across the uneven ground. He could hear the heavy breathing of Josh as he reappeared by his side, ran ahead, and grabbed the handlebars.

'Got you!'

John's Christmas present had been bought from a friend of Dr Everitt. It was a good model but required attention; the back tyre was almost flat, the chrome was pitted, and it needed a coat of blue paint.

'Can we do it again, Josh?'

John turned the bike ready to go back.

'In a minute... let me get my breath.'

John waited with his foot ready on the pedal.

'Right, once more, but this time when I push you off, you carry on around the track on your own and I will meet you over the other side.'

He ran alongside the bike and gave it one last push. Then he turned around and ran in the opposite direction to the other side of the duck pond. John pushed down on the pedals as fast as he could and continued around the track. The ducks murmured and shifted in the reed bed. Josh grabbed the handlebars and pulled the bike to a halt. Their gasps filled the air.

'Do you think you've got it now?'

He panted, his hands on his knees.

John nodded.

'Have a go on your own...see how you get on. We'll get that back tyre replaced and sort out the chrome and paint.'

Afterwards, they walked back to the farmhouse and left the bike outside the scullery.

'Would you like a cup of tea, Josh?'

Annie moved towards the kettle.

'No thank you, Mrs Hadley. I need to get back home. The in-laws are coming for Sunday dinner today.'

She smiled.

'John has done well. He will be able to ride on his own in no time at all. If he needs any more help let me know.'

'That is very kind of you, Josh. Thank you.'

He raised his arm.

'Well, I must be going. I will see the guv'nor in the morning.'

Eloise pushed the pram hood back, picked up Tommy

and kissed the top of his head.

'My sweetest boy.'

She cradled the baby in her arms and smelt the honey sweetness of his skin. Tommy focused his eyes and studied her face.

When Eloise first visited the park with Tommy, she took him earlier in the day. Then, young mothers gossiped in groups as their children fed the ducks and tottered about on reins, whilst men sat on park benches, smoked their cigarettes, or dozed in the sunshine and waited for opening time. However, she felt vulnerable after the birth and the bustle did not suit her. She preferred the latter part of the day when the park was quiet, the benches were empty, and she had a clear, unobstructed view of the woods and parkland.

She stood up and repositioned Tommy in her arms.

'There you are! Now you can see!'

She pointed to a flitting bird and the late daffodils as she cooed and cuddled him. His cheeks became red from the cold and his eyelids closed and opened. She placed him in the pram and covered him with a blanket.

She took the same route home. Sometimes she nodded to a neighbour, at other times she walked in silent happiness. She fumbled in her pocket for the key and opened the front door. As she manoeuvred the pram over the front step Tommy remained asleep, his face turned to one side. She stroked his cheek and checked the blanket.

The clock struck four and the kitchen door opened.

'Hello, love. Did you have a nice time in the park?'

'Yes, thanks. Still, it is chilly out there.'

She hung her coat and scarf on the coat stand.

'I have lit the fire and made us some tea.'

She smiled and opened the lounge door. The fire flickered gold and burnt umber, and the flames danced shadows on the walls. She pulled a chair towards the warmth and sat down.

'Here you are, love.'

'Thank you.'

'Is Tommy, okay?'

'Yes, he is fine. I've laid him down. He'll sleep for an hour.'

She smiled and drank her tea.

Kind concerned eyes scrutinised her face.

'You look a little flushed, darling. Are you tired?'

'A little, but I am fine thanks.'

'Maybe it's coming in from the cold and sitting in front of the fire that's done it. I will give Tommy his tea if you want to have a lie down.'

'Thank you. Yes, I will.'

She rose from the chair and lay on the sofa. Coal was shovelled on the fire and a blanket tucked around her feet and pulled over her body. The lamp was turned off and the door closed. She lay on her side, repositioned the cushion under her head and placed her arm over the top of the blanket. The flames danced high on the walls vigorous from the loaded coal.

She felt a surge of guilt as she recalled the confrontation with Fred, the anger and bitterness in his voice and the unforgiving way he looked at her.

The birth had been straightforward, but it had drained her of physical strength and emotional resilience. Every day she felt a searing rawness as if she might not cope with the smallest thing. Then something within her changed, and she stepped onto a different path. She smiled to herself.

I have made the right decision.

62

'Hello, my dear.'

Anita squeezed Annie's hand and sat beside her.

Margaret Barling arrived, followed by Ed Simpson, Dickie Byers, and Frank Thomson. Margaret Barling smiled at everyone around the table.

'Well, thank you for coming today. It is so lovely to see you all.'

She tapped a finger on her open notepad.

'Now, we discussed the allocation of jobs last time we met, but we will go through them again, and if anyone has any questions, please do ask.'

She turned towards Ed Simpson.

'Now, Mr Simpson, the marquee tents please.'

Ed Simpson shifted in his seat. Aware he was employed as the farm manager by Mr and Mrs Barling, he spoke in a formal tone, his easy banter gone.

'We will put the marquee tents up on Friday evening, Mrs Barling. May I ask what time the entrants are due to arrive for the flower and vegetable competitions on Saturday morning? We need enough time to set out the stalls.'

'The entrants will arrive from nine o'clock on Saturday morning, but there are bound to be some who arrive early.'

'Very good, Mrs Barling. In that case, we will get the stalls set out on Friday evening too. Mr Barling has given the workers permission to leave work early on Friday.'

'That's wonderful, Mr Simpson. Thank you.'

She ticked her list.

'Annie, I think you are buying the prizes for the hoopla stall and the lucky dip?'

'Yes, that's right, Margaret. I will go across to the mainland in the next few days and get those purchased.'

'Excellent, thank you.'

Dickie Byers raised his hand. He looked at Annie, knowing, purposeful; he glanced away and turned towards Margaret.

'I can provide some prizes, a jar or two of something.

'That is so kind, Dickie, thank you.'

She ticked her list.

'Dickie and Frank, I have both of you down to run the beer tent.'

The two men nodded.

'Annie and Anita, you will be organising the baking competition. What about the tea and cake stall? Who's running that?'

'That's us too,' replied Annie.

'Once the entrants have arrived and the cakes set out, there will be nothing further to do until the judging starts. Doris and Edith are going to help with the tea and cake stall. They will come in early, fill and heat the urns and set out the tables and chairs. They will also help us to serve teas.'

'Jolly good and thank you. It is wonderful we can have the summer fete this year. I know the islanders are looking forward to it, especially members of the Horticultural and Flower Club. Many have been trying to grow their own vegetables and flowers again.'

'Yes,' said Annie. 'This will be our first fete for two years and there's a lot of excitement about it. Oh, I almost forgot; "Bowling for the Pig," George will oversee that stall.'

'Excellent. Please do thank him.'

A few days later Annie drove to the mainland. She purchased jumping jack sets, dice, and colouring books. She also bought some crepe paper to finish Val's outfit for the fancy dress competition. On her return, she decided to visit Moses and Emma.

'Hello, Annie! Shall I get Moses?'

Emma kissed and hugged her.

'I am on my own,' replied Annie. 'I thought I would pop in and see how you are.'

The old lady acknowledged the reply, but her expression was one of dissatisfaction.

They sat in silence and drank their tea. It was a strange ritual, but one they had developed over the years when they were alone together; tea first followed by a few words of conversation.

'How are the children?'

'Very well, thank you.'

'I just wondered...I mean...is George all right?'

'Why, yes, he is, thank you, Em. Is there a reason why he shouldn't be?'

'Well, he has not been around here for a while, not since Moses drove the heifers across.'

They reverted to silence. Annie felt a button had been pressed within her. They could not escape their lack of money. She knew George veered from appreciation of his father's helpful gesture to embarrassment at not having money to buy his own cattle.

After several minutes, she glanced at Emma and picked up her bag.

'Well, I really must be going.'

'So glad you came over, Annie. Do get George to visit. His father will be pleased to see him.'

63

The day of the fete dawned fine and warm.

Five marquee tents stood erected in the field. The three competition tents each had a single row of stalls placed inside their perimeters, and a further line of stalls positioned down the middle. Next came the beer tent, and then the fifth tent, allocated for the sale of tea and cakes.

'Mind your backs please!... I am sorry, Sir, but this section is for main crop potatoes only. Other vegetables must go over there...Please move your carrots...thank you, Sir... My word, that's the biggest marrow I've ever seen! What have you been feeding it to get it like that? ... Pretty sweet peas, wonderful fragrance... Those cabbage roses are beautiful...Who do you think will win the best flower competition?'

The baking entrants arrived with their cakes and biscuits. There were towering Victoria sponges oozing with raspberry jam, rich Dundee and fruit cakes, delicate Maids of Honour, robust jam tarts, and moreish honey and oat biscuits. Recipes were jealously guarded. It was an unspoken rule not to ask.

'That looks lovely,' said Anita.

Daphne Ditchin moved forward, as if to hand over her fruit cake, but she hesitated.

'Are you sure it is going in the right class, dear?'
'Yes, I am sure, Mrs Ditchin. Once the fete is open you

will be able to come back in and view all the bakes. So, if you would be so kind...'

Anita took the cake and placed it on the stall.

'Will the judges see it from there, dear? I don't want them to miss it.'

'Yes, Mrs Ditchin, of course they will! The tent will be shut whilst the cakes are being judged. The judges will cut and taste each cake, so they will get a close look. Now, if you please, Mrs Ditchin, if you want to enter the competition, please leave your cake!'

George arrived with the piglet. He placed it in a small run and set up the stall.

'Bowling for the Pig' was a popular game with the villagers. George erected a wooden board, supported with an easel-type stand. The board was a yard wide and four feet tall with a curved top. The front of the board advertised the game; 'Bowling for the Pig. Six Pence a Go - Five Balls a Game.' In the middle, at the bottom of the board, was a hole in the shape of a horseshoe, big enough for a ball to roll through. The player who succeeded in getting the highest number of balls through the hole in one game, was the overall winner and announced at the end of the day. If they were unable to 'grow the pig on' and feed it until it was big enough to be slaughtered, they received a compensatory prize of ten shillings.

'Morning, George,'

Eric approached the stall and leant over the run.

'That's a fine piglet you have there.'

'Aye, we should get a good turnout today.'

'Yes, I reckon you will. My men, well, they have been talking about the fete all week.'

'Yes, so have mine.'

Eric steadied the top of the table whilst George positioned the stall legs. He counted the small change in the box.

'You heard anything about your compensation claim?'

'No, nothing.'

He topped up the piglet's water bowl.

'I must say they are taking their time. I never dreamt it would take this long. It is making life difficult.'

'Yes, same here,' replied Eric.

'I am guessing but I think some farmers won't be able to hold out much longer.'

George did not reply.

He gave the piglet a final check.

'Right, all done. Let's go for a beer.'

It was two o'clock in the afternoon and a large crowd waited by the entrance gate. Pennies and tickets exchanged hands and the crowd entered the field. By half past two, the stalls in the field were surrounded, and the marquee tents full.

Olive bent down towards the children.

'We will go and see Mummy first and then look at the stalls.'

She squeezed Val's hand.

'The children's fancy dress competition is later this afternoon.'

Val nodded and jigged up and down. She wore a turquoise and white shepherdess dress, a bonnet of crepe paper and held a small wooden crook made by George.

'There is no mistake about it, that is a short carrot.'

The man placed his hands on his hips.

'No, no that's not right,' said another.

'You can see it is a long carrot. It's got no place in this competition. It should be in the other competition over there.'

'I don't agree. Anyway, it is too late for me to enter that competition. I'm staying put.'

The judge looked from one carrot to the other and pointed at one of them.

'Right, gentlemen, this one is the winner.'

He held up his hand.

'That is my decision. And it's final.'

Dorothy looked past Derek.

'Why that's your brother over there.'

'Yes, I saw him earlier.'

She shaded her eyes and frowned.

'I don't understand. He is with Eloise!'

Her mouth opened and closed, like a fish taken off the hook.

'You told me they were getting divorced!'

'I thought I had told you what happened... I...'

'Don't be ridiculous.'

She spat out her words.

'Do you think I would have forgotten if you had told me what happened? You did not tell me!'

She stared across the field for several seconds.

'They are coming over! Oh! There's a child with them!'

Fred wore cream, baggy trousers held up by bright striped braces. His white shirt was open at the collar and the sleeves were rolled up. He carried a baby in his arms. The baby held a toy and was absorbed in its shape and colour. Eloise walked alongside them. She fanned the brim of her straw hat across the baby's face and over his body.

Suddenly they stopped.

'Hello,' said Fred.

He repositioned the baby in his arms.

Eloise looked at Dorothy, her gaze unwavering.

'Hello Dorothy, Derek.'

The adults stood as if frozen in time, their limbs still, their mouths silent. Only the baby's babble filled the void. He let go of his toy. Eloise caught it.

'Here you are, darling.'

'Well,' said Dorothy. 'Look how things turn out when you don't see people for a long time!'

Her mouth slammed shut into a hard, thin line.

Derek flushed.

The baby put one end of the toy in his mouth and fixed his gaze on Dorothy.

She looked into the baby's eyes. They were beautiful, the darkest brown, with sweeping black eyelashes. She paused as if to say something. She looked at Fred. His eyes were pale blue. She looked at Eloise. Her eyes were bright blue.

'Why, I do believe...'

Fred stepped forward.

'Dorothy, it's been a while. This is our son Tommy! I can't believe you haven't met him!'

'Time goes so fast,' said Eloise. 'Are you enjoying the fete? Fred just won a prize for his cabbage roses!'

She stroked the baby's hair and smiled at Dorothy.

Derek patted his brother on the shoulder.

'Well done.'

'Thank you,' said Fred. 'Well, we must be getting on. We want to take Tommy to see the rabbits.'

The two brothers nodded. A look passed between them; it spoke of knowledge, conspiracy, and the promise to keep a secret.

Fred clasped Tommy and began to retreat.

'We must get together some time... perhaps tea at our house?'

Eloise smiled, turned away and caught up with her family.

George and Eric stood outside the beer tent. The aroma of hops invaded their nostrils and lay on their lips like salty sea air.

George raised his glass.

'To old times!'

'Yes,' said Eric. 'To old times.'

They chinked their glasses and gulped their beer.

The local band struck up a tune.

'It's good to see the islanders enjoying themselves again.'

George nodded. He inclined to a group of young men to their left.

'The soldiers are here too.'

Some of them wore their uniforms. It was clear from their voices they had not strayed far from the beer tent.

'George!'

George dipped his mouth away from his beer as he was slapped on the back.

'Gordon! You old bugger! It's good to see you! Gordon, this is Eric. Eric, Gordon.'

The men shook hands.

'It's good to see you too, George,' said Gordon. 'Is your family well?'

'Aye, we are, thank you. We all survived. We've had a bad time of it, but we're getting through it now. I have started growing crops again.'

George drew the glass to his lips.

'That is good to hear, George. The flood devastated so many people's lives.'

'Yes, it did, but we were lucky'

Gordon looked around him, then back at George.

'Did you know the emergency services said there were no survivors on the island after the flood?'

'Yes,' replied George. 'I did hear that, although it was sometime later when I found out.'

'But you see, at the time, I didn't believe it,' said Gordon. 'I just could not accept that everyone on the island was gone. I had to see for myself. So, on that Sunday I took my light aircraft up and flew over the island. I saw people in boats and on rooftops. They waved and shouted as I flew over. I went straight back to headquarters and told them. Thankfully they found you and got you off.'

Gordon placed a cigarette into an expensive holder.

'By God,' said George. 'I didn't know that.'

His voice quavered.

'You saved our lives, Gordon...all of us. If you had not flown over, we would have been left to our fate...I'

George's glass began to shake. He placed his free hand around the top and tried to steady it. Gordon put his arm around George's shoulders.

'It's all right, old boy. You would have done the same.'

Eric stepped forward.

'Can I get you a drink, Gordon?'

'Why thank you. A pint of the same please.'

Barrett placed his empty glass on a table and stepped away from the group of soldiers.

There were plenty of girls at the fete. He watched them as they linked arms and sashayed in their fashion slacks and full skirted dresses. Several looked in his direction, but none caught his eye. He had listened as his friends spoke about the local dance scheduled for the following weekend. He was not interested. Maybe, nearer the time, he would decide who to take.

He moved between the tables with his unlit cigarette. A lighter was held to its end. He nodded, inhaled, and exhaled. The smoke curled around him, soft and white. Then, as the haze of smoke cleared, he saw Daisy. She sat alone at a table near the tea tent.

The sergeant felt his body flood with small, convulsive twitches. He wanted to hurl tables and chairs out of the way to reach her but forced himself to approach in a casual manner.

'Hello, Sergeant Barrett.'

Daisy smiled and lowered her eyelashes. She wore a blue gingham dress and white open toe sandals. A closed, pale blue parasol rested beside her chair.

'Hello, Daisy.'

He extinguished his cigarette behind his back and dropped it to the ground.

She nodded towards the group of soldiers.

'Are you with your friends, Sergeant?'

'No, not really.'

His body was tense, rigid.

Daisy looked around at the fete.

'Everyone is having such a lovely time, don't you think? It is so nice to be able to do something that's well, normal.'

She smiled again.

What could he say? He had not seen Daisy since the day in the graveyard before she left for London. Yet all she wanted to do was engage in polite conversation. Well, he didn't. It was now or never.

'I wondered if you would like to...'

'Excuse me'

A well-spoken voice came from behind him, a male voice, educated, entitled. Barrett stood to one side. The man wore navy blazer and cream pressed trousers. He placed a tray on the table.

'Here we are.'

'This is Sergeant Barrett,' said Daisy.

'Sergeant Barrett, this is Peter Roberts'

'Jolly nice to meet you.'

The man did not make eye contact. He placed a cup of tea in front of Daisy and sat at the table.

Barrett dug his fingers into his palms.

'Nice to see you again, Sergeant.'

She turned to her companion.

Barrett felt his body sway.

Somehow, he managed to retrace his steps, but he did not return to his soldier friends. He was in no mood to talk about the dance, nor was he interested in placing bets as to which of the women would be fair game. Every woman he met he tried to like in his pursuit of love. But even if they had the dark, wavy locks and porcelain skin of Daisy, all he felt was a cold numbness.

She is the one I want, but she will never be mine.

He strode to the back of the beer tent and placed his hands on his knees. Perspiration sprung across his face and leaked from his armpits. He knelt beside a bucket of water, dipped in both hands, and sluiced the cold liquid over his face and body. After several minutes he stood, shook himself like a wet dog and left.

The sun shone late into the afternoon.

The children's fancy dress competition was a success. Only one child cried when he did not receive a prize. Val received a packet of fruit pastilles for best bonnet and John won the junior painting competition with his night picture of a wildfowling man and his dog. When the flower auction began, Gordon bid for two voluminous bunches of pink and white roses and presented them to Annie and Anita. The hoopla stall gave out the last of its jumping jack sets. The baking tent heaved with mothers desperate for a last cup of tea as their children clamoured for more cakes and biscuits. The men had one last beer and talked about their ferrets and pigeons.

'Madam, congratulations, you have won the piglet,' said George

'Would you like to come forward and collect her?'

Daphne Ditchin approached the stall. George picked up the piglet. He had not seen Daphne since the farmer's meeting. His smile was nervous, hesitant.

'Here you are, Madam.'

The piglet wriggled and squealed.

Daphne shrunk back from the animal.

'I can't possibly take that home. I have nowhere to put it. And besides...it's a pig!'

'She is indeed a pig Madam, albeit a young one. That's why the game is called "Bowling for the Pig".'

'Well, that's as maybe. But I will not take it home.'

She sniffed and glared at George.

'Very well, Madam. That means you are entitled to the compensatory prize of ten shillings.'

He pulled the note out of his pocket, and with a flamboyant flourish, placed it in her hand.

At the end of the day, George took the piglet back to the farm and gave it to John to 'bring on'.

John called the piglet 'Tig'. He fed her barley meal, cabbage leaves and potatoes. He scratched her back, watched her play in her fresh bedding and jumped aside when she ran in and out of her pigsty.

One day when he came home from school, Tig was nowhere to be seen.

'She's gone,' said George. 'Gone to the slaughterhouse. We can't afford to keep her for nothing.'

64

August 1954

George and Josh walked the field and surveyed the barley crop. It stood tall and strong. Even better, it was malting barley, which could be sold at a higher price for whisky and beer.

'It is not overripe,' said George. 'But that's good for the binder. We will get in here on Thursday.'

The following morning George met his farm workers in the bever hut. They had heard the crop was ready and high-spirited conversation rose amongst them.

George raised a hand to quieten the men.

'The barley is fit, and the weather looks good and settled. We will have that barley in tomorrow. Get everything ready, men, and I will see you in the morning.'

'There is a letter for you.'

Annie nodded towards the kitchen table.

George eyed the envelope positioned against the marmalade jar. It was addressed to him and bore a government stamp in black ink. He sat and picked up the letter. He turned the envelope over and slit open the top. It was a short letter, its type uneven and faded and the signature a black squiggle. It contained his compensation claim number in a heading across the top of the page.

He began to read.

Annie stood by the sink drying a plate. When she saw his body twitch, she held the plate and waited. He gave the letter a shake and began to read it again.

'Why the...?'

He placed the letter on the table, smoothed it out and with a trembling finger followed the text.

'Oh...Oh!'

'George...what is it? What does it say?'

Annie placed the plate and cloth by the sink. She picked up the teapot and took a step towards the table.

'It's the compensation...the government...they have refused our claim!'

'But I don't understand George, we were told...'

'Annie...I don't know...I...'

The words were a jumble on the page.

He held the letter at arm's length. The words were still muddled but two words jumped out from the typed lines; 'compensation' and 'unsuccessful.'

He placed the letter on the table and put his head in his hands.

'They slaughtered our livestock ...maimed our pigs ...and now they refuse our claim!'

He scraped back his chair and shoved the table to one side; the crockery jumped up and down on the surface. Annie dropped the teapot. It shattered into a dozen fragments and a puddle of hot tea spread across the flagstones. He sunk back in his chair and pressed his fingertips into his temples.

'George, let me see the letter.'

She stepped over the fragments of the teapot. He pushed the letter across the table towards her. She read the letter twice. It was clear the claim had been refused. She read out loud.

'Due to noncompliance with government requirements namely, the growing of crops without permission.'

'The growing of crops without permission? But George, that is not true! You have not grown crops without permission!'

'It's outrageous, Annie! We have grown one field of barley, twenty-five acres of barley, that's all.'

He ran his fingers through his hair.

'It's a mistake, George. It must be a mistake.'

He pointed to the letter.

'This isn't right, Annie. Keep quiet about it. Something big has gone wrong and I am going to get to the bottom of it. But today we get the barley in. Nothing is going to stop that.'

'The dew and damp have gone from the earth,' said Josh. 'We can start work.'

'Righto, men.'

George pulled on his cap. The men stood in one synchronised movement and left the bever hut. They had worked until dusk the day before when they sharpened the cutter in the binder, repaired one of its wooden sails and ensured the binder string was ready for tying the sheaves.

They stood in the yard whistling and talking whilst Jake and Reggie hitched the binder to the tractor.

Josh drove the tractor and binder out of the yard, George and Jake followed in the farm truck and the farm workers came on their push bikes. Josh stopped the tractor on the edge of the field and turned in his seat.

'Ready when you are, Jake.'

Jake climbed onto the binder. He adjusted one lever, to ensure the barley was cut at the right length and excess stubble was not left in the field. Then he adjusted another lever, which controlled the wooden sails and tipped the cut barley onto the canvases.

The farm worker raised his hand and Josh pulled away.

George watched as the binder cut the barley and the golden stems began to fall. The canvasses took the cut barley up to the knotter. The knotter bound and tied the barley into individual sheaves and flicked them down on the ground.

How wonderful.

The sweet, stinking chamomile smell of the scented mayweed filled his lungs.

You can, you have.

He felt like a small speck on the vast landscape of earth, smaller than the smallest creature and less significant than a grain of sand. He was surrounded by the power of nature and in awe of her ability to overcome the destructive forces of the salt. But even then, he knew nature was not finite and that she required help to feed them all.

'Let's get them stacked, men.'

Reggie worked with the men to ensure they stacked the sheaves into traves, so they were not left to absorb moisture from the ground overnight. By late morning, dozens of traves stood like small wigwams in regimental rows across the field.

'See you after dinner,' said Josh.

The farm workers cycled back to their homes whilst George, Josh and Jake climbed into the farm truck. As George drove down the track, he noticed three teenage boys in the distance.

'I wonder what they are up to.'

He stopped the truck, but before he could alight from the vehicle, Moses appeared from a field entrance and stood in front of the boys. He wore his familiar trilby hat and pieces of string were tied above each trousered knee to prevent mice running up his legs. The old man struck his stick on the ground. George opened the truck door and jumped down. Moses walked with an uncomfortable, lumbering, rhythm and waved his stick at the boys. George knew what his father would say to them.

'Go home, lads. Get off the farm, right now.'

He smiled. Despite everything, his father's habits did not change. The boys ran back down the lane and out of sight. George walked towards his father.

'You all right, Dad?'

'How's the crop running, lad?'

'Yes, it is good. It's quite clean, not too many weeds considering what the soil has been through. The women and children will be able to glean soon. They will like the grain for their chickens.'

The old man nodded.

'Are you coming back with us, Dad?'

'No, lad, I am going to walk home.'

An hour later, the farm workers reappeared in the field. They worked through the afternoon and when they stopped for tea at five o'clock, hundreds of traves stood complete in the field. The men sat with their backs to the machinery. They soaked up the sun, ate bread and cheese and drank cold tea.

'Tis good to be back in the field.'

Jake pared off a slice of cheese and placed it on top of his bread.

'Aye, it's grand,' replied Reggie.

'Yep. Tastes good out here in the field.'

'We will be knackered this evening. We've not been used to this work.'

'That wife of yours, she will be "bulling" for you

tonight, and you'll be knackered.'

'Tis true, I will be knackered, but not that knackered!'

The men laughed and then fell silent. Since the flood, they had feared for their livelihood, that the soil would not come good, and the crops would fail. But they were back with the rhythm of the harvest and working on the farm again.

At last, they could provide for their families.

65

George drove across the road bridge onto the mainland.

The top end of the high street was quiet. He parked outside a large, double-fronted house and alighted from his vehicle. The path to the door was set with black and white tiles in a diamond pattern. George raised the large, brass door knocker and gave it two resounding raps. An internal bolt shifted, and a key turned in a lock. The man wore a paisley dressing gown and blue slippers. He stared at George.

George removed his cap.

'Mr Browning?'

'Ah...Mr Hadley...Butterwood Farm...Yes...of course.'

George recognised the man's voice, an English accent inflected with Scottish dialect.

'Please, come in.'

George entered the hallway.

'Can I get you some tea?'

'No, no thank you, Mr Browning.'

He rotated his cap between his hands.

'Look... I'm sorry, Mr Browning to come here on a Saturday morning and disturb you like this, but I need your help. I don't know who else to turn to I...'

'Do come through, Mr Hadley.'

They entered a sitting room and sat around a small table. George produced the letter and smoothed out the creases. Mr Browning glanced at the government stamp at the top of the letter.

'Ah...'

'Would you read it please.'

Mr Browning removed a pair of glasses from the top pocket of his dressing gown. When he had read the letter, he looked over the edge of his glasses.

'Yes, I see.'

George drew a deep breath.

'You can imagine how I felt when I read it.'

'Well, it is rather odd Mr Hadley, but I must ask you, have you grown crops without government permission? If you have, well as you know, your claim will fail. The government is very strict about such matters.'

'Of course not! Why would I do that? Why would I want to destroy my claim for compensation and ruin my only chance of getting back on my feet? If this is not sorted out, Mr Browning, the farm won't survive. Without that money, I won't be able to carry on. It must be a mistake, or someone is out to ruin me.'

Mr Browning frowned.

'That is a serious allegation you have just made, Mr Hadley.'

'Yes, it is! But unless there has been a mistake that is the only other possibility as far as I can see.'

'It is more likely to be a mistake, Mr Hadley, but I cannot rule out the other possibility. Leave the letter with me. I will make enquiries and let you know.'

'Thank you. I appreciate your help.'

'As I said, Mr Hadley, it is probably a simple administrative mistake and nothing more. However, I cannot rule out at this stage the other possibility you mention. In the circumstances, I advise you in the strongest terms not to divulge the content of this letter or tell anyone about your visit this morning. I need a free rein to establish what happened.'

'Yes, of course, I understand. My wife knows about it. She was present when I opened the letter. I will remind her to say nothing. In the meantime, I will try and carry on as normal until you contact me.'

When George returned to the barley field the men fell silent. Josh gave him a curious look and the men whispered in hushed tones, but nothing was said, and they continued to work until dinner time.

George stopped the truck outside Josh's cottage.

'I will bring John back with me.'

'He will enjoy that.'

Josh jumped out.

George turned the truck towards Butterwood Farm. Since the spring he noticed an increase in the rabbit and hare population.

Growing the barley helped and there will be more of that next year.

He had seen the odd gamebird too when a pheasant or partridge flew across to the island from the river or mainland. Many of the predatory birds had drowned in the flood and given the game birds a good chance of regeneration, but he knew it would take some years until there was a sustainable supply again.

He sighed.

However, the wild fowling birds had not been affected by the flood, and as the temperature cooled in the coming weeks, he expected to see the odd widgeon and teal fly in from the northern hemisphere ready to access their winter food source. He knew they would roost further north along the east coast, and in the early evening fly down to the island and feed on the zostra weed or eel grass. Although some wild fowlers sold their bag to Frank Thomson, or the London restaurant market, he took his bag home to feed the family.

It will be good to go again.

He smiled as he remembered Annie's refusal to cook sparrow or rook pie despite Anita's attempts to persuade her.

He noticed some of the fields had been harvested, although many still lay empty of crops. He felt trapped.

Just as we were starting to get back on our feet.

He wanted to run across the barren fields, scream and shout, and vent his frustration at the paucity of the crops and lack of progress.

When he returned to the farm, John sat at the kitchen table. Annie did not question George about Mr Browning, but their glance between them confirmed his visit.

'Hello, son. Once I have eaten, we will go back to the field together. Some of the farm workers are bringing their children to the field this afternoon. You will be able to help pick up the traves, unless you want to join the younger children and play further down the field?'

John's fork stopped midway between his plate and his mouth.

George chuckled.

'Don't worry, you can help with the traves.'

Annie placed a plate on the table.

'Have the women and girls started gleaning the grain yet, George?'

'No, not yet. They will be allowed to enter the field tomorrow.'

'What will we do if we don't get our compensation, George? If it turns out there was no mistake, or we can't prove you did comply with government requirements? What then? Will we be able to keep the farm?'

Annie twisted the bedcover until her knuckles showed white in the moonlight.

'We must wait for Mr Browning, my darling, let him investigate the matter on our behalf.'

He did not add how he hoped Mr Browning would get a hurry on with his enquiries or the reaction of Josh and the farm workers earlier in the day. He was down to a few pounds. The seed bill and other bills remained unpaid, and he needed to buy cattle.

'And what if someone has made a false claim against you, George? Who would do such a thing?'

'If that has happened, I will find out who it was, make no mistake about that.'

George pulled her close. He pressed down on his own worries, kissed the top of her head, and stroked her hair.

His breathing was as tight as a drum.

66

Three days later, the men completed the traves.

On the fourth day the men arrived in the stack yard. Whilst the sun dried the dew from the traves out in the field, they began to prepare the corn stacks. The men laid a deep base of old straw on the ground, to prevent moisture reaching the bottom sheaves, and repeated the same for the second stack. After they had prepared the bases, they ate their bever and returned to the field.

The tractor and trailer were already in the field. A short distance away stood two shire horses Daisy and Dixie, on loan from a neighbouring farmer. They were hitched to a wagon ready to start work. The men gathered around the horses and patted and stroked them.

Josh separated the men into two gangs, one gang to work with the tractor and trailer and the other gang to work with Daisy and Dixie. One man climbed onto the trailer and another onto the wagon. All the men had pitchforks, although most of the pitchers stayed on the ground.

Josh drove the tractor.

As they progressed through the field the two gangs worked in two rows. They separated each trave out and pitched the sheaves onto the trailer or wagon. The men on top pitched and placed the sheaves with their heads of barley facing inwards.

The loads got higher.

Josh slowed the tractor and shouted to the man on the wagon.

'Hold tight, water lock here.'

A water furrow dug out the previous winter stretched across their path. The man on the wagon pulled the horses to a halt and a pitcher took hold of Daisy's bridle.

'I've got them. Keep it steady.'

The pitcher pulled at the bridle and guided the horses across the furrow. A short while later the men completed the first load.

'That's it,' said Josh. 'Let's get back to the stack yard.'

When the tractor and wagon reached the stack yard, the pitchers placed ladders against the loads and the men on top climbed down. They kicked the loose straw away from the stack area, formed a gang line and waited for Roger, the best stacker and thatcher on the farm.

The men passed the sheaves along the line to Roger who started the first tier. He laid the sheaves on the longer rectangular, outer edge of the stack, and ensured the outer edge remained slightly higher. He placed the cut bottom of the sheaves outwards, and the heads of barley inwards to protect them from the elements. As the men unloaded the sheaves, Roger repeated the tiers until the trailer and wagon were empty.

The men worked on. Again, and again they carted the sheaves from the field, returned to the yard and passed them to Roger to build the stacks.

When the field stood empty and the stacks complete, Roger climbed to the top of each stack and thatched a ridge across its top.

George looked at the completed stacks.

'It is good the barley's in. We can leave it alone now

until we start threshing later in the year.'

He thanked his farm workers and returned to the farmhouse.

The following morning, George took John for a ride in his tractor. He let him sit on his lap and take the steering wheel.

They stopped in the cut barley field.

'Smell that stubble, son.'

He waited whilst the boy looked out across the field. After a while he started the tractor.

'Let's go and have a look at the corn stacks.'

They drove back to the yard.

The two corn stacks towered above them magnificent and golden, like rural works of art.

'That's a truly wonderful sight, son'

George said a silent prayer.

67

The barley fields were shorn of their crops. They showcased spikes of turned stubble, and the pungency of fresh, aerated soil hung in the air. Curlews and golden plover roosted inland and circled the fields with the lapwings; they dug up earthworms and gobbled down bugs and insects. Hares abandoned their nocturnal habits and played on patches of brown and smudges of ochre. But when a bird of prey appeared in the sky, they squatted and froze in the field, their camouflaged bodies invisible to the eye.

The ploughing match was organised by the Agricultural Society for the third Saturday in September. Farmer Turner hosted the event. He had an arable farm on the mainland and good accessible roads for the tractors.

George drove off the island just before eight o'clock in the morning. As he got closer to the host farm, he overtook a variety of tractors.

John turned in his seat.

'Dad, where are the big horses?'

'They will come in the lorries, son. It is too far for them to travel on the road.'

They pulled into the farm.

'There's Daisy and Dixie!'

John pointed to a large lorry; it's open back revealed the rears of the two cart horses.

'I believe you are right, son. Old Dick will guide and steer his single furrow plough which Daisy and Dixie will pull between them.'

They parked up, opened the doors, and unwrapped their bever.

'You got here nice and early.'

Eric appeared beside the truck.

'Good morning to you, Eric. Aye, we made good time. Which class have you entered?'

'I have brought along my three-furrow mounted plough. It's my first competition in two years, so I will see how I go.'

'I am pleased with my barley crop,' said George. 'It's a shame it's only twenty-five acres, but we will sow a full Autumn crop in a few weeks. Then we can get ploughed up for winter, which will give us time to thresh the barley.'

'I will probably do the same. I better get back to my tractor, we start in five minutes.'

'Good luck! We will come over and give you a look.'

More tractors arrived. George placed the bever tins in the grub bag.

'Now, let's go and see how Eric is getting on.'

They walked to the first field and watched the tractors and ploughs as they trucked to their allocated plots.

George pointed to the second tractor along.

'There's Eric.'

He pulled John's arm down.

'No, son, don't wave at him. He needs to concentrate.'

He bent down towards John.

'See, son, they must plough one chain per furrow and complete all the furrows on their plot, about half an acre overall. Each furrow must be good and straight, and the weeds and stubble buried.'

John pointed to the fourth tractor along the line.

'There is a lady on that tractor.'

George recognised the unmistakable uniform of the land girl; fawn cord breeches and a green, cropped cardigan.

The woman turned in her seat.

'Well, I never, it's Margaret! One of Eric's girls! He must have let her bring that tractor.'

George chuckled.

'Eric won't be able to show his face if she beats him.'

George and John visited the other fields.

'Daisy and Dixie are working well,' said George.

Old Dick walked behind the two horses as they pulled the plough and turned the soil. It was a slow, painstaking business and two hours given to complete the task never seemed enough.

A man to the left of George pointed and spoke to another as they walked past.

'There is a rabbit over there.'

'Dad, it's not a rabbit! It's a hare!' whispered John.

'You and I know it is a hare, son, but town folk don't always know the difference.'

John's forehead wrinkled.

'But they are different. Rabbits live underground and have kittens, and hares live overground and have leverets! Why don't they know?'

'Some folks that live in towns, they don't always know things about the countryside.'

He looked across the field.

'Well now, there's a face I haven't seen for a while.'

'George!'

Farmer Buckle's voice boomed across the field as he lumbered towards them.

'It is good to see you, George. It's been a while.'

The men shook hands.

'It must be three years,' said George. 'If my memory serves me correct, the last time we met was at the cattle market in Chelmsford.'

'Yes, I remember. I bought my Hereford prize bull, from there. He's done me proud.'

The farmer turned towards John.

'Is this young man Master Hadley?'

He winked at the boy.

John stepped behind his father, his blue eyes hesitant, curious. George put his arm around the boy and pulled him back beside him.

'Aye, this is John. He is my eldest boy.'

'Does he like tractors?'

'Yes, God blast, he is tractor mad.'

'How's the rest of your family, George?'

'Very well thank you.'

'There is some good farm machinery for sale in the next field.'

'Thanks, we will have a look. Some farmers have talked about buying a combine harvester. I suppose mechanisation is the way forward.'

'Well, I must be going. Good to see you.'

Farmer Buckle raised his hand and walked towards the judge's tent.

The competition finished late morning. George and John ate Cornish pasties and returned to the first field. It had been transformed; instead of stubble and weeds, chain lines covered the terrain. Some were straight, but still showed stubble where the furrow failed to turn the soil. Other chains possessed a military precision, the soil clean and turned in, and no sign of stubble or weeds.

Eric stood by his completed plot.

'That looks good, Eric. I reckon you might be up for

a prize there.'

'Maybe, but we will have to see what the judges say.'

George laughed and nodded towards Margaret.

'You have some stiff competition.'

Margaret waved and turned back to the farmers circled around her.

'She's caused quite a stir,' said Eric. 'But she knows what she's doing. She is one of the best workers I have ever had.'

The prize giving took place at two o'clock in the afternoon. Eric won first prize and Margaret received highly commended.

68

'Good to see you, Mr Browning.'

The men shook hands.

George gestured towards a seat and Annie placed an extra cup of tea on the table.

'Sorry for the delay.'

Mr Browning removed documents from his briefcase.

'It took a little longer than expected but I can inform you where the Ministry stands on your claim.'

George gave a tight smile. Annie pulled her chair closer.

'About a week after your claim came in, a report was received that you had sown and planted crops in your fields. The report came from an islander who gave a detailed eyewitness account. There is a note on the file recommending a visit to that islander and to you before a decision was made on your claim. However, that was not done. I can only think it got overlooked due to the sheer number of claims that came in across Essex.'

'I can't believe what I am hearing,' said George.

He drummed his fingers on the table.

Mr Browning continued.

'You may not be aware, Mr Hadley, but when I come down for the weekend and stay at the Old Post Office, I often come across to the island to walk and birdwatch.'

'I'm surprised I haven't seen you.'

'Well, there you are, Mr Hadley, but the point I want to make is that apart from my visits to you last year, I have often walked around the island and know the location of your fields.'

'We have sown the one field of barley, that's all. We have done nothing to the other fields apart from spread them with gypsum, just like the government directed.'

'After your visit to my house, Mr Hadley, I came onto the island and took some random soil samples from the fields. I also took some photographs. I gave the samples and the photographs to Mr Cuthbertson and requested he run some tests. He confirmed this week, that although the soil has a gypsum content, it has not been disturbed. I passed this information on to my superiors and yesterday they approved your claim. You will receive the full amount claimed within the next week.'

George tried to speak but no sound came from his mouth.

'Why, that is wonderful news,' said Annie. 'Just wonderful!'

She clasped George's hand.

'Thank you, Mr Browning. I will be able to pay the bills and buy more seed. And some cattle!'

George hesitated, then continued.

'Just one thing, I am curious as to who made the false report. As far as I know I have no enemies, but I can only think it came from someone who has an intense dislike of me and bears a grudge big enough to want to ruin me.'

Mr Browning eased the collar of his shirt with his fingers and shuffled his papers.

'I think that is best left alone, Mr Hadley.'

He picked up his briefcase.

'I will leave you to it. Oh, and good luck.'

69

It was early evening and Reverend Peak was alone.

The committee members had been busy all day. They arrived early, cleaned the church, and decorated the nave with fresh flowers. Just before noon the islanders came with their harvest gifts. Some brought fresh produce grown in their gardens or allotments, whilst others purchased items from Dickie Byers and Frank Thomson. All the islanders contributed: fresh flowers, eggs, apples and pears, bags of flour, tins of ham, corned beef, spam, and fruit.

He crossed the church with silent footsteps and looked at the displays.

They have given so much when they have so little.

He emitted small grunts of satisfaction as he admired the islander's efforts.

He pulled the door shut.

The church hushed silent.

'Thank you, my darling.'

George took the plate of fruitcake from Annie and placed it beside his cup of tea.

'The nights are starting to draw in again, but we have a harvest moon tonight.'

Annie sat in the opposite chair.

'Busy in the church today?'

'Yes, but it's all ready for the harvest festival service

tomorrow.'

She smiled and half closed her eyes.

'Have something to eat and go to bed.'

Her head nodded like a bobbing toy.

'Annie!'

Her eyes blinked open. She looked at George and down at her plate.

'Yes...I think I will. Busy day tomorrow.'

Sunday arrived bright and cloudless blue.

The islanders experienced a joyous predictability: ablutions, a good breakfast, Sunday best clothes, and off to church. They undertook their journey in a variety of ways, an open back farm truck packed full of children, an occasional car, a tractor, or a brisk walk.

George parked in front of Dr Everitt's car.

'Everyone out please.'

Annie and the children scrambled out of the car and followed George into the church.

'Good morning, Dr Everitt.'

Annie ushered the children along the pew.

'Good morning to you, Mrs Hadley, Mr Hadley.'

The church was full. Babes in arms wriggled and young children sat between their parents. Older folk were helped to their seats and farm workers sat by the door, ready to leave for liquid refreshment.

The islanders sat or stood in the pews and chatted to neighbours and friends; their conversations rose to a crescendo, around the nave, along the aisles, and up to the vault.

Daphne Ditchin sat in the gallery in front of the organ. For the last week, Reverend Peak permitted her to enter the church every morning to practise the hymns. She felt nervous, excited, and moved her fingers above and across the keys in a last silent practice.

Reverend Peak surveyed his flock. His face flickered with delight at the full house. He cleared his throat. A hush swept through the congregation.

The service was traditional, collective in its message of resilience and determination, and beautiful in its delivery. Reverend Peak blessed the harvest, and the islanders sang loud and joyous, and said prayers with earnest thanks.

Annie dropped coins into the collection box and passed it to Dr Everitt.

'Master John looks well.'

'Yes, he is thank you, doctor. He made a full recovery'

'Where has Daddy gone?'

Val turned in her seat and eyed the empty pew.

'I expect he needs to speak to someone. We will meet him by the car.'

They joined the queue and inched their way along the nave.

'Lovely service, Reverend, thank you.'

Reverend Peak beamed.

'Thank you, Mrs Hadley. Jolly nice to see you and your family'

Annie and the children stepped out into the warm sunshine.

The islanders were reluctant to leave and continued their conversations in small groups. George stood on a grass verge with four other farmers, their enthusiastic gestures and hearty laughs accompanying their booming voices.

'Mrs Hadley?'

Annie turned towards the voice.

A man of older years stood in front of her. He had a roughhewn face. His suit was clean but cheaply made, his shirt collar threadbare, and his boots worn and scuffed.

Annie recalled a distant memory. She recognised his face but was unable to recollect when or where.

'Do you remember me, Mrs Hadley? My name is Bill. I was a foot rescuer with Arthur during the flood. We rowed you and your children across to the sea wall.'

The man's voice possessed a soft neutrality, but his eyes were haunted, distant.

'Ah, yes, of course! Of course, I remember you, Bill.'

She touched his arm.

'It has been a while since that day, but I will never forget it. You and Arthur, you saved our lives. How is Arthur?'

She pressed the man's arm as if the movement would produce answers to her questions.

'Arthur, well...now there is a sad story...'

His face contorted.

'Arthur caught pneumonia. He was admitted to hospital and died.'

Annie's eyes filled with tears.

'Oh Bill, I am so sorry to hear that. He was a good man but so young! May he rest in peace.'

She took out her handkerchief and dabbed at her eyes.

'Was Arthur married? Did he have a family?'

'No, Mrs Hadley, he was not married, but he has a widowed sister, who has three children. Her husband drowned in the flood. Molly is here somewhere. I spoke to her earlier.'

He scanned the small groups.

'There she is. Do you see? The young woman with the head scarf, with the two boys and a girl.'

Annie followed Bill's line of vision. She let out a cry.

'I have met Molly, Bill. She came to the house one day with crockery to sell. That's right, she came in for tea and cake. She told me her husband drowned in the flood. She also mentioned her brother, but I didn't make the connection. George employs her from time to time to work on the farm.'

Annie did not mention the welfare committee's involvement with Molly and her children. Some women saw it as a matter of pride to be independent and fend for themselves.

'I can fetch her over if you like?'

'No thank you, Bill. Now is not the time, but I will pay Molly a visit soon. She needs to know her brother was a hero and saved our lives.'

The harvest supper took place in the village hall the following Saturday. The farmers attended with their wives. Food was plentiful and alcohol flowed. To ensure a good crop the following year, corn dollies made from the last sheaf of their small harvest were placed on each table.

George squeezed Annie's hand.

'Just like old times.'

Speeches were made, prayers said. Stories were told and retold, some sad, some incredible, all worthy of a place in the island's history.

70

Autumn arrived early. Leaves of gold fell from the trees and red rosehips and berries repainted the landscape. The bird population on the island remained below normal, but the annual winter migration from the northern hemisphere began in earnest and hundreds of widgeons, waders, ducks, and Brent geese migrated to the island for the zostra grass. Bright, still weather still visited the island, but the daylight hours shortened, and the nights brought a heavy dew or a shock of frost.

George inhaled and exhaled the cold air. Much of the soil had been ploughed, lifted, and turned and the weeds and stubble dug in. It was the first time in two years he had been able to prepare his land and sow a full crop of barley and wheat.

Two years. Two years out of our lives. But time never stands still. We must learn and move on.

Male voices came from the bever hut.

George smiled to himself and opened the door. His farm workers were a lively lot, but they were loyal and worked hard.

'Morning, all.'

The men quietened.

'Today we finish ploughing and start on the seed beds. The ground will be dry enough by ten.'

George looked around the hut.

'Harry and Mike, you plough the bottom two fields.

Keep going with those and get them turned.'

The men touched their caps.

'Jake, you go discing.'

'Righto.'

'Reggie, you go rolling.'

'Yes, guv'nor.'

'And Jake, when you have finished discing, come back to the yard, collect the duck foot harrow and go behind the roll.'

'Will do.'

'I will come and check the soil later today.'

George allocated the remaining jobs.

'Josh, you stay with me. We have jobs to do here. Some of the seed will be delivered this morning.'

Josh nodded.

George adjusted his cap.

'The weather looks dry for the next week or two, so we should be able to get on. We need good seed beds men. Right let's get on.'

The seed arrived just after eight 'clock. George finished greasing the seed drill and walked over to the lorry. The driver wound down his window.

'Morning guv'nor. I have your first delivery of autumn seed; forty bags of barley seed and twenty of wheat. Where do you want it?'

'My trailer is the same height as your lorry,' said George. 'If I bring it alongside, we can wheel it across.'

The driver nodded, climbed down from his lorry, and let down its sides. The sacks were stacked in vertical rows and weighed a hundred weight each. George parked the tractor and trailer beside the lorry.

The driver untied the ropes and rolled back the sheets. One at a time, the driver slipped his sack barrow under a sack and wheeled it across to the trailer. George and Josh stacked the sacks and covered them with a sheet.

'All done.'

George thumped the bonnet of the lorry.

'Mind how you go. See you next week.'

George drove the tractor and trailer to the shed store and opened one of the sacks.

Lovely.

The seed had been dressed and the quality was excellent.

The following morning George drove the tractor and trailer out of the shed, whilst Josh hitched the seed drill to another tractor. They drove in tandem down to the fields. When they arrived, one worker stood on the trailer and moved each sack into position, whilst a second worker heaved the sack onto his back, carried it across to the seed drill and laid it on the seed box. Then, he cut the strings of the sack and sprinkled the seed along the box. As the seed drill sowed the seed into the soil, the rooks and pigeons appeared and picked off the exposed seed. By lunchtime a third of the field stood complete.

The men worked each day and every Saturday morning until all the seed was sown.

George and Josh visited each field in turn.

The fine, tilled earth stretched before them.

'Lovely seed beds,' said George.

'And the weather held,' said Josh.

'Our prayers have been answered. We should get a good crop of barley and wheat next year.'

71

'Mum!'

John's voice broke into Annie's thoughts.

'Sorry, John, what were you saying?'

'I said do you think Dad will take me to flight when he goes wild fowling this year?'

'I am sure he will, John. Why don't you ask him?'

The boy turned as his father entered the kitchen.

'Hello, my darling,'

George kissed Annie's cheek and squeezed her arm. He winked at John and sat at the head of the table. He ate a sandwich and talked to Annie. But when he placed his empty cup on the table, the boy could wait no longer.

'Dad, can I go to flight with you next time you go?'

'Of course, you can, son.'

The boy jumped up and down and ran up the stairs.

'He's been wanting to go with you for a while.'

She cleared the plates and sat next to him.

'All the fields are tilled and drilled now?'

'Aye, they are.'

She touched his hand.

'George, I can't stop thinking about it.'

She gave a small sob.

'I know, Annie. I have seen how it has affected you.'

He squeezed her hand.

He recalled Annie's elation at confirmation of the compensation claim after Mr Browning's visit, but after that, she began to wring her hands again, and at night, her body jerked with convulsive twitches as she slept. They were gestures he had not seen since the early days after the flood.

I can't bear to see her like this.

Annie wiped her tears.

'There is someone on this island who wanted to ruin us, George, see us finished on the farm.'

'I don't understand why someone would want to do that, Annie. God knows I have racked my brains as to who it could be and have made discreet enquiries of the other farmers and the islanders. But nothing, no name or clue.'

Later that night in bed, George trawled through his mind again. Most of the islanders were too busy with their own problems to be interfering in other people's lives. Suddenly, a person's name flickered into his head. It was something Eric said.

'Oh, I meant to tell you George, I had a visit from Paddy Watkins last week. Do you remember him? I sacked him after the incident when Maisie was locked in the bull pen.'

'Aye, I remember him.'

George had not forgotten the young man's sneer before he punched him to the ground.

'He turned up with his father and asked for his old job back. His family had severe money problems. Of course, I refused to take him back. He and his father didn't like it, but I can't afford to have troublemakers like that loose in my yard. The lad's a mischief maker.'

'Well, Mr Hadley, if I tell you his name, you must understand it will be strictly off the record.'

'Of course, Mr Browning, I understand.'

When George heard the name, his eyes widened and

for several seconds he did not speak.

'Not Paddy Watkins? Are you sure?'

'Yes, I am sure, Mr Hadley. There was no mention of a Paddy Watkins or anyone by the name of Watkins.'

72

George did not hire contractor gangs on his farm. He owned his threshing machine and always used his own farm workers. But he took nothing for granted. A few years earlier, a farm worker on a neighbouring farm lost his hand in a threshing drum, and he recalled the story of a land girl who lost a leg in a similar way. George was fortunate, he had experienced staff.

Josh parked the tractor and threshing machine alongside the first corn stack.

'Let's get it level, men!'

The farm workers surrounded the threshing machine. Spades hit the earth, pressed in by body weight and heavy boots. The men rearranged the reluctant turfs and smoothed them flat.

Josh checked the spirit levels on the main carriage.

'Nearly there.'

'A bit more here.'

George stamped his foot to the ground.

'And here!'

The men continued with their spades.

Josh raised his hand.

'That's it.'

'Get the blocks under it, men. And Josh, get your tractor. Let's get this belt on.'

Josh climbed onto the tractor and started it up.

Two workers secured the belt between the tractor

and the threshing machine. The men waited whilst Josh reversed the tractor, tensioned the belt, and applied the handbrake. Then they stepped forward and placed blocks under the tractor wheels.

Josh turned off the engine.

'Bever now, men.'

The men each made their own seat from loose straw fallen from the corn stack. For a few moments there was silence as numbed fingers opened bever tins.

'You've got your "pozzy" then.'

'Yep!'

The man laughed and pushed the remains of the jam sandwich into his mouth.

The wind whipped up the debris and chased it across the yard.

'Not the best weather for threshing,' said Josh.

He tightened the silk scarf around his neck. Some men had similar scarves. Others had goggles tucked in a pocket. None of them wanted barley hale in their eyes or next to their skin.

'Okay, men.'

Josh closed the lid on his bever tin.

'Let's start the drum up'

He climbed onto the tractor.

'All ready.'

The men placed the stack ladder up to the first corn stack. One man climbed the stack and removed the thatch whilst the band cutter clambered onto the threshing machine. The men on the stack pitched the sheaves to the band cutter. The band cutter cut the strings and fed the sheaves into the drum. After the barley was separated, it got shaken through the sieves and the chaff was blown out onto the ground.

George was impatient.

'Come on, bagger. What are the samples like?'

'It's all right, guvnor. They are good and fine.'

As each sack filled with barley, the bagger shut the shutter and tied the bag. The men on the ground braced themselves, lifted a sack off the sack lift and stacked it on the tumble cart. When the cart was full, it was hitched to a tractor and taken to the granary.

'There is a weasel's nest here.'

A farmworker pointed to a depression in the corn stack alongside a dung pile and two pieces of mouse tail.

'Aye, he's been working the stack.'

'Good. There should be less mice when we get to the lower levels, not three or four hundred like we had before.'

The men joked and sang as they worked. Only the chaff cleaner complained. But the chaff cleaner always complained even when he wrapped his silk scarf twice around his neck and across his face. However, his job was the dirtiest job of all, and when he removed straw residue from under the middle of the drum, the choking dust permeated his clothing, penetrated his eyes, mouth, and nose and travelled deep into his lungs.

It took three days to thresh the corn stacks. When the men had finished, they moved their limbs slow and quiet. And when they returned home, they washed the dust off, ate in silence and crept into their beds.

73

George stepped inside the cottage and removed his cap.

It was quiet. He felt the warmth of the fire on his skin and the smell of roasting meat came from the kitchen. He noticed a change in Alice Wright too. Her breasts and hips had filled out and her skin was less sallow.

'The boys are out on the shore. They will be back soon.'

She wiped her hands on her apron.

'How are the repairs to the back wall?'

'Fine. Come and see for yourself.'

He followed her through to the kitchen. Five plates were stacked on the table and a loaf of bread lay untouched on a board.

George surveyed the wall and ceiling.

'You won't have any more trouble with that.'

'Thank you.'

She looked around the kitchen.

'We are gradually getting straight, and thank you again, Mr Hadley, for repairing the wall.'

'That is quite all right, Alice.'

He changed the subject, aware of the imminent return of her boys.

'Did you manage to get a tenant for the forge, Alice? I did mention it to one or two men here on the island.'

'Yes, I did thank you, Mr Hadley, and the

73

George stepped inside the cottage and removed his cap.

It was quiet. He felt the warmth of the fire on his skin and the smell of roasting meat came from the kitchen. He noticed a change in Alice Wright too. Her breasts and hips had filled out and her skin was less sallow.

'The boys are out on the shore. They will be back soon.'

She wiped her hands on her apron.

'How are the repairs to the back wall?'

'Fine. Come and see for yourself.'

He followed her through to the kitchen. Five plates were stacked on the table and a loaf of bread lay untouched on a board.

George surveyed the wall and ceiling.

'You won't have any more trouble with that.'

'Thank you.'

She looked around the kitchen.

'We are gradually getting straight, and thank you again, Mr Hadley, for repairing the wall.'

'That is quite all right, Alice.'

He changed the subject, aware of the imminent return of her boys.

'Did you manage to get a tenant for the forge, Alice? I did mention it to one or two men here on the island.'

'Yes, I did thank you, Mr Hadley, and the

arrangement is working well. I get a regular income from the rent and Ronnie has started his apprenticeship. They reckon he will be ready in a year or two.'

'That's good to hear, Alice.'

He scratched the top of his head.

'When we last spoke, I got the impression your brother was not a favourite choice for the forge?'

'Oh, Willy. No, he wasn't. He wanted the forge, wanted it bad, but I knew he would be unreliable and mess me about with the rent. I told him it was your idea about the tenant. He was blinding angry about it I can tell you, but I had to think of my boys. I couldn't be favouring him when I needed money to feed my boys.'

'Ah...yes.'

He nodded. Suddenly, a great weight lifted from his mind and a feeling of freedom liberated his very being.

'Do you know where I might find him?'

'I am not sure, Mr Hadley. Come to think of it, I haven't seen him for months.'

'Well, when you next see him, Alice, please give him a message from me.'

'Yes, of course, Mr Hadley.'

'Tell him to leave the island and never come back. Tell him if he does return, he will get a visit from me.'

She gasped.

George Hadley's eyes bore a look of menace few had seen.

Her lips clammed shut like a clamp, a guarantee against enquiry.

He smiled and replaced his cap.

'Well, I must be going. I am glad it's worked out for you here. If you need any help, let me know.'

74

'Today's the day, my darling.'

George kissed Annie on the cheek and squeezed her waist.

'How long will you be gone?'

'I will drive over to Eric first. We will be out most of the day. It will be good to see everyone.'

He hummed and whistled as he sat at the table.

'Here you are.'

She placed a large plate of bacon and eggs in front of him.

The cattle market at Chelmsford took place every Friday and livestock came from all over the county and beyond. The auction was due to start at eleven o'clock. George intended to arrive early and have a good look at the cattle. Although some of the heifers his father gave him had been served by Eric's bull and produced calves, he wanted to increase his stock.

As he drove towards Eric's farm, he looked across the landscape at the brown, tilled rows of hope.

I am a lucky man Some farmers have lost so much but I have still got Annie, our children, and my parents. And the farmhouse has dried out and the soil is coming good.

His eyes pricked with tears, but he was in no mood for sadness. He had money to buy cattle and the reduction of salt in the meadows enabled him to get a good cut of hay for their winter feed.

'Morning.'

Eric slid onto the seat and pulled shut the door of the truck.

George drove towards the mainland.

'The year is spinning away from us,' said George. 'But we have made progress and we will get a full crop next year.'

'Yes, it is a grand feeling. My men have worked well. I was concerned at one point as they had quite a break, but they soon got back into it.'

'Same here. We finished the threshing last week, so I can concentrate on my cattle now.'

'What are you after today?'

'Well, cattle are the first thing. I want a bunch of stores that I can add to my existing bunch, but I will see what's there.'

'The foot and mouth disease closed the market for a while and the stocks got low, but I think the numbers are back up again. They should have a full stock today.'

'Aye, I heard about that. What about you, Eric? Are you looking to buy?'

'I'm not sure. I might get some more heifers and maybe some pigs. I am pleased with my pure-bred Hereford bull. He's got a good temperament not like the Friesian bulls.'

'Ah yes, the Friesian bulls, they can be tricky customers.'

'Did you hear about the Friesian bull owned by Farmer Buckle? It turned on one of his workers. Luckily, the bull's horns had been cropped, otherwise it would have killed him. The worker had a few broken ribs but that was all.'

'It is important to remember bulls weigh a ton and

are dangerous even in play.'

'I agree. They require respect and careful handling.'

They drove in silence for several minutes. Cattle floats appeared ahead of them.

'Looks promising,'

'Aye, should be a good day.'

George had forgotten the size of the market. It was spread across a twenty-acre site with its corn exchange at one end, and an area for the sale of agricultural machinery and parts at the other. However, he did not need to look for the cattle, pigs, and poultry. He tasted the smell of their fur, skin, feathers, and dung, and he laughed with joy at the sound of the beasts as they pushed and shoved in their pens and stalls.

Within a few minutes of their arrival, George and Eric received enthusiastic greetings, several handshakes and banter from the other farmers. George checked his watch.

'We'd best be getting on.'

They walked towards the cattle pens. The varieties of breed for sale were impressive: Friesians, Short Horns, Herefords, Aberdeen Angus, and Ayrshire.

George pointed to a group of cattle to his left.

'The beef cattle look good.'

The familiar markings of their red bodies and white faces indicated they were Hereford beef cattle.

'You can see those ones were born and bred in Hereford and Worcester,' said Eric. 'They're bigger and thicker than the ones from Wales. They will do you better.'

He pointed further along the pens.

'You could go for the Aberdeen Angus, but they will be a lot dearer.'

'Aye. They are beauties. Whatever I do buy, I have got to keep them through the winter months. I got a good cut of hay from the meadows for winter feed, and I got some barley straw for litter from the threshing, so that will help.'

'What about those two pens of Hereford, Friesian-cross over there?'

'They look solid. They are a possibility, although one bunch looks more forward than the other. Let's finish those pens down to the right.'

The two men walked past the remaining pens and retraced their steps.

'Which ones are you going for, George? I don't want to bid against you and push the price up.'

'I like the look of the two pens of Hereford, Friesian-cross we saw earlier. They will make a good bunch of twenty stores. They will do me just fine, if I can get them right.'

'The lot that's more forward will be more expensive.'

'Yes, I think you're right.'

'That might raise the price of the second lot, if the bidding on the first lot gets run up.'

'I will take that chance.'

'Shall we look at the pigs now?'

'Not for me, thanks. I have my eye on those twenty stores. I will leave the pigs for another time.'

When they entered the sale ring, the auctioneer gave them a nod. He was a rotund man of middling years, wore a country tweed suit and stood by the bidding table surrounded by farmers and butchers.

The auctioneer opened with the fat cattle. Bids came in from the butchers. The next lot were the store cattle.

'There are quite a few, including yours, George.'

They waited for the auctioneer to announce the

bidding for the Hereford, Friesian-cross store cattle.

'Here we go.'

George straightened up and focused on the auctioneer.

'Here we are, a nice little bunch.'

The auctioneer looked around the ring to gauge the interest.

'They have come out of Worcestershire. There are ten here. There will be another ten to follow. You've seen them in the pens. How you going to start me...'

The bidding began.

In less than a minute, the gavel came down and the auctioneer announced the buyer.

'George Hadley.'

The second group were brought into the ring.

'Here we go again. Same lot but not quite so forward. Where are we with these.'

Eric nudged George.

'You might do well with these, if you can get 'em.'

A minute later, the gavel came down and George was announced the buyer.

'You were lucky with those, George. They did not run up so bad. Shall we stay and see the cows being sold?'

'No thanks. Let's go for a cup of tea. I will square up with the office afterwards. I am just going to talk to the drivers.'

George strode off towards the cattle floats. The drivers stood around their vehicles smoking and chatting as they waited for jobs.

George approached the men.

'Can one of you run twenty stores back to the island for me?'

A driver stepped forward.

'Yep, I'll get them loaded. It will take me half, three quarters of an hour.'

'Good on you. Thank you.'

When George and Eric left the market, George's stores had not been loaded.

'That's good,' said George. 'I want to get back before he does, make sure everything's ready. It will be good to get those cattle settled in.'

He changed gear and pressed the accelerator.

'I spoke to my men yesterday. I told them I was going to buy a bunch today and to get the yard ready.'

They crossed to the island and drove to Eric's farm.

'You've done well, George. You have a good bunch there, and a fair price too.'

He slapped the bonnet of the truck.

George drove the last mile to his farm.

Ah, there he is.

The cattle float was behind him.

He pulled into the yard. The bottom half of the yard was covered in barley straw. The racks were stocked with hay and the water troughs were full.

He opened the main yard gate. The driver reversed the lorry whilst George and two farm workers stood on the opposite side to the open gate. The driver opened the back of the lorry, unbolted the tailboard, and scattered it with straw. He opened two interior slatted gates and moved to one side. The first of the cattle walked down the tailboard, off the lorry and into the yard. He unbolted the next gated section and released four more cattle. After ten minutes all the stores had left the lorry and stood in the yard.

George watched his cattle as they pulled at the hay and went to the water troughs. He felt proud and full of life.

It's been a good day's work. Good for me, good for the farm.

75

John looked out through the window again. The yard was quiet, still. He wandered around the kitchen. The hands on the kitchen clock appeared frozen. He touched the berries and leaves arranged in a vase, picked up the butter pats and turned them over.

Annie shooed him away.

'You are getting under my feet, John. Go and play until they arrive.'

He went upstairs and knelt on his bed. Half an hour later he heard the familiar sound of the car enter the yard.

He raced down the stairs.

'Grandad! Grandad!'

John ran across the yard towards him whilst his father helped Emma out of the car. The old man stopped and smiled at the boy.

'Why lad, you have grown!'

He ruffled the boy's hair.

'You are feeding him well, Annie.'

John turned towards his father.

'Can I show grandpa the cattle now?'

'Not yet, son. Let's have a cup of tea first.'

The kitchen smelt of roast pork. Cabbage and carrots lay prepared on a wooden board and a large pan filled with water contained peeled potatoes. A pie stood on the table. Its golden crust encased a sweet apple compote.

John tried to sit still whilst the adults spoke, but after a while their voices mingled and became a far-away murmur. He placed his elbows on the table and slumped his chin into his hands. He couldn't understand why adults took so long to do everything.

He let out a sigh but quietened when he felt his mother's eyes on him. He studied the grain of the kitchen table, the metal of the cutlery. He looked up at the ceiling, dragged his eyes across to the window and out to the yard. He flickered his eyes back to the table, over the stacked plates and the folded cloth beside them.

At last, his grandfather stood up.

'You going to show me the cattle, John?'

John turned to his father.

'Can we take Sam with us?'

'Yes, you can, but you make him mind.'

It had rained overnight, and the late Autumn sunshine reflected on the puddles in sharp bursts of fragmented light.

John and Moses crossed the yard. Sam trotted behind them. His winter coat lay thick on his body and his legs were streaked with mud.

The cattle lay chewing the cud. They cast a curious eye over the boy and old man but became watchful when Sam looked from under the gate. After a few moments the dog lost interest and moved away. The cattle relaxed and returned to their digestive reverie.

John climbed onto the lower rungs of the closed gate. His grandfather stood beside him. He pointed with his stick and moved it from left to right.

'Your father has bought a nice bunch, boy.'

John manoeuvred himself on the bars of the gate and faced his grandfather.

'I helped to feed them this morning.'

'Good, lad.'

'They can't go out to the meadows and eat grass in the winter. We give them hay and they've got their barley straw.'

'That's right, boy, they must be kept in during the winter months.'

He pointed at the hay racks.

'You made a good job with the hay, boy, it's almost gone. Can you tell the difference between them yet? Which one is your favourite?'

John studied the animals for a moment or two.

'I know some of them.'

He pointed to a large heifer.

'I like that one. I call her Margaret. Dad says she's the bossy one.'

'Ah, yes there's always a bossy one. She keeps the others in order.'

Two of the heifers rose to their feet and lumbered towards the water trough. Margaret came up to the gate. She sniffed at John's outstretched arm and licked at the cloth of his sleeve with her large, rasp of a tongue. John stroked her forehead and ran his fingers down her nose. She shook her head and turned away.

His grandfather gave a satisfied nod.

'Tis good to see a herd back on the farm.'

As they watched the cattle, small, incessant droplets of rain fell from the sky, and a slight breeze brushed their faces.

'Come on boy, let's go back. I can smell that pork crackling from here.'

76

December 1954

Dawn broke over the horizon in the east. The sea was covered in a white, foaming spume and the waves rode unforgiving and rough. Most of the migrating birds from the Tundra had arrived and established their winter feeding grounds. The ditch bank grass swept sideways and gave shelter to rabbits and hares. Inland it was bright and freezing cold.

George parked his truck on the side of the lane and waited for Eric's truck. They wound down their windows and faced each other.

'You finished now?'

'Aye,' replied George.

He placed his elbow on the open window.

'We are all done up for the winter. I will be looking after my cattle now.'

'Same here.'

Eric looked at the sky.

'Looks like a good moon tonight.'

'Yep, we are due a full moon in two days.'

'You goin' on the shore to see if you can shoot a widgeon or two?'

'Aye, I'll be there. Wouldn't miss it for the world.'

'It will be rough tonight. They'll be flying low.'

'Aye. Should get a good bag.'

Eric moved away.

The birds appeared fast and low as the high-pitched whistle of the male widgeons and the purring females chased across the sands. George half stood, then sat and rose from the box.

'Look at them, Sam!'

He swung his gun in front of the bunch. Again and again, the crack of the gun echoed across the sands. Sam streaked back and forth, until a pile of birds lay at his master's feet. An hour later the birds were bagged, and the flight was over.

'Come on, Sam. We've done well. Let's go home.'

George returned to the farm early evening and hung ten birds in the coal shed.

The house was quiet, the children in bed.

'John was upset this evening.'

Annie placed a sandwich on the table.

'He so wanted to go with you.'

'Aye, I know. But there'll be other times for him.'

She toyed with the spoon in her saucer.

'It was a wonderful flight. I think I'll go back tide time. It's not often you get weather like this.'

Two hours later, he left the farm for the second flight. There was no sign of Eric and high tide was due in an hour. George knew when the tide rose, the widgeons would be disturbed from their feeding ground and take flight.

He waited.

An intense, strong wind blew from the south and the tide began to flow. Waves splashed against the edge of the saltings and covered him with spray.

'Here we go, Sam.'

The dog's ears pricked up, his eyes darted, and his nostrils quivered.

'Cronk. Cronk.'

A long skein of Brent geese swept over the top of George's head. He lowered his gun; Brent geese were a protected species. A Dunlin battled head to the wind as he flew along the shoreline. Suddenly the bird hit George's coat.

'Well, I never!'

The small bird had dropped into his pocket. He waited for it to revive and let it go. As the tide got higher, bunch after bunch of widgeons took flight in their quest for a sheltered bay. The crack of his gun came again. Sam lurched out into the tide; it was not straightforward, but he knew what to do. He swam with the tide, let the wind take him and disappeared. Minutes later the dog reappeared along the top of the sea wall with the dead bird in his soft mouth. Back and forth he went, his body silhouetted by the moon, until he retrieved fourteen birds.

'Good, boy. Good, boy.'

George picked up the birds and placed them in his bag.

This lot will feed a few mouths.

He thought to whom he would distribute the birds. The best brace would go to Annie, some would go to those who were widowed and others to elderly folk on the island. If there were any left, the rest would be sold to Frank Thomson at half a crown a brace.

He turned to Sam. The dog's fur lay matted and wet. His eyes were sunken and fixed, and his tongue hung out to the side of his mouth.

'You've been a damn good boy. You are tired out and you need to dry out.'

He picked up the dog and lay him on a bundle of straw in the back of the truck.

John stood at the window all evening and listened to the muffled shots. The weather was rough and exciting, and he knew his father would go for the second flight. Despite the late hour John stayed awake until the kitchen light was extinguished, and his parents retired to bed. Then, he dreamt of the wild fowl and the Brent geese. He flew with them across from the Baltic states as they continued their search for the zostra grass in their unceasing quest for survival. He dreamt he owned his own gun and hunted for food, like his father, grandfather, and the generations before them. When he awoke it was silent and black, but he knew dawn was on its way. He slid out of bed and crept into his parents' bedroom.

George stirred and opened his eyes.

'How many did you get, Dad?'

He turned his face away from his father and looked out the window.

'Morning, son.'

George put his hands behind his head and rested back on the pillow.

John stayed by the window.

'We got ten and then fourteen. Plenty enough for a good food supply.'

The boy approached the side of the bed where his mother lay. She raised her hand and touched his arm. He slipped between the covers.

'Don't be a baby, son. You will get plenty of opportunities.'

'He's had a tough time,' said Annie. 'Give the boy a chance.'

She stroked his hair.

George softened his tone.

'Things are getting back to normal, son.'

Sometimes he forgot how young John was and how

he wanted to live with nature and be on the land.

'The flood has taken its toll on all of us, son, but we must take nature's setbacks in our stride. Give her a chance, give the land time to heal; let the animals reproduce and respect the sea and its wild ways.'

He touched John's face.

'It is all here, son. There's no rush.'

Foaming, white waves embrace me,
Your lunar tides lull and soothe me,
Feeds my soul, gives life.

'Are you going to make mud decoys?'

'I won't bother. It will be so rough. It will be fine without'

George looked at his watch.

'I reckon it's time for breakfast.'

George stepped into the scullery. The voices of Annie and Olive travelled through from the kitchen. He removed his jacket and boots and hung up his cap.

'Good morning, Mr Hadley.'

Olive placed cutlery on the table.

'Good morning, Olive.'

He pulled out his chair.

'Cold out there.'

Annie smiled.

'The children didn't want to go to school today. We had to force them out the door.'

George laughed.

'The scamps! They will do anything to avoid leaving the farm.'

Annie gave the porridge one final stir and removed the pot from the cooker. She placed it on the table and ladled the contents into two bowls.

'I will get on with the beds, Mrs Hadley.'

'Oh yes. Thank you, Olive.'

George and Annie ate their porridge. They looked at each other and smiled.

George drained his cup.

'Must get on.'

George put his head around the kitchen door.

'I am going to flight. I will be a couple of hours.'

Annie nodded.

He pulled on his thigh boots, picked up his gun and canvas bag. He called out to Sam and opened the tailgate of the truck. As he started the truck, John and Val turned into the yard. John ran up to the truck. His satchel banged against him, and his cap sat askew on his head. George wound down the window.

'Let me come, Dad. Let me come with you.'

The boy's face was red with cold, and his scarf had fallen loose and exposed his neck.

'No, not this time, son. I am going now. You can come another time.'

'But Dad! Please! I want to come! You said I could!' The boy's eyes filled with tears.

'Come on, son. Not this time. I'm going to be late.'

When he reached the sea wall, he let Sam out and collected his bag and gun. They climbed up and over the wall and dropped onto the saltings.

'Now, Sam, flotsam and jetsam. Let's see what we can find.'

The dog sniffed the air and put his nose to the ground. As he ran ahead, his fur stood up in straight tufts. George found a wooden box. He placed it on a spartina knoll and took out his gun.

'Perfect.'

The moon lit up the sand and the black shimmer of water beyond. A squall of wind rushed over his face and whipped around his legs. He steadied his cap.

Eric appeared to his left.

George shouted above the wind.

'Isn't this beautiful?'

'Yes, it's perfect.'

The two men stood together and scanned the sands. They knew the birds would fly low in such weather. Sam pricked up his ears and smelt the air. He wagged his tail slow then fast as he stood square to the invisible sight.

'They're coming,' said George.

'I am going to go out further.'

Glossary

Nissan huts: individual, prefabricated buildings in the shape of a half cylinder. They were made of corrugated iron with brick ends, had windows along the sides, and additional windows either side of each front door. They were built after the second world war as a temporary solution to the housing shortage.

DUKW vehicles: tracked vehicles made for use during the second world war as a landing craft.

King Canute Rescue Operation: name given to the rescue operation from the mainland.

Farmer's teeth: wooden landmarks, used for centuries as a guide in coastal areas

A drag: a long fork with four prongs for clearing silty rubbish or straw blocking sluices or drains.

Track Field Marshall tractor: a single cylinder tractor which was an icon in its day. Some had tracks instead of tyres for use in difficult terrain.

Captive bolt pistol: before this pistol was legally required to be used on livestock, they were often killed using a knife during full consciousness. On 16th November 1950 Lord Dowding raised the issue of the humane slaughter of animals in the House of Lords (Hansard). He proposed that except for religious reasons, animals must be stunned before being killed by a knife or gun. To protect food rationing, a private owner could not kill his own animals without authority from the Food Officer. But authorised animal welfare officers had stocks of captive bolt pistols and used them to prevent the animal suffering unnecessarily during the slaughter process.

Spring tides: tides that occur once a fortnight throughout the year. Spring tides in May and June are called bird tides. These tides do not have much depth, so they do not wash the nesting gulls and terns off the saltings. Bird tides are a natural phenomenon.

Marsh weed: a generic term for any plants that normally grew on the shore but were displaced by the flood and swept inland.

The Lord Mayor's Fund: a fund set up by the government to provide financial assistance to flood victims.

Commemoration booklet: children of school age were given a commemoration booklet to celebrate the Queen's coronation. They were inscribed with the royal motto – 'Dieu et Mon Droit – God and my right.'

Stack yard: a convenient spare area on high free draining soil in the farmyard or an appropriate field, where hay and corn stacks were created so that water would run off and keep the stack dry during the winter wet months. Some stacks survived the great flood.

A sea waller: a colloquial term for having sexual intercourse on the sea wall.

Ringing the Bull: a game or pastime for farm workers which was played on inclement days. It comprised of a hook in the wall. String about four feet long hung down from a beam. A ring tied to the end was spun around in a curve to catch the hook. The players had several tries each.

Binder: a piece of machinery that is linked up to the tractor. It cuts and binds the barley and throws the finished sheaf onto the ground.

Sheaf: barley that has been cut and bound with string by the binder. The heads of the crop are at one end and the cut ends at the other.

Trave: between four and six sheaves make a trave (or a stook). Pairs of sheaves are placed against each other to provide mutual support. The head of the barley is never put on the ground, always at the top. At this stage each sheaf is in the exact same state as in the field except it has been cut and stood up.

Gleaning: done by the women and children. They had a legal right to go on the field and collect the remains after the harvest

Bulling: a colloquial term for wanting sex, usually attributed to the female despite its male connotations.

Corn stack/rick: a way of storing a crop. Corn stacks that survived the flood were used to feed the livestock.

Corn: unlike the American term, in this country corn is a generic term (like the word grain) for wheat, barley or oats.

Pitchers: men using pitchforks and working on the ground during the harvest.

Kedger/cadger bag: fisherman's bag.

Cam: a circle in the sand with a hole in one corner to drain the water away and made for digging logworm.

Kiddle/keddle net: colloquial term for a commercial V shaped fishing net. The fish swan in but could not escape.

Pan hole: a puddle of salt water, left behind by the tide.

Chain per furrow: old measurement term – twenty-two yards in a chain.

Discing: done by a disc harrow, normally eight feet wide. Attached to a tractor, it slices and tills the soil and levels it ready for the roll or harrow.

Duck foot harrow: often six feet long and twelve feet wide. It is like a giant garden rake. It is attached to a tractor. It lifts the ground up, pulls the weeds out and levels the soil.

Rolling: the roll has a ground coverage of eight or fifteen feet in width according to the power of the tractor. It is attached to a tractor and follows the disc harrow or duck foot harrow. It consolidates the soil and breaks the clods down.

Pozzy: colloquial term for a jam sandwich.

Hale: hair or bristle like appendage that grows out from the end of the barley. It is covered in minute one-way hairs and causes severe irritation to the eyes and the skin.

Chaff or cavings (includes barley hale): the residue from any crop that is too fine to be carried to the straw stack.

Stores: cattle that are between calves and fat cattle in size and development.

Widgeon: wild duck shot for food

Mud decoys: made with a spade, dug in the mud and the sod turned up on top of the sands. Two yards apart and numbering twenty or so, at a distance under the moon, they look like a large bunch of wildfowl. It decoys the ducks towards the wildfowler. Anything that flies into the area will be silhouetted against the moon.

Saltings: an area of coastal land which is a mass of green growth and about a yard higher than the sands. It provides a drier area for longer until the tide covers it.

Spartina knoll: a raised and irregular mound of reed.

Zostra grass: a colloquial term used by the islanders for zostera or eel grass.

Printed in Great Britain
by Amazon